King Edward the Last

Graeme Ratcliffe

King Edward the Last

Prologue

The hospital was surrounded by a chain-link fence; topped with razor wire, this created some protection from the surrounding slums. An ambulance splashed past the armed guard at the front gate. It slithered across an empty parking lot and pulled up at the emergency bay. Dirty rain flayed the asphalt as paramedics opened the back doors of the ambulance and wheeled out a female patient.

An hour later the grey-skinned woman was deposited alone in a pre-op chamber at the palliative care unit. She was unconscious, her chest wired to a heart monitor. It emitted a string of irregular bleeps. But for a rusting chair, and the bed on which she lay, there was no furniture. At the door stood a man and a woman, their presence silhouetted by the glare from the outside corridor. The man wore a lab coat and buzz cut blond hair. His small eyes flicked from side to side as he scanned the printed form on his metal clipboard. 'Bessie Stuart. Hmm, any family?'

The woman shook her head. 'No, Doctor, none that we know of.'

The doctor looked at Bessie's once beautiful face, her body emaciated and her head, now bald, wrapped in a scarf. 'Alright, Nurse, euthanasia module?'

The nurse nodded. 'She's first in. Tomorrow morning at seven.'

The doctor grunted as he checked off the last box on his form and signed it. 'They must be expecting a big day down there.'

'It gets busier every week.'

The doctor took out a well-used handkerchief and blew his nose. 'Keep her on the monitoring equipment and stick to standard procedure. If she becomes distressed increase the medication. Might as well enjoy her last night.'

The nurse flicked off the light and closed the chamber door.

Several hours had passed. The room remained enveloped in the grainy tones of night. The only source of light came from a lamppost out in the alley. It shone through the window's security grill, casting stripes across Bessie's bed. Lightning flashed and from the back of deep sockets her sunken eyes broke open. She glanced toward the window and saw the rain. It still fell—relentless as when she was last awake. It overwhelmed the clogged gutters and poured backwards onto the sooty pane.

For months Bessie had dreaded this day, holding fast to her council flat until the neighbourhood captain ordered her removal. Despite increasing frailty she had fought with all her tiny might to stay in the cluttered space that had been her refuge for ten thin years. Even when the estate committee upheld the captain's ruling, she held on, stubbornly refusing to accept the inevitable. When the end came, Bessie's residue of strength was insufficient to do much more than offer mild resistance. For the medics who held her down, her eviction was routine, the sting of their needle muzzling the attendant din. Not till hours later would she rouse from beneath the tranquilliser's shroud.

Strapped to a gurney, Bessie had been transported to the hospital, the removalists free to enter her home and dispose of its ragged contents. As with those who had gone before, Bessie knew the hospital was her final destination, a place where the patient rarely spent more than a day.

There was another bolt of lightning. She blinked, but in the bleaching instant of sudden white she caught a hint of her. Thunder rolled as Bessie struggled to face the old lady who sat in the steel chair to the side of her bed.

'Hello, my Darling.' the woman said, her voice as soft as the night was hard.

Bessie gazed in disbelief. The familiar voice was a caress, the words a balm. 'Mummy?' she whispered.

'Just call me Alice. You haven't called me Mummy since you were a toddler.'

Bessie struggled to lift her head. 'You're back?'

Alice's eyes twinkled, reflecting the dim lights emitted by the medical equipment. 'Yes, it's me, a ghost from Christmases past.' She chuckled before becoming serious. 'I'm sorry for taking so long; I got here as soon as I could.' Feeling the temperature of Bessie's forehead, she asked, 'Are you in pain?'

Her daughter shook her head. Alice squeezed her hand. 'The drugs here are good… Much better than the décor.' Observing the heartless room, its peeling paint a shade of institutional green, Alice continued, 'I've come to read you a bedtime story. Would you like that?'

Bessie nodded like a child.

Alice switched on the bed lamp and picked up her handbag. She removed an old, leather-bound book. 'This is a story about a girl who had the power to capture the heart of a handsome prince.'

Bessie's voice was hoarse. 'Cinderella?' she asked wryly.'

'No,' said Alice. 'This is no fairy tale; this girl was real.'

Alice opened the book and the leather binding creaked, the odour of mouldy vellum escaping. She rested its weight on the bed covers and tilted the pages toward Bessie, revealing a black and white photograph of a young woman. Shifting her chair closer and peering over her daughter's shoulder, the old woman explained. 'Here she is. Her name was Wallis Warfield Simpson.'

Alice allowed a moment to pass before turning the page. 'And this is the handsome prince.'

Bessie saw a second photo. It showed a fair-haired man of boyish appearance, but with smile lines that not only hinted at the approach of middle age, but the fatigue born of a bemused youth rendered comically senseless through a desultory obedience to the absurd. She couldn't comprehend why, but he appeared to Bessie as the most beautiful man she had ever seen.

Squinting through her spectacles, Alice nodded as she read the caption. 'David Windsor— '

'David Windsor?' Bessie queried; the name sounded familiar.

'Yes,' Alice agreed, still nodding, but now with eyebrows raised, 'his family called him David. He was the Prince of Wales. Later he became King Edward the Eighth.' She turned to the next page. It featured a photo of an older, bearded man. Alice continued reading aloud. 'In 1936 he succeeded his father, King George the Fifth.'

The old woman ran her bony hand over the page, its surface soft and rich beneath her fingertips; she loved this ancient book. As an antiquarian, Alice had spent her life devoted fervently to the discovery and preservation of such valuable artifacts. It was a love affair with the better part of humanity's bequest. Not the vicious ebb and flow of greed and vanity, but the intimate world of people who toiled to craft a beauty so much greater than themselves, a humble replication of the wonders that nature could create by accident or grand design. She had married a man who shared her passion: their work in antiquities, a love that enriched beyond riches their love for each other. Asthmatic, he died young, their daughter, a lasting legacy of that blissful time and a treasure more fascinating than anything she'd ever liberated from a dusty attic or crowded flea market. 'Want to see some more?' The old woman asked.

'Yes,' Bessie murmured, responding to her mother's warmth and energy.

'Alright then, let's lift up your head a bit.' Alice cradled her daughter's chest in the crook of her arm, plumped the pillows then eased her back down. 'Yes, that'll be a bit more comfy,' she assured. Turning another page of the musty book, she chuckled again. 'Oh, this is good.' It was an informal photo of David with his date at a cocktail party. Alice's tone became dreamy as she read aloud the accompanying text. 'David, when he was still the Prince of Wales, pictured with Lady Thelma Furness.' She glanced at Bessie and crossed her lips with her finger. 'Thelma was his mistress.'

Bessie didn't care. She surveyed the picture and felt herself transported to another time and place, a ballroom in a grand English country house. It was as though she could see David and Thelma break out of their pose after the flash bulb snapped, saw them walk back into the crowd, waving in acknowledgement to other guests. She fancied she could hear David complain, as she herself would have done, 'God, I hate flashbulbs. All I can see is a great, blue blob that flashes white when I blink.'

Bessie broke from her reverie, hearing again Alice's voice as the old woman turned another page. 'In 1934, David met Wallis for the second time. Her presence thrilled him. All the memories of the ball at Burrough Court came surging back, flooding in as surely as the blood that raced through his heart, the flush as dizzying as three years earlier; but this time, even more acute. He remembered how she seemed to read his thoughts, answered questions not yet put, and with a wit that charged his brain. At their first meeting, he had just embarked upon an affair with Thelma, making his introduction to Wallis as untimely as it was profound. Now fate had caused their paths to cross again, and in the throes of Thelma's farewell party. The sudden return of distant, tender feelings left David paradoxically becalmed. Thelma saw none of this, putting his vagueness down to what she knew to be her lover's eccentricity.'

Bessie floated deeper into the book. The effect was hypnotic. She was there, a fly on the wall of history, writing that history in her imagination. Then her inner eye saw Thelma lean toward the prince and ask: 'Are you okay?'

'Yes,' she heard David say, 'I think the champagne is going to my head.'

Thelma gave him a knowing smile. 'I told you not to skip lunch. You have to take better care of yourself. You're only flesh and blood.'

'Even if your blood is blue.' said a different voice.

The words were like a gun discharged. Bessie saw David look up to find Wallis in front of him. She was just like in the photograph: jet black hair, porcelain skin, dangerous eyes, smoky dark and sizzling with irreverence. Bessie heard the prince laugh, the sound pure and rich: a geyser of pent-up feelings, a release from a life informed by boredom, small talk and the fawning of everyone he met. From the depths of a dying woman's fantasy Wallis Warfield Simpson had fired off six words, and Bessie knew, that for David, no scholar could have penned a dissertation more pure.

Listening again for voices escaping from between her mother's spoken words, Bessie heard Thelma ask: 'David, darling, why don't you rustle up some drinks?'

'What?' she heard him respond, shaking his head as though his thoughts were returning from a pilgrimage. It took a moment for the request to sink in. 'Oh yes, of course,' he belatedly agreed, and rushed away to grab the butler.

Bessie then saw Thelma take Wallis aside. 'Sweetie,' she

whispered, 'I think the prince is in one of his moods. He's upset that I'll be gone for two months. Be a darling and keep an eye on the boy while I'm back in the States.'

Alice propelled the story forward, turning yet another page of the mildewed book. 'Thelma trusted Wallis; they were close friends. They had met through their husbands, both of whom were shipping company executives. The women were now divorced and had traded in their former, greenback grooms for British sterling. As a result, both now lived in England.

'Wallis told Thelma she would do her best to watch out for David during her old friend's absence, and honoured the promise with an enthusiasm her friend had not anticipated. How could Wallis help it? The emotional craving and animal lust David felt for her, she reciprocated with equal zeal. At the confluence of need and opportunity their eyes met, as glorious to each other as polished diamonds thrust together on an endless belt of coal. In that instant, David knew he'd met his match. She knew it, too. Both sides of the Rorschach inkblot, perfectly reflected. Few couples could ever be so privileged. Their love would be unqualified, intoxicating, complete.'

Bessie looked up from the yellowing pages of the timeworn book and stared at her mother. 'Thank you... thanks for coming to see me.'

Alice touched her daughter's cold cheek and fought to hold back her tears. 'How could I stay away?'

'I don't deserve this,' Bessie whimpered. 'I was never there for you. The cells eating me to bone are born of guilt. My life has been travelled blind to the needs of those around me.'

'Oh Darling, no, you're wrong. Don't be so hard on yourself. We are made what we are. There's no shame in that.'

With a sigh, Bessie released a rivulet of teardrop from a reservoir of remorse. 'I wish I had this life to live again. To live it better.'

Alice's chin quivered. With a quick sniff she tried to quell her own tears. Tilting her head upwards, she saw the cracked ceiling and tried to deduce how deep into the concrete the crevasses split, tried to think of anything but the tragedy of her daughter's self-reproach, Bessie's loathing for the life she had chosen to live.

Alice forced herself to smile. 'Your life is a life, my darling—nothing more, nothing less.' She returned to the book. 'Want me to keep reading?'

'Yes,' answered Bessie, so softly she could barely be heard. 'I love your stories.'

Chapter One, the Crisis

He shouldn't have, but David couldn't resist glancing at his great-grandmother. Cast in bronze, her stern face returned a glare of disapproval; protocol and respect decreed the new king should keep his eyes straight ahead. He immediately looked away, gripping the hilt of his sabre as though needing its steely reassurance.

Queen Victoria's statue disappeared into the distance as the cortege trudged through the streets of Windsor. Beyond a forest of naval ratings, David could see the gun carriage and his father's flag-draped coffin; and from behind, he could hear the footfalls of three princes—his father's other sons. He knew that following them came the dignitaries, drawn as iron filings to a magnet, from home and abroad: foreign heads of state, generals, admirals and senior members of the Cabinet. Among these walked the prime minister, Stanley Baldwin. All evinced solemnity, but unbeknown to David, Baldwin's mood had darkened. Having trodden in household cavalry horse manure, the prime minister's gait lurched in three-quarter time as he tried to wipe the sticky mess from his boot.

Finally, after the prime minister and the files of other important men, a royal coach lumbered. Glistening in the rain, it shrouded within its misted windows the black-veiled presence of the dead king's widow, Queen Mary. Impossible to be seen as anything more than a darkly blurred silhouette, she seemed as much an emblem of death itself as anything mortal.

A flurry of rain buffeted the marchers and the watching crowd. Grimacing against the bite of the droplets, David caught sight of his Royal Standard being run up the flagpole, atop the Round Tower. Even though a king was dead, the next king lived, the flag, as always, raised to full mast. However, quickly made sodden by the rain, his colours struggled to fly.

Sounding in the distance came the deep-pitched boom of the King's Troop, Royal Horse Artillery firing another salvo in salute. The rain flurries subsided, but relentlessly as the slow beat of the march, the pewter sky still drizzled damp. The glacial moisture weighed down David's greatcoat, January's icy fingers knifing through his uniform, passing flesh and bone to marrow. Every nerve said shiver; but only a man could shiver, not a king.

Edward Albert Christian George Andrew Patrick David Windsor was 41, but looked years younger. He had been, by the Grace of God, King of all the Britons, Defender of the Faith and Emperor of India for eight days.

His first name was in honour of his Uncle Eddy, the imbecilic Duke of Clarence, second in line to the throne when he died of typhoid fever without leaving an heir. His next name was in honour of his great-grandfather, Albert, on the insistence of Queen Victoria. This necessitated a third name in honour of a great-grandfather from the family's other side, King Christian of Denmark. Finally, for good measure, the different nations of Great Britain were honoured by the inclusion of the patron saints of England, Scotland, Ireland and Wales. It wasn't until he was four that he could recite his name without stumbling. Family and friends called him David.

He entered the world at White Lodge, a royal residence in Richmond Park. The eldest child of George, the then Duke of York, and his cousin, Mary of Teck, he was schooled by private tutors before entering naval college, and was the first Prince of Wales to be invested in that land. During the Great War David served with distinction on the Western Front and was awarded the Military Cross. Dubbed a Knight of the Garter in 1910, he had since been conferred an additional nine knighthoods. Over the years he had also been awarded the Croix de Guerre as well as seventeen other foreign decorations; had been appointed a privy councilor of both the United Kingdom and Canada; had received a princely scattering of university degrees from both home and abroad; had variously been proclaimed Duke of Cornwall and Duke of Rothesay; and was bestowed, at his father's pleasure, the Royal Victorian Chain. From the time of his birth, all this and more was woven like a Bayeux Tapestry, leading remorselessly to the throne. But a person can be burred by too much grooming. He was thought to be a handsome man, but his baby blue eyes glowed with the light of a candle that he burned from both ends, and his boyish blond hair disguised streaks of grey. He was one of the world's most recognised faces and its most eligible bachelor, but though popular with the people, he was seen in high places as a loose canon, King George once confiding: 'After I am dead the boy will ruin himself in 12 months.' But that didn't matter much anymore; his father was in a mahogany box.

Two hours after George had been laid to rest in the royal vault, a chauffeur driven Rolls Royce pulled up outside a country mansion, Fort Belvedere. It was David's official residence. Located at the southernmost point of Windsor Great Park, it was his sanctuary, private and unseen, deep within a forest of elms and oaks.

A footman rushed from the house to open the back door of the car. David emerged, still dressed in his Royal Navy uniform. He walked up to the front entrance to be greeted by Watson, his butler. 'Sir, Mrs Simpson awaits you in your private apartments.'

Once inside the hall and before climbing the stairs, David handed his chapeau, great coat, sword, scabbard and gloves to a row of attending footmen. Seconds later, he entered his bedroom and found Wallis lying naked beneath the covers of his four-poster bed. Closing the door behind him, he asked: 'Why, madam, are you indisposed?'

Wallis stretched luxuriously. 'Naughty Boysie, you should know better than to enter a lady's chamber unannounced.'

The king approached the bed and kissed her. 'Please forgive me ma'am, in future I shall remember to knock.'

David and Wallis had now been together two years and were seldom out of one another's sight. He had fought to have Wallis at his father's funeral, but his mother had forbidden it. Queen Mary could still remember her husband's outrage on hearing that David had introduced Wallis to her at Buckingham Palace. Wallis was divorced and divorced people were not supposed to be presented at court; the king would have spun in his coffin if he had known Wallis was sitting in the pews nearby. Out of respect for what she knew would be her departed husband's wishes she kept Wallis away and endured her son's wrath for her trouble.

David's love for Wallis had if anything intensified since their second meeting. He remembered vividly that fateful night, and how they'd slipped away. It was January, impossibly cold in the stables and dangerous in the stalls. Spooked by the banging on its stable door, his horse had reared several times, its hooves stamping on the limestone floor, inches from David's feet. Wallis was safe, her feet were in the air, and neither noticed any danger. Stripped of fear, the thrill of reckless disregard for protocol drove both to parts unknown. It was so impromptu, so urgent and so inappropriate, the thrill intensified by the sure knowledge that the other found it just as thrilling; their love, their lust, their greed as unbridled as the horse's mouth that whinnied in their ears, the flighty gelding disturbed by commands not recognised as anything the beast had ever heard in dressage school.

David's taste in women had always been unorthodox. As a handsome prince and future king his desirability was such that he could have found and wed a great beauty, but beauty can be boring if the woman is bereft of a single peculiar quality, save her beauty. For him, idiosyncrasy trumped perfection because it was unpredictable. Wallis was nothing if not idiosyncratic. David was a man who'd lived and loved but he'd never encountered anything like her. She was that wondrous toy that had always been beyond his grasp, up on the highest and most unreachable shelf; but now, here the toy was, bright and shiny in his fondling hands.

The toy's beauty was more Gothic than Baroque. Wallis was from an old Baltimore family that could be traced back for almost as far as David's. Disastrously, while still a baby, her father died, and with him, his income. The money was gone, leaving only the memory of its smell. Life for mother and daughter was not as easy as it might have been. The privileges they enjoyed became dependent on the charity of a wealthy uncle. If these straightened circumstances had caused her pain she gave no sign of it, her easy wit and charm disguising a grim determination to be happy, and David made her very happy.

Wallis watched David closely as he crossed to the drinks table and poured them both a scotch. 'I hope the funeral wasn't too maudlin. Lousy weather.'

'Papa would have considered it perfect for the occasion— brooding clouds, weeping rain, all that added dramatic effect. Mama, of course, loved every last bit of it.'

'And our friend, the prime minister?'

'Mr Baldwin's missed his true calling in life; he should have been an undertaker. Nothing like a corpse to bring out the colour in old Stanley's cheeks.'

David walked back to the bed and handed Wallis her drink. 'Chin-chin,' he said as he sipped his scotch, but she didn't move. She stared at him with bedroom eyes and murmured: 'Strip!'

David raised an eyebrow and put down his drink. He undid the brass buttons of his bemedalled jacket and let it drop to the floor. Wallis turned away as if suddenly disinterested and looked out the window at the muddy day.

'I can't believe that George is actually gone.'

David undid his tie. 'Oh, he's gone alright, no curtain calls allowed in this Wagnerian opera; the old Teutonic king took a tumble down the trap door.'

With casual indifference, David removed his braces, trousers and shirt, his shoes and socks and the garters that kept up his socks, letting them fall wherever they might.

Wallis took a sip of her drink and placed the glass delicately on the nightstand. 'Mr Windsor would never have approved of being called Teutonic.'

'Correction,' said David as he dragged off his shorts. 'You mean Mr Saxe Coburg and Gotha!' He threw his underwear to the end of the room and jumped into bed.

Wallis recoiled. 'My God, your hands are freezing.'

David smiled playfully. 'Then tie them up.'

She gave the king a deep kiss, then broke away. 'You forgot to say please.'

Twenty-five miles to the east, Stanley Baldwin and the Chancellor of the Exchequer, Neville Chamberlain, were sharing a drink. They sat together in the Cabinet Room at Number 10 Downing Street.

Chamberlain raised his glass. 'God save the king.'

Baldwin, a gruff man at the best of times, clinked his glass against Chamberlain's, but kept his eyes fixed firmly on his boots. 'Yes, Neville, to the king... without a queen.'

Chamberlain nodded. 'Indeed, Prime Minister.'

Baldwin sighed and sipped his whisky. The prime minister

was in the midst of his second term at Number Ten. He had been the leader of a Conservative government that was voted out of office seven years earlier. However, upon the fading health of the Labour leader, Ramsay MacDonald, and the election of a national coalition, he managed again to seize the keys to Downing Street. It was rare for a British Leader to get two bites of the cherry but Baldwin was a formidable player, no stranger to the rough and tumble of politics and never one to roll down his sleeves and step away from a stoush. Now he feared he might be on the verge of an epic battle with no lesser entity than the king. He put down his drink on the Cabinet table. 'I suppose we should be grateful for small mercies. At least he didn't invite that American divorcee to the funeral. That really would have been the limit.'

Chamberlain ran his index finger around the rim of his glass. 'I am reliably informed that his ardour for Wallis Simpson is undiminished by the heavy weight of the crown.'

'A crown still in his hand,' snapped Baldwin, 'not yet on his head.'

'Stanley, my fear is that he might one day wish to marry Mrs Simpson.'

'Good God, Neville, the woman's a whore. A respectable whore, I grant you, but a whore all the same.'

Chamberlain shook his head regretfully. 'The man is besotted.'

Baldwin rose from his chair and paced the room. 'But she is married, her second marriage at that. He quite simply has no choice but to do the fit and proper thing and keep her as his mistress.'

'Oh dear, this is a sticky situation,' fussed Chamberlain. 'He's a stubborn man. Last month, I pleaded with him to relent on the currency portrait, to adhere to a centuries-old tradition, yet he still insisted on showing his left profile on the coinage. He claims it to be his better side. I mean, the vanity!'

Baldwin thrust his fists into his pockets and growled: 'The Nation and the Dominions could never endure a Queen Wally. Is there anyone who might bring him to his senses?'

Queen Mary lived at Marlborough House. Built by the architect, Sir Christopher Wren, it was, for a hundred years, the London home of the eponymous dukes. Taken over by the Crown in 1817, it was now the official residence of the old widow. It contained many staterooms, including a sumptuous saloon, replete with murals depicting the Battle of Blenheim, but Mary rarely saw them. She preferred to remain in the comfort of her drawing room. Here, she could sit in her wing-backed armchair, stitching her embroidery; but today the hoop lay untouched on a side table. She was in the middle of an unpleasant meeting and her demeanour transformed her cosy chair into a throne of iron.

Before her sat Horace Wilson, a man as small in bearing as in thinking, he had risen through the ranks of the civil service to become chief industrial adviser to the government and seconded for special service to the office of the prime minister and Cabinet. His special service this day was to elicit, on Baldwin's behalf, the support of the queen dowager in the government's attempts to control her son.

Mary sat ramrod straight, her hands lacing the sides of her

chair like guardian lions at the entrance to a shrine. Wilson had been speaking uninterrupted for some time and she had tired of him.

'Please, Mr Wilson, you are belabouring the point. There is no need to go on.'

'But, Your Majesty, it is of vital importance that you understand that the king must abandon any thought of marriage to Wallis Simpson.'

'Mr Wilson, I understand all too completely.'

'Yes, Ma'am.'

Mary took a deep breath and spoke with disdainful finality. 'Give to Mr Baldwin my assurance that the young king will do his duty.'

A month later, the steamship, the Nahlin, sat at anchor off a sun bleached island. A smaller craft sat close by, a reporter and a news photographer standing on the deck. The photographer took a series of shots of a man who was swimming through the pellucid water. It was the king. He had decided to escape the misery of the English winter by taking a cruise to the Aegean Sea.

David made his way to the Nahlin and climbed on board. Across the quarterdeck, lay Wallis, sunning herself on a deckchair. She turned and watched through dark glasses as her man towelled himself dry, the hard Mediterranean light accentuating his wiry, athletic physique.

'Are those reporters still here?' she enquired.

'Yes,' said David as he approached and reclined on a deckchair beside her, 'it seems we'll be enjoying their company all day.'

Wallis sat up and removed her glasses. 'Do you think we'll be famous for living in sin?'

'I frankly don't care,' he pronounced. 'They can publish and be damned.'

'David, Darling, you're very well liked. You could even say the public... I would say they love you. And I don't want to play a part, any part, in damaging that.'

David's face broadened into a cheeky grin. 'What, do you think I might lose the next election?'

'People may talk,' said Wallis with mounting concern.

David got up and walked to the side of the ship. 'Let them talk, I'm the King; I'll do as I please.'

Wallis leaned forward. 'Charles the First did that and they chopped off his head.'

David gave a little wave to the newsmen. 'Charles was married to a Catholic. You, on the other hand, are an Episcopalian.'

'Why, Boysie,' said Wallis, startled by this new turn in the conversation. 'Would you have an Episcopalian, an American, a commoner as your queen?'

'Yes,' he said, walking back toward her, 'and to hell with the Fleet Street hacks, to hell with the politicians! Once the people meet you, grow to know you, see your beauty, your intelligence, your passion, they will fall in love with you as I have, madly. Behind every great man is a great woman. I want to be great, but I need you with me.' David knelt down beside her. 'Wallis, my darling, will you marry me?'

Wallis allowed herself a guarded smile. 'That is one hell of a marriage proposal.' She kissed him and looked into his eyes; they were as open and clear as the surrounding sea. 'You're quite a guy, but you seem to have forgotten the small matter of my husband.'

'I'm the King. I'll have him shot at dawn.'

'Your Majesty, I think you're making me moist.'

'I'll take that as a yes,' said David, suddenly up on his feet. 'Sun's past the yardarm, time for champagne.'

Queen Mary sat in her conservatory, eating breakfast. Behind her, the first rays of spring sunshine slanted through the French doors, illuminating an explosion of potted daffodils. She sipped her tea and was about to take a bite of toast when her butler entered.

'Ma'am, the American newspaper that you requested from the foreign office.' He carried a silver tray to the table. On the tray was a copy of the New York Times.

When the old widow saw the headline she lost interest in her toast. In bold type it read: 'King Edward Wallis Simpson Romantic Cruise'.

Mary picked up the newspaper and cleared phlegm from her throat.

An hour later, Baldwin conferred with Chamberlain at the Cabinet table. Like other British prime ministers before him, Baldwin had no official study and therefore worked from the Cabinet Room. As usual, his mood was sour.

'Why must the unions be so truculent?' he declared. 'Many mills have shut down, many mills and mines, but they have my assurance, things could still be a lot worse.'

Chamberlain adjusted his pince-nez. 'These are hard times, especially in the North and—'

'Wales! Yes, I know,' Baldwin interrupted.

Chamberlain ignored the prime minister's rudeness and tidied away his papers, placing them in their red box. 'One last matter before I go. There are rumours the king has proposed marriage to Mrs Simpson.'

Baldwin's face contorted into a deep and well-practised frown. 'How can he propose marriage to a Mrs Anybody, be it Mrs Smith, Jones, or for that matter, Simpson? The last time I looked, bigamy was illegal in this country.'

Divorce proceedings between Mr and Mrs Simpson have been brought at Ipswich Assizes. That means she'll be free to marry the king upon receipt of a decree absolute.'

Baldwin's face darkened. 'Oh, blast it all, when does he return from his Mediterranean tryst?'

'Tomorrow,' said Chamberlain resignedly.

That next day David travelled from Fort Belvedere to visit his mother at Marlborough House. Ever since his proposal to Wallis he had been dreading this meeting. There had been no announcement of their marriage because that would be out of the question until after Wallis had obtained a divorce, but in spite of this, rumours had begun to circulate. Although the British papers had exercised a self-imposed censorship on any mention of the matter, David knew his mother would have already heard all there was to know. The information could have been learnt in a variety of ways, but he suspected it was more likely as not the intelligence would have been relayed through his own loose talk to friends and acquaintances. His royal court leaked like a sieve, but he didn't care. He thought it better to have his mother softened up, her hard earth made friable by rumours. Better that than arriving as the bearer of unforeseen and unwelcome tidings, the seeds of his enthusiasm falling on stony and unbroken ground.

While being driven through the grey streets of Hammersmith, David's contemplation of his impending confrontation with his mother was halted abruptly by the sight of something he'd not noticed before. 'Michael,' he said to his chauffeur, 'slow down a bit. There's something up ahead that looks rather odd.'

David stared out his window as the Rolls Royce approached Queen Caroline Street. 'Michael, have you any idea what that's all about?'

David's chauffeur was a Londoner of Irish descent, and had been with David since serving as his valet during the war. As with Watson, his butler, David trusted completely Michael's loyalty and discretion. 'It's to do with Saint Paul's,' he answered. 'That's the church across the road there. They run the place. It's open every day of the week—even Sundays.'

David rolled down his window to take a closer look. A long line of pale, thin people extended down the sidewalk, their worn boots scraping on the cold pavement as they slowly shuffled forward. David quickly rewound the window.

After passing King Street Michael sped up and soon the car was turning off the High Street to Kensington Palace. There they collected Georgie. The Duke of Kent was the youngest of David's surviving brothers and a close adviser. Unlike stammering Albert, the Duke of York, or quietly boozing Henry, the Duke of Gloucester—whom David liked to call 'The Unknown Soldier'—Georgie was handsome, athletic and articulate. He climbed into the back of the car. 'Whatever is the problem?' he asked after observing the gloomy expression on David's face.

'I've just seen a soup kitchen. It's opened on Great West Road. You should have seen the length of the queue. Hundreds of people without work.'

Georgie nodded. 'The papers have taken to calling it the Great Depression.'

'It's appalling,' said David, working his fingers into his forehead, trying to rub out the knots. 'Something must be done.'

The young king forced himself to smile as he and Georgie entered their mother's drawing room. They each gave Queen Mary a kiss on the cheek, then headed for the drinks' table. Georgie poured a scotch for David and himself. 'Anything for you Mama?' he asked with a sunny smile.

'No, nothing, Georgie.'

'Not even a teeny-weeny pink gin?'

Mary brushed an imaginary piece of lint from the arm of her chair. 'Please, hurry up and be seated.' Her sons settled down on the sofa. She put on her glasses and squinted at David. 'You have a sunburn from your cruise!'

David snuck Georgie a quick glance and rolled his eyes. 'It's called a tan, Mama.'

'Coco Chanel has made it all the rage,' added Georgie, coming to his brother's defence.

'It makes you look like a farm labourer,' she sneered, 'a common man, lacking the cares and obligations of a king.' The old queen looked upwards as if God were listening in the attic. 'You have failed to attend to your royal duties, preferring instead to loll about in the Mediterranean.'

David stopped smiling and withdrew his cigarette case from his jacket.

'I wish you wouldn't; they killed your father.'

David took no notice of his mother's advice and lit up. 'During the cruise I attended official engagements, representing British interests in both Greece and Turkey.'

'Yes, indeed you did, and in the company of Mrs Simpson. *Mrs* Simpson!'

'She is the love of my life.'

'As were all the other married women with whom you have been associated.'

'That's not true.'

'David, I have been informed you have made a proposal of marriage to Mrs Simpson. Can you confirm that?'

'Yes, I can,' he replied without hesitation. 'I arranged this meeting to inform you of my plans, and in the hope we might receive your blessing.'

'My blessing?' The old queen snorted in the midst of sudden fit of coughing, not sure whether she was more horrified by the naivety or the temerity of her son's request.

David's gaze sank to the floor in disappointment. He had suspected this would be the Queen's reaction. She was a remote figure of authority. No closer to him than a strict and unsympathetic school master. 'Yes, if we might obtain your blessing,' he whispered, secretly harbouring the uncharitable wish that his mother was already lying beside his father in his crypt; he would never be his own man until his mother was dead.

Mary could see her son's loathing for her. The emotion flowed both ways; she had never really felt affection for her son. During their growing years the Queen rarely saw her children more than once a day. Her instructions were precise: as with all his siblings, his nanny was to present him to his mother at six o'clock each evening. At such times she would look him over, make any criticisms she felt necessary and then have him dismissed. Now the boy had grown up and grown out of control, her restraining chains cut loose. She sighed and looked longingly at her needlepoint and the escape it offered from the outside world that again entrapped her. 'You must put the past behind you,' she stated matter-of-factly. 'Soon you will be crowned king, your head anointed with holy oil—'

Georgie got the giggles. 'Oh, really, Mummy, holy oil?'

Mary carried on regardless, 'and created Defender of the Faith, head of the Church of England. Mrs Simpson will be a twice-divorced woman. Divorce is against the teachings of the Anglican Church. You cannot—must not—marry her; she is unsuitable.'

David put down his drink. 'If you might talk to Wallis, just the two of you, in private, I'm sure you would realize your fears are unfounded.'

'No, I do not agree with divorce. A vow made before God

cannot be unmade. I have no wish to see her. I will never agree to see her.'

'And what of my marriage proposal to Wallis?'

'The Church would never allow it.'

David took a deep drag on his cigarette. 'I need Wallis.'

Mary pushed her head back into the depths of her armchair and lifted her nose in the air. 'You need to do your duty.'

Sir George Downing was a soldier of fortune and a notorious spy employed by both Charles the First and his mortal enemy, Oliver Cromwell. In 1684 he built a row of townhouses for 'persons of good quality' on a street that came to bear his name. Forty-five years later, the house at number ten was purchased by King George II. He gave it to William Walpole as his official residence for the duration of his incumbency as prime minister and first lord of the treasury. Following Walpole's retirement, it passed on to succeeding prime ministers; however, very few ever actually lived there. Most were wealthy and owned more substantial London homes, seeing Number 10 Downing Street as a perk of the job and subletting it to friends and colleagues.

Built on loose landfill where once a stream had flowed, Number 10's structure was inherently unstable, its foundations well above the bedrock and prone to sinkage. It had been necessary to refurbish the building several times, raising the footings and plastering over the cracks. This work had been ongoing for the preceding three centuries, but the original façade remained; the bricks, once yellow, stained burnt umber by years of pollution.

Behind Number 10 was a courtyard. To the west of the yard, and at right angles to the front building was 'The House at the Back'. On its upper floor, connected to Number 10 by Treasury Passage, was the Cabinet Room. Over the years, the walls of this modestly proportioned chamber had borne witness to many dark moments: ruthless greed and ambition, cynicism and cruelty, plotting and betrayal. Around its table, men in powdered wigs or bushy beards had fought to defend child labour, limited suffrage, slavery and the lash. Here, a mighty empire had been built and partly lost, the departure of the American colonies, a wound still weeping, the hatchet from the revolutionary war still waiting to be fully buried. Today, another layer, dark as the carbon on the outside bricks, was added to the room's stale breath of intrigue.

Stanley Baldwin glowered at the members of his Cabinet. 'The implications implicit in his proposal to Mrs Simpson are immense. Their marriage could undermine the broader public morality and the constitutional integrity of the nation.'

Around the Cabinet table sat other men who like their leader had scrabbled to high office; for their efforts, enjoying the reward of privilege and power that a ministry of the crown bestowed. Along with Baldwin and Neville Chamberlain, the senior members of His Majesty's Government included the handsome, ill-tempered and possibly illegitimate son of a baronet, the Foreign Secretary, Anthony Eden; the energetic but widely disliked Secretary of State for War, Leslie Hore-Belisha; the barrister and son of a puritan minister, the Home Secretary, Sir John Simon; and the Lord Privy Seal, Lord

Halifax, an ardent right winger, born with no left hand. All were unusually quiet, sensing they would be in for a bumpy ride. There had still not been any engagement announcement from the Palace, but Wallis's divorce application presaged the possibility, and the rumours floating around the royal court and Westminster left little room for doubt as to the king's marriage intentions. Halifax subconsciously demonstrated the dexterity of his single hand by twirling his fountain pen around his fingers. 'I disagree, Prime Minister,' he countered. 'The king is very popular. I believe he would carry the people with him.'

'But at what cost?' asked Eden. 'He already has strong views on his right to intervene in matters of state—welfare issues, unemployment and the like. If we allow this marriage he will see it as a victory. He would become yet more adventurous, more demanding.'

Eden turned to Baldwin who took the baton. 'Thank you, Anthony, well said. The king presents the government with multiple threats of which his marriage plans are just one part. I don't mind telling you, gentlemen, that on top of the fact that Mrs Simpson is not only divorced once and married twice, she is also in possession of a reputation that is quite notorious. The woman has, for many years, flaunted a decadent love life, indulging in a cavalcade of torrid affairs, not caring a tinker's cuss as to whom she may offend. I have even been reliably informed that she is sent seventeen roses every day by no less a personage than His Excellency, Joachim von Ribbentrop; one rose for each of their sexual encounters. To say this is outrageous is to put it mildly.'

'Dear God,' muttered Chamberlain, 'has this woman no sense of decency?'

Baldwin grasped the lapels of his jacket. 'I'm afraid, Neville, that it would seem not. If the public at large were to learn of her licentious cavorting, the outrage would be such as to threaten the very existence of the crown. With such a woman as consort to the king we would be condemned to return to the darkest days of the regency. I'm sure that given time for reflection, all of you around this great table will find yourselves agreeing with my view that we must nip this marriage business in the bud. We must be rid of Wallis Simpson.'

David perused the letter on his desk. Its content seemed to him particularly pessimistic. He looked up at his guests who sat on the other side of his desk. 'Would either of you care for a coffee?' he inquired.

'No thank you, Sir,' said the younger of the two men.

'Perhaps something stronger,' said David, pointing to the drinks table.

Both men shook their heads. The king turned to the older man. 'Walter, your letter provides interesting reading. I thought it might be a good idea to see you in person, so thank you for dropping in.'

Walter Moncton rubbed his hands together. 'It's a pleasure, Sir. It's good to see you again and I think vitally important that we go over, in person, the details of my advice.'

'Good,' said David, 'I've never been much at translating all this legal jargon.'

Moncton's lower lip pushed up defensively, almost touching the tip of his hawk nose as he involuntarily emitted a deep grunt. David quickly backed away. 'Not that I'm suggesting anything obfuscatory in the language of the law, you understand?'

Moncton's lip relaxed and stretched into a wry smile as he defended his profession with a deft reply. 'I understand perfectly, Sir, but with respect, articulation and economy of expression can be awkward bedfellows.'

'Yes, I understand. I'm sorry, I did not mean to sound abrasive,' said David, embarrassed he may have unwittingly revealed the level of his concern. He had been worried ever since his torturous meeting with his mother. It was only after departing Marlborough House that David realised the true nature of the resistance his marriage plans might instigate. He had discussed the matter with Georgie and they had agreed it would be a good idea to be forearmed with solid legal advice as soon as practicable. David contacted Walter Moncton. He was a well-respected barrister and a highly decorated veteran of the Great War who was running a large and lucrative legal practice. Several years earlier, he was approached by David to become his legal adviser. The two men had been friends at Oxford University, and since that time, Moncton had become a trusted aide.

'Walter,' David continued, indicating the lawyer's letter, 'do you really think matters could get so bad as to warrant this action?'

'Yes, Sir, I'm afraid they may well do. It is incumbent upon me to warn you that the Church's case is very strong.

Wars have been fought over less. Under the Act of Succession and possibly the Bill of Rights, or even Magna Carta, the Government has powers to dictate your choice of queen; powers based in legal precedents set by the courts, and in particular, laws created in pursuance of parliament's removal of James the Second. These powers were enacted due to fears regarding the possible political and religious persuasions of his successors as kings or queens of England and Scotland, and the threat that the Pope or any so-called papist country might pose to British sovereignty, both here and abroad.' Moncton paused to catch his breath.

David leaned back in his chair. 'So this was all brought about because James the Second converted to Catholicism?'

Moncton knew he would now have to wait for his client to vent his frustration with the arcane ways of the law. 'In essence, yes,' he concurred, hoping David wouldn't come out with a trite response about the law being an ass; always an insult to those who practised it, and an affront only made tolerable by the extra time it added to the ever-ticking meter. Moncton's general rule of thumb was, the deeper his client's pockets, the longer he'd allow them to rant at their wallet's expense.

Unaware of his lawyer's rumination, David shook his head and continued unabated. 'Bloody James Stuart! Embracing the Church of Rome didn't stop him from dying of syphilis or losing the western half of New York to the governor of Jersey in a poker game, but it prevents me from marrying the woman that I love.'

'Yes,' Moncton said firmly.

'But that is the thing,' protested David. 'Wallis isn't Catholic.'

'No,' agreed Moncton, 'but she is divorced.'

'And that amounts to the same thing?' David asked, brow raised in amazement.

Moncton's earlier self-assurance waned and his expression grew overcast; he feared the king might shoot the messenger. 'With respect, Sir, I cannot say how events would play out. From the time parliament took unto itself the right to dictate who could or could not be sovereign there has been a crack in the levee controlling the river of the succession. Once created, such a crack can easily be widened. If the parliament feels the law has grown inadequate, that law can always be augmented by parliament to the parliament's satisfaction—if you take my point. I also feel compelled to warn you with a respectful reminder that no English king has ever married a divorcee or has ever been himself divorced.'

David leaned forward. 'I cannot believe my ears. If memory serves me well, Henry the Eighth was divorced twice!'

Moncton braced himself and calmly corrected his client. 'That is unfortunately not correct,' he said. 'Henry's marriages were annulled.'

'All right then,' agreed David. 'Then if Henry could split hairs why can't I?'

Moncton straightened up, confident now in his argument. 'Your powers have been constrained by the passage of time and events. You could no more cause her marriages to be annulled than order her husbands, Spencer and Simpson, beheaded. You well know you haven't your ancestor's powers.

They have, rightly or wrongly, been taken by parliament. Your Majesty's government could well force you to abdicate, and failing that, certainly has the power to depose you.'

David scratched his head, perplexed. 'It seems odd that my actions might be controlled by decisions made such a very long time ago.'

'The law has a very long memory,' replied Moncton. 'But I grant you, there are matters of more immediate concern. Mrs Simpson's divorce to her first husband, Earl Spencer, was granted in America on the grounds of emotional incompatibility—under English law that would not be recognised. Here, the only ground for divorce is adultery. Her American divorce could be challenged in our courts. Her marriage to Ernest Simpson and therefore any subsequent marriages could be ruled as invalid on the grounds that they are bigamous.'

'I think I need a drink,' David rose and carried to his desk the whisky decanter.

'Nevertheless,' Moncton leisurely observed, 'the law is anything if not malleable when great powers are locked in dispute—'

'Sir,' the younger man interrupted. 'Walter has found a loophole—a possible solution to the problem.' Peregrine Cust, Lord Brownlow, David's lord-in-waiting, had thus far looked on in silence, but now, seeing the moment as apt to upstage Moncton, was quick to be the first to mention the most positive aspect of the lawyer's advice.

'Ah, excellent,' said David, his confidence returned. 'Where there is faith, there is hope.' He poured himself a drink.

'Are you both sure you wouldn't care to join me in a tipple?'

'Actually, I wouldn't mind,' said Peregrine, jumping up and grabbing a glass; he and the king often shared a drink together.

David poured another scotch as he glanced back to Moncton. 'Walter, are you sure I cannot twist your arm?'

'I'm certain,' said Moncton, ever business like, and annoyed by Peregrine's intrusion. 'It will, no doubt, come as no surprise to you, Sir, that other royals have found themselves in predicaments similar to your own. My research has revealed a number of cases concerning European royal houses that could serve as precedents in support of our case.'

David sat down and sipped his scotch. 'Walter, before we go into the legal detail, I have to tell you that the government would be very brave to take me on. This, in the end, must surely be considered by the people of this country as paltry, and obviously a private matter for their sovereign.'

'Not so,' said Moncton. 'You are the people's voice, the physical embodiment of the nation. The British are intensely conservative when it comes to the bedchamber and divorce is, therefore, inevitably—if not lasciviously—seen as a major source of concern. Wallis will be thought of as a fallen woman, not worthy of their king and therefore not worthy of them.'

'My God,' muttered David. He threw back his drink and poured another.

Moncton rushed forward to his point, fearing its power may be lost on the king due to the rapid onset of inebriation. 'Whereas the matter might be seen in black and white terms by the people,' he said quickly, 'the law may see a shade of grey.'

'And your precedent suggests such a shade,' said David, lifting the letter of legal advice.

'Perhaps,' Moncton advised, 'this dispute with the government and the Church of England over their acceptance of Wallis as queen could be mitigated by my proposed legal mechanism.'

'A morganatic union?'

'Yes, Sir,' Peregrine interrupted again. 'This was successfully employed by your own great-grandfather, Duke Alexander of Wurttemburg.'

Moncton regarded the young man with barely disguised contempt before continuing his argument. 'In a morganatic union, Wallis Simpson would be your wife, but not your queen.'

'Oh dear, how tedious, embarrassing, humiliating,' David sighed as he placed Moncton's letter into a manila folder. 'I thank you for your thoroughness, Walter. I'm sure that as learned as your advice may be, it is advice that I take with little pleasure. It is also advice that I would only accept as a last measure when all other avenues have failed.'

'I understand your reluctance,' nodded Moncton.

'Good,' said David. 'This compromise must remain absolutely confidential. I have no wish to mention it to the government or the Church at this early juncture. It might be misconstrued as panicking. Right now, Baldwin and his cronies are more afraid of me than I of them, and that is a situation I should like to maintain.'

'With respect, Sir,' said Moncton. 'I understand your point

of view, and would therefore advise that you keep the option up your sleeve in case or until it becomes necessary to use it.'

The meeting had ended on that note, but as time wore on, Moncton's words echoed more and more loudly in David's ears. Days were soon passing into weeks and Baldwin was proving increasingly obstinate. No matter what he did or said, the prime minister refused to budge. This challenge, if anything, made David even more determined to marry Wallis, but he now felt that if forced into a corner he might have to accept Walter and Peregrine's advice. However, Wallis would have to agree. By the end of September David realised the time was fast approaching when he would have no choice but to broach the matter with her. He picked a sunny afternoon.

David was still living at Fort Belvidere and did not plan to move to Buckingham Palace until after his coronation. It was while walking with Wallis in the fort's wooded grounds, taking in the bracing autumn air, admiring the season's many shades of red, yellow and copper that he finally decided to speak. 'Damn the Church of England!' He picked up a pebble and hurled it into the lake.

Wallis had been watching with equal concern the standoff with Baldwin. 'Boysie,' she said softly, 'I don't want to see you hurt. We don't need to marry. I'm happy just to be with you.'

'Really? You don't want to become Her Majesty the Queen?'

Wallis cocked her head whimsically. 'Hmm, when you put it that way.' She paused, kissed David and continued, 'But I can live without it.'

'Alright,' he said cautiously, 'have you ever heard of morganatic marriage?'

Wallis stepped away and pouted. 'You're going to get me to a nunnery?'

David ran his tongue along the inside of his cheek. 'We don't do that anymore.'

Wallis picked up a pebble of her own, small and flat. 'That's a comfort,' she said as she bent sideways, and like David, threw it across the lake; it skipped over the ripples of water like a fawn in flight.

David was impressed. 'Very good,' he observed, and picking up another pebble, added: 'Morganatic means a compromise—we marry and you become Duchess of Lancaster, but not my queen.'

Wallis frowned before murmuring: 'Duchess of Lancaster—lucky Lancastrians.'

'Yes, Her Grace the Duchess of Lancaster, Countess Merioneth and Baroness of Greenwich.' David threw his second pebble over the water, seeking to emulate Wallis's trick. It went plop, his attempt unsuccessful. 'Hmm,' he sighed, 'it seems my rock has sunk like a stone.'

A London bobby stood at his usual position by Number 10's modest front door. His face remained stern as he endured the humiliation of having his photograph taken by a group of giggling schoolgirls. Inside, in the Cabinet Room, there was no such mirth; a discreet meeting was taking place between Baldwin, Chamberlain, Anthony Eden and the press baron, Lord Beaverbrook.

Eden stared at a pile of foreign newspapers. They all featured stories covering the romance between Wallis and David. 'This damned business is all over the international press. People are talking, rumours are rife.' He turned to Beaverbrook. 'Is it only a matter of time before the British papers run with the story?'

Baron Beaverbrook was a Canadian who had started life in Maple, Ontario as Max Aitken. By dint of hard work, good luck and utter ruthlessness he had built a newspaper publishing empire. As a former minister for information he also had been responsible for government propaganda in the final year of the Great War. Beaverbrook smoothed down what remained of the hair on his shiny head.

'Anthony, to date, I've managed to persuade my press colleagues to stay silent, but they won't keep a lid on this forever. It's only a matter of time till—'

'Till what?' interrupted Baldwin, his face flushed with mounting anger.

'Until a comment on the crisis is made by a person of note, someone important. Once that happens, the blood will be in the water. The Fleet Street sharks will go into a feeding frenzy.'

'Oh, my God, scandal,' whispered Chamberlain.

The government didn't have to wait long for the scandal to break. On the following Sunday, two hundred miles to the north, Alfred Blunt, Bishop of Bradford, listened to hymn number 122: 'Where Can I Turn for Peace'.

As the congregation laboured through the final bars of the

hymn, Blunt solemnly ascended the spiral staircase to the pulpit.

The congregation sat back down in their pews. In a silence broken only by an occasional cough, Blunt opened a massive bible to where he had placed the notes for his sermon. He spoke in the quavering voice of the ecstatic.

'The benefit of the king's coronation depends upon the faith and prayers of the king himself. To commend him to God's grace, he needs to do his duty faithfully.'

The congregation muttered to one another, confused by the bishop's message.

Blunt lowered his voice and looked sternly from over his glasses. 'We hope that the king is aware of this need. Some of us wish that he would give more signs of that awareness.'

This was all the excuse that was needed. On the Monday the barkers were holding aloft the morning news, crying out: 'Hear all about it—king in world's greatest romance!'

On the buses and the trains the people of Britain buried their scowling faces in their different papers. The headlines were worded to attract their divergent readerships but they all screamed the same story: 'FATE OF THE EMPIRE IN HANDS OF MRS SIMPSON', 'KING TO MARRY MRS SIMPSON', 'AN AMERICAN QUEEN', 'MONARCHY IN CRISIS'.

Winston Churchill lay in bed, head propped up by a pile of pillows, absentmindedly stroking his overweight cat and puffing on a fat cigar. He tossed aside the last of the morning papers, all of which he had read with mounting despair.

Churchill was over sixty years old. In the far off past he had been referred to as a young man in a hurry, but his rapid early rise to fame had been gradually weighed down to a dead stop.

He started his working life in 1895 by graduating, a cornet, from Sandhurst. While still a young cavalry officer, he soon augmented his military pay with lucrative work as a war correspondent. This led him to seek out and find those places where he was most likely to see action. He was a veteran of campaigns in Afghanistan, Sudan and the Boer War. During the relief of Khartoum he had taken part in one of the last significant cavalry charges in the history of the British army, and in South Africa he had come close to winning the Victoria Cross for his actions in defending an armoured train that had been ambushed by Boer guerrillas. During this skirmish he was captured, but later made a bold escape, travelling 300 miles to Delagoa Bay in the Portuguese colony of Mozambique. Press reports of his adventure made him a celebrity. Upon his return to Britain, he successfully ran for the House of Commons, winning for the Conservative Party the seat of Oldham. Four years later he crossed the floor, joined the Liberals and entered the ministry, becoming in turn President of the Board of Trade, Home Secretary, First Lord of the Admiralty, Minister of Munitions, Secretary of State for War and then for Air and then the Colonies. In 1924 he left the Liberals and rejoined the Conservative Party, becoming Chancellor of the Exchequer in the first Baldwin ministry. He had won and lost the parliamentary constituencies, not only of Oldham, but also Manchester North West and Dundee. Now he was the member for Epping, just outside London, in rural Essex.

His had been a chequered career of ups and downs. As it is with men of ambition, he had made many good friends, but also a host of great enemies. Counted among these were several members of Cabinet who believed him to be headstrong and untrustworthy. Following the Conservative defeat of 1929 he was denied a shadow portfolio. When his party returned to power in coalition with Labour he was again ignored and relegated to the backbench.

Now it was frosty morning and he was a rank outsider with little influence on the affairs of state. Frustrated by his fate and dispossessed of his usual energy, he got up, put on his robe and wandered out onto the roof terrace. His flat, which he had purchased from the Liberal leader and former prime minister, David Lloyd George, was in a building called Morpeth Mansions; it was just a short walk to Victoria Station and handy to the Palace of Westminster. On the balcony, six floors above the street, Churchill could enjoy an excellent view of southwest London. Gazing out over the rooftops, he breathed deep and once again took inspiration from the sight of Westminster and the clock tower that housed Big Ben. It was a tonic.

From within his flat he heard the doorbell ring, it was answered by his butler, Inches. A moment later Churchill was joined, still out on the balcony, by an old friend, Brian Gorton. The men had known each other for twenty years, having first met in the army on the Western Front. Soft featured and disarmingly mild mannered, Gorton's outward appearance disguised an unbreakable will and unerring patriotism. He had been an artillery officer until he was shot in the heart at the Battle of Arras. After making a remarkable recovery from his injury, he returned to the army, serving as aide de camp to Field Marshal Sir Douglas Haig. Since then he had been drawn into intelligence work, eventually becoming head of the Industrial Intelligence Centre of the Committee of Imperial Defence. He still carried the bullet in his heart, but this didn't prevent him from enjoying a drink, doing so often and mostly with his old comrade, Churchill.

'So, Brian, your agents have an ear to the ground. What's the word from the Whitehall insiders?'

'Winston, they don't like her. She's considered a hussy.'

Churchill turned back to his view of the tower of Big Ben. A finger of lemon sunlight broke through the heavy clouds. It illuminated the tower's clock face, the hour and minutes radiating from the city's grey skyline.

Night had fallen on Fort Belvedere and despite the fire that crackled in the library's fireplace the atmosphere was pierced by an icy tension. Stanley Baldwin had just arrived and had refused the offer of a warming brandy. Sitting uncomfortably on an upright, armless chair, the prime minister faced his king and announced without preamble: 'The people are opposed to your marrying Mrs. Simpson. If you did so, it would be against the advice of your government. I'm afraid we would be left with no other choice but to resign en masse.'

David appraised his prime minister from behind the polished expanse of his desk. To his right sat Peregrine Cust, to his left, Walter Moncton. This was a vitally important meeting with constitutional ramifications. David made a point of having his key legal advisers on hand for he didn't trust Baldwin or his ability to interpret correctly the finer points of the proposition he was about to present. The king lit a cigarette and blew a perfectly formed smoke ring. 'Resign en masse?' he inquired. 'My dear Mr Baldwin, is that a threat?'

Baldwin squirmed and couldn't bring himself to answer one way or another. David leaned back in his amply upholstered chair and continued. 'I intend to marry Mrs Simpson as soon as she is free to marry me. If the government is opposed to our marriage then I'm prepared to go.'

Baldwin's jaw dropped. 'Sir, are you suggesting you'd rather abdicate?'

'Yes, I would,' he sighed, twirling his cigarette case on his desk mat.

'You must forgive me, Sir,' Baldwin spluttered, 'but I'm truly at a loss for words.'

'Unusual for a politician.' David's eyes homed in on the prime minister. 'Especially one of your pre-eminence.'

Baldwin coughed and cleared his throat. 'Sir, with the deepest respect, you fail to comprehend the gravity of the situation—no British monarch has ever abdicated of their own free will.'

David could sense the nervous sweat percolating in Baldwin's armpits. 'I am aware of the proclivities of my ancestors,' he smiled, 'after all, they're family.'

The prime minister was a deep-purple plum, bursting with ripeness and ready for plucking.

David leaned his head to one side and considered:

'Perhaps there is a solution to our predicament.'

Baldwin ran his finger under his starched collar. 'Yes?'

David tapped his cigarette on the side of his silver ashtray. 'Prime Minister, there are three options that you can take to Cabinet: one, that I abdicate; two, that I marry and Wallis becomes queen; or three, that we marry and she not become queen; that is to say, a morganatic marriage.'

Baldwin's cockscomb eyebrows quivered, betraying his scepticism. 'Morganatic? Is Mrs Simpson accepting of such a proposal?'

'Yes, she is.'

It had been a fine performance but behind the edifice of a serene Britannic majesty, David's heart had been racing. 'Do you think we have him?' he asked Walter, following the prime minister's departure.

'Hard to say, Sir, he's a wily piece of work. You don't get to his position on beauty alone.'

Peregrine laughed. 'If poor Stanley had ever been dependent on his looks he'd still be an iron monger in Worcestershire.'

The king didn't see the humour in his counsellors' banter. David stared at the smoke, rising in lazy spirals from his cigarette. He was worried and well knew that Baldwin's temper was as hot as the iron that his family forged. Baldwin would have to be handled as if with a blacksmith's tongs, perhaps with the hammer as well.

A day had passed, then two and then three. Now a week had gone by, and David had still heard nothing. There had been no response: spoken, written or implied from the government to his proposal, just silence. That night David walked into the bedroom to see Wallis at her dressing table, packing her jewellery. He had to step aside to allow the footmen room to exit with her suitcases. 'This is madness.'

'No, it's smart,' she shot back. 'We need the government to be more flexible, but my being here is a red rag to a bull.'

David stepped into the room. Piles of clothing and half-filled cases cluttered the floor and bed. 'Those ruffians were caught and arrested, you do realise?'

'Yes, I know.' Wallis snapped shut a box of diamond earrings and placed them into a portable strongbox. 'But please don't press charges. Goodness knows people dislike me enough already without my being seen as vengeful.'

'But, Darling, they threw rocks at your car.'

'So what? I don't care!'

'Alright,' David agreed, alarmed by Wallis's show of temper. 'I'll ask that they be released without charge.'

She pressed her head into her hands, embarrassed by her loss of control. 'Thank you,' she whispered before returning to her packing.

David moved behind her and looked at the reflection of her eyes in the mirror. 'I don't want you to go to Paris.'

'Boysie, it's only for a while. Sometimes to win you have to make sacrifices.'

'I can't live without you.'

Wallis stood up and took David in her arms. 'Nor I without you, so just remember, all things come to those who wait.' She kissed him softly, sat down and returned to her packing.

He leaned against the back of her chair. 'This is all the prime minister's doing.'

'Yes,' she agreed, 'Baldwin, wants you to dance to his tune.'

'Do you think he'll ever accept a compromise?'

'I don't know, but he's hardly going to make you abdicate.'

David suddenly felt unsteady on his feet. He walked across the room and flopped down in an armchair, despondent. He knew Wallis was right, but he hated it all the same. Walter and the other lawyers were the first to suggest that it would be a good idea for her to sit out the crisis in France. David had rejected the advice outright but Wallis said she would think about it. Now, with her car attacked by demonstrators, abusive graffiti appearing on tube station walls and scores of other threats, written and spoken, she had decided to go.

'How long will it be before I see you again?' he asked forlornly.

Wallis swivelled around, saw David's face and read his mind. She got up again and knelt down beside him. 'I'm not taking this move lightly. I'm leaving the country because I have to for both our sakes. It's the right thing to do. Deep down you know that.'

Two days later a cab drew up outside Number 10 Downing Street and Winston Churchill emerged. He had been trying for days to see the prime minister, but his face showed no indication of annoyance. He waved and bid good morning to the police constable on duty at the entrance, and was immediately recognised.

'Good morning, Sir,' said the bobby as the former minister entered the building.

'Season's greetings,' Churchill replied, seeming to be cheery. The Christmas wreath, hanging beneath the brass knocker, wobbled as the door closed behind him.

Churchill crossed the chequered floor tiles of the entrance hall and continued through the inner door to the staircase that led up to Treasury Passage. A moment later he was looking out the Cabinet windows, observing the office workers going every which way across St. James Park. He turned to face Baldwin, Chamberlain and Horace Wilson.

'The king and I are old friends,' he began, gazing solemnly across the all too familiar table, 'and I have known Mrs Simpson from the time she first arrived from America some five years ago. In that period I have seen that when the king is with her he is a changed man, he delights in her company. Their relationship has been branded as a guilty love but I see it as most natural, completely free from impropriety or grossness.'

Baldwin glowered. 'Winston, do you mean to say that you approve of the king marrying a divorced woman?'

Churchill remained unruffled. 'I do not, but there's no reason why they should not continue to see each other outside marriage.'

'I agree,' said Baldwin, 'but he is intent on marrying. Although he mentioned that this arrangement might be, hmm—'

'Morganatic?' asked Churchill helpfully.

'Yes, that's it, morganatic. He dragged me out to Windsor to bully me with it, but I shan't be bullied. Morganatic! Such a move would be unprecedented in Britain, and frankly, very awkward. I have talked to the Dominions and the Cabinet and all agree that they will have nothing to do with such messiness. If he insists on marriage he must abdicate and he must do so at once.'

Taken aback, Churchill protested: 'There's no need to act with such haste.'

Chamberlain entered the conversation in support of Baldwin. 'This business must be finished before Christmas.'

Churchill continued to remonstrate. 'If he could be given time to weigh the whole matter, I am sure that he would come around to our thinking?'

Chamberlain remained unmoved. 'This continued uncertainty must be put to an end. As Chancellor of the Exchequer I can assure you that it is hurting the Christmas trade.'

Churchill slipped a cigar from his breast pocket. 'My dear Neville, it is with heavy heart that I acknowledge the risk that this year Father Christmas may prove less generous.'

The Chancellor snorted. Churchill lit his cigar and puffed thoughtfully for a moment before turning to Baldwin. 'Allow me time to talk with the king.'

Baldwin's mood had not improved and he was of no mind to be conciliatory. 'Cabinet meets tomorrow morning. We must have a final decision by then.'

That night, Churchill drove his Daimler out to Windsor. As he entered the hall at Fort Belvedere, he was filled with a deep sense of foreboding, but not for himself. It was a fear for his comrades around him. A fear he hadn't experienced since fighting in the trenches of Flanders. Georgie appeared at the top of the stairs and rushed down to greet him.

Churchill and the Duke of Kent had never been close; Georgie felt a pang of jealousy for how much his brother put in store by the word of the former Cabinet minister. Churchill and the king had both served on the Western Front. This was a boast that youth had denied to Georgie and it gnawed away deep in his bowels. But, right now, the duke could ill afford such self-indulgence.

'I'm so pleased that you're here,' he said, shaking Churchill's hand.

'Why, Georgie, what's the matter?'

'David isn't well. He's not himself at all. He's lost without Wallis. I fear he may do something rash.'

When the two men entered the library David was motoring steadily through a bottle of scotch. He paced the room, smoking feverishly and gulping his drink. 'They are not listening to reason,' he said, spitting out the words, 'not Baldwin, not the Cabinet, nobody. They won't have anything to do with any kind of compromise solution. Not even our proposal that Wallis be my wife but not my queen. They will do nothing to help us. I'm driven to the last extremity of endurance.'

Churchill took in every detail of what he was witnessing.

'They're impatient men,' he agreed.

David failed to acknowledge that his old friend had conceded his point. 'I mean Wallis's divorce doesn't even become absolute for another twelve months. Why must they rush me so?'

'Because they fear that prolonged uncertainty would weaken the crown irrevocably.'

'But surely a king must be given some period of grace?'

Churchill's face grimaced into that of a determined mastiff. 'The government demands an answer by the morning. You must promise to end any thought of marriage to Wallis or you must abdicate.'

David glared skyward. 'By the morning?'

Churchill knew the question to be rhetorical and remained firmly silent.

David drained his glass. 'I cannot live without the woman I love.'

'No man in the government is suggesting that you cannot see her,' said Churchill, alluding to the brighter side of a compromise.

David was having none of it. 'Oh, of course, so she must slink around in hiding, never to be noticed in public with me, never to be my wife, a faceless, nameless nothingness.'

'She would not be left with nothing,' Churchill protested.

'What would she have?'

'Your undying love; that should be enough.'

'Not enough for me.'

'But enough for her,' Churchill countered, becoming avuncular and moving in closer. 'If she loves you as much as you love her, she will understand. After all, you must bear the responsibilities of a king.'

'I've less power over my personal life than any of my subjects, what kind of a king is that?'

'A king who would give up the woman that he loved for the nation and the empire that he loved more.' Churchill threw out his chest in pride of what might be. 'A king who had sacrificed on the altar of duty his personal happiness for the happiness of his people.' He shook his finger and wished he had a lit cigar with which to gesticulate. 'We live in challenging times, and I fear that as your successor, your poor stammering brother, Prince Albert, would not be in any way equal to the task.'

David put down his empty glass. 'And what should I do?'

'Give the people the leadership they will sorely need. Galvanise the nation and they will reward you with their enduring support and—' Churchill paused before continuing more cautiously '—and the authority that you crave. Be a king in deed as well as in name.'

David ran his hands through his hair, thrown by Churchill's change of tack. He turned to his brother and asked: 'Georgie, what's your advice?'

The Duke, grateful to be suddenly part of the discussion, took up the argument with enthusiasm. 'We are in the midst of a depression. People are suffering. They need a champion.'

Churchill put his thumbs in his braces. 'If you are going through hell, keep going.'

David looked out the window, suddenly deep in thought. His silhouette could be seen from outside, the light behind him shining brightly, illuminating the gravel drive and Churchill's Daimler, parked several yards away.

'What would you do?' asked Alice.

Bessie lifted her eyes from the book. 'Me?' she asked, squinting as if woken from a dream.

Alice leaned forward. 'Yes, you.'

Bessie took a deep breath. 'I wouldn't submit to the church or the government, I'd fight.'

'How?'

'Wear them down. Play for time.'

Alice smiled like a person who'd just asked a riddle, relishing the fact that only she knew the answer. 'Play for time—it's interesting you should put it that way. Let's keep reading.' The two women returned to the old book.

David was still at the window, staring out at the drive and the dark woods that lay beyond. This was a turning point. The Baldwin government was forcing him to make a decision that was carved in stone, but there was no reason why he had to play by their rules. He was still the king. David looked away from the window and was confronted by the faces of Churchill and Georgie, their countenances frozen in expectation.

'Thank you, Winston,' he said. 'If I could have a moment with my brother, alone?'

Churchill looked across to Georgie, alarmed the king might really be choosing to abdicate. The duke responded with an expression of nervous puzzlement. Realising them both to be equally baffled, Churchill turned back to David, bowed his head ever so slightly and left without saying a word.

David waited until the door was closed and poured another drink. 'Georgie, I'll play for time.'

His brother's mood immediately lifted. 'Does that mean you won't marry Wallis?'

The king looked him in the eye and repeated his words, but this time with immensely greater resolve. 'It means I'll play for time.'

The next morning Baldwin rushed from Horace Wilson's office and into the Cabinet Room. Chamberlain, Eden and the other members of the ministry were already there. The prime minister caught his breath before sitting. The room was silent with expectation; they could even hear the distant sound of the traffic on The Mall.

'Gentlemen,' he announced, 'my apologies for being late. I've just been on the phone to the Palace.'

Eden grabbed the edge of the Cabinet table. 'And?'

'And it is with great pleasure that I can inform you that the king has decided to abandon any intention of marrying Mrs Wallis Simpson.'

The Cabinet ministers exhaled in relief. Chamberlain shouted 'Hear, hear,' as the room broke into applause.

The headlines that afternoon heralded the news: 'EMPIRE IN SAFE HANDS', 'MRS SIMPSON GONE', 'KING PUTS DUTY BEFORE LOVE', 'COURAGEOUS DECISION BY OUR KING'.

Commuters on the buses and the trains smiled as they read the story in their evening papers. Meanwhile, Churchill sat in his flat in Morpeth Mansions. On reading the news, he too smiled as he petted his overweight cat and puffed on his Cuban cigar.

Chapter Two, the Lady

It was winter, but Paris was beautiful any time of the year, and there was no better place to stay than the Hotel Ritz. Wallis's suite opened onto the Place Vendome, and was decorated in antique furnishings from the reign of Louis XVI, its walls panelled with gilded mouldings and draped in ornate tapestries. The décor of soft greens, salmon and pearl grey evinced a calming sense of patrician continuity and regal certainty. At any other time Wallis would have revelled in such luxury, sleekly gliding and purring amidst the satins and the silks, but this day it might as well have been a wretched garret. Wallis could think of nothing but her phone; it was the portal to the rest of her life and it sat silent, or at least when it rang, it failed to resonate with the only voice she wished to hear.

It had been over a week since she and David had last spoken. All Wallis knew about his decision was what she could glean from the papers and they gave no reason for optimism. Before her escape from Britain, David had arranged for her to be accompanied by Peregrine Cust. They had left for Paris by air, and during the flight Peregrine had taken it upon himself to draft a statement on her behalf indicating her readiness to give up the king. David and Wallis had often stayed at Peregrine's country estate, Belton House, but Wallis had never enjoyed the young man's company. People called her ambitious, but she considered her behaviour nothing in comparison to the Custs of this world. Wallis politely thanked him for his efforts and then ignored him.

Upon her arrival in Paris she had been hounded by a press pack. They had hovered in the Ritz's foyer until ordered out into the street by the hotel management. There the reporters and photographers huddled in the cold until David's announcement of his decision to abandon his marriage plans. Since then the story had run cold, cooling as fast as the season, the sidewalk quickly reclaimed by the city's bustling crowds of Christmas shoppers. Likewise, Peregrine had disappeared back to England, deserting her, but determined to remain within the king's inner court.

Wallis was lying fully dressed on top of her bed, staring at the ceiling, when the call finally came. Though taken by her maid, Wallis was there, grabbing the phone as quickly as decorum might allow.

'Allo, Madam Simpson?' inquired the operator.

'Oui,' she answered in her best Baltimore French.

A click came down the line and an English voice spoke. 'I have a Mr David Windsor on the line. Will you take the call?'

'Yes,' said Wallis and she waited.

'Hello. Hello, Wallis? Wallis, are you there?'

'Hello, David,' she replied, her tone distant.

David was phoning from his library desk at Fort Belvedere. 'I assume you've heard the news.'

'I've read about it.'

He noted the hurt in Wallis's voice. 'Darling, I'm sorry,

news travels so fast and I must admit I've found it difficult to make this phone call.' He hunched over his phone as if that might draw them nearer. 'Wallis, it doesn't matter what you might see or hear or read. Just remember, I still love you.'

'David...' Wallis paused to wipe away a tear, any hint of irritation exhausted. 'Boysie, you've done your duty. That's what matters.'

Though many miles away, he could sense that he had been forgiven. 'You've always been so… so very…' He struggled to speak. 'Your being so understanding only makes me love you more. I don't know how I'll get by without you.'

'What?' asked Wallis, at once more fearful than at any time before.

David cleared his throat, knowing that he had now reached a critical juncture. Everything hung on Wallis's reaction. 'I need you to stay in France. Could you postpone your return?'

'Till when?' she asked reflexively.

'I'm required to stay in Britain and not be seen abroad until things have settled down. It's also thought best that you not return until after your divorce is absolute.'

'I see,' said Wallis, though she didn't really. There was a dull ache in her heart as David raced to argue his case before she had time to think.

'Look, you're in Paris,' he said, 'so much more fun than dreary old London. Take this chance to enjoy all the gaiety of the place. I shall, of course, continue to cover all your expenses.' David stopped, knowing full well that wasn't the point. He moved forward with a new angle and said, 'Wallis, be assured the fight is not finished; this is just a truce. I will marry you. Do you hear me? I will marry you. I just need to hold off Baldwin for a short while yet. It's like you said, all things come to those who wait. Just a little time and I promise we will have it all.'

Wallis carried her phone to the couch and flopped down. 'David, please, let it be.'

'No,' he said, 'I won't be satisfied with second best. I love you more than life itself and I will marry you, and you will be queen, the queen of Britain and the empire. We fight this till we win.'

It was the dead of winter. Snow fell on Sandringham House as the Royal Family gathered in the main dining room. The chamber was lined in Spanish tapestries, the flames that danced in the fireplace reflected in the collection of fine porcelain that adorned the surrounding shelves. A team of liveried footmen served a meal of several courses. There had already been a clear and a thick soup, oxtail bouillon and shellfish bisque. This had been followed by an entrée of lemon sole and now a main course of roast goose with dumplings and apple stuffing.

Illuminated by candelabras, David sat at the head of the table, Queen Mary, in regal splendour at the other end. To David's right sat Elizabeth, Duchess of York. To her right sat her husband, the eldest of David's brothers and first in line to the throne, the Duke of York. Called Bertie by the family, the duke had been a sickly child, but despite suffering from bleeding stomach ulcers and a profound stammer, he managed to serve in both the Royal Navy and the nascent Royal Air Force. He had fought at the Battle of Jutland where he was mentioned in dispatches, and had worked hard at all his duties, both civil and military. He had also, through long hours of coaching, managed to reduce his painful stammer to a slight hesitancy, barely noticeable except when he had to speak in public. In 1920 he met Elizabeth Bowes-Lyon, and after a long courtship, they married. Although a descendant of a Scottish king she was in law a commoner. This made the marriage unusual in that it would normally be arranged for him to marry into royalty. That he was allowed to make his own choice was considered at the time to be a modernising gesture. The duke and duchess had two children, Elizabeth who was referred to as Lilibet and her younger sister, Margaret.

Also at the dinner were Georgie and his wife Marina; Henry and Alice, the Duke and Duchess of Gloucester; David's sister, Princess Mary, given the title of the Princess Royal, and her husband, Henry Lascelles, the Earl of Harewood.

One of the footmen refreshed the Duke of Gloucester's bottomless wine glass. Henry's ruddy face was deepening in hue. Holding down a belch, he watched the claret pour and pronounced through a straining throat: 'Jolly good show.'

Elizabeth turned to David. Her eyes were penetrating but twinkled as if a good joke had just been told that only she had heard. The effect was at once alarming and flirtatious. 'I believe there will be many attractive debutantes in the upcoming season.'

David recognized the danger implicit in her observation.

He covered his alarm by effecting a bored disdain. 'Not another tiresome presentation at court.'

'Faint heart never won fair lady,' Elizabeth scolded.

David bowed his head before his dinner like a bull about to charge a prancing matador. 'There is nothing faint about my heart, as you well know.'

Mary intervened. 'You must be getting on with it, David. You can't let the recent past become a distraction. You need an heir. I don't want poor Bertie at the head of the queue forever.'

Elizabeth grasped her husband by the hand, his fork slipping onto the table. 'I for one,' she pronounced, 'am haunted by the thought that my poor Bertie should ever have to take the reins.'

David inhaled sharply. 'Oh dear, heaven forbid that I drop off my perch too soon.'

Behind her veil of unfeigned sweetness, Elizabeth was as stern as any Scot, and as sturdy as the granite mountains from which her family hailed. 'We have our Lilibet to think of, David. We don't want the succession hanging over her young head like the sword of Damocles.'

'I d-d-dare say, my dear.'

The table suddenly turned quiet, everyone embarrassed at the recurrence of Bertie's stammer. Marina broke the silence. 'Things seem to have settled down in Germany.'

'More's the pity, my dear,' said Georgie, acknowledging her fretfulness. The duke loved his beautiful wife, and was much affected by the princess's political views and her concern for the welfare of her many close relatives in Europe, although this didn't prevent him from indulging in the occasional affair.

Elizabeth released Bertie's hand. 'Don't worry, Georgie,' she advised, before taking a mouthful of peas, 'they're still rearming at a pace.'

Her husband chimed in again. 'I d-d-dare say.'

She continued without hesitation. 'Churchill won't stop going on about it.'

'Yes. I know,' Georgie protested. 'I wish he'd shut up.'

'Steady on,' said Bertie, gallantry eradicating his speech impediment.

'No, I'm not going to bloody well "steady on!"'

'Georgie!' ordered Mary. Her voice brought the room to attention with the efficiency of a regimental sergeant major.

'I'm sorry, Mummy, but the stronger Germany becomes, the safer we are from the barbarity of the Bolsheviks.'

The old queen dowager became wistful. 'Oh, yes, poor cousin Nicky.' Her fading grey eyes pored over sepia memories of holidays with her cousins, the Romanovs, all murdered in a cellar in the distant Ural Mountains. For a second her iron will seemed tempered by something softer.

David sipped his wine. 'As a boy, he had an enormous set of toy soldiers.'

Marina looked surprised. 'The Czar?'

'No,' said David. 'I mean Churchill. He told me that he used to play alone in his room with battalions of lead for hours on end. He was known to be very shy, an introvert.

'I wish he still was,' said Georgie. 'Now, instead of little tin soldiers he wants to get his hands on the war ministry.'

David nodded in acknowledgement of his brother's point

but countered: 'All the same, it must be frustrating for such a great man to be left for so long out of the Cabinet, left for years in the wilderness.'

Georgie laid down his knife and fork, threading his fingers together in a defensive wall. 'David, it's because his fellow Conservatives don't trust him.'

Queen Mary weighed in again, this time almost pleading, her strength corroded by all the follies of the world. 'Can we please not speak so much of politics?'

There followed another, much longer pause in the conversation, a silence punctuated only by the dull scrape of sterling silver on bone china, a percussive accompaniment to the slow but steady disappearance of everyone's serving of goose.

Though slim, Marina was a fast eater and the first to finish. 'I suppose, David, you must be run off your feet with all the preparations for your coronation?'

He frowned. 'Yes, I think all this fuss is designed to keep me distracted from the real business of the nation. People out there have lost their livelihoods—they're starving, for God's sake—while I am forced to concern myself with the seating arrangements at Westminster Abbey.'

'Enough!' said Mary, leaping back into the cut and thrust of the moment, her anger genuine.

David threw his napkin down on his plate. He felt suffocated by his overbearing mother and was gripped by a wave of nausea. He closed his eyes and pinched the bridge of his nose, as if to shield his mind from a kaleidoscope of confused emotions. A footman took away his unfinished meal.

Marina sliced gaily through the sulphurous air, suggesting brightly: 'David, would you like to get away for a weekend?'

'What?' groaned the king, his eyes still closed.

'Marina and I have been invited to ride to hounds at Blandford Castle,' said Georgie. 'Old Dorset always puts on a splendid show, I'm sure he'd love to see you there.'

'Fresh air would do you good,' added Marina.

Elizabeth grasped the opportunity to take the subject of conversation back to where it had started. 'David, have you met the Earl of Dorset's daughter, Lady Susanna?'

He looked at his sister-in-law, immediately recognising the wide smile and cherubic cheeks that so neatly disguised her sly and agile mind. A beguiling, almost bucolic, bonny face that lulled the unwary into the shadow of her ruthless instinct to protect the ones she loved. The king knew he orbited the outer limits of that coterie.

The hunt surged across the fields and hedgerows. Lady Susanna de St. Croix stared at the master of foxhounds as he galloped just yards ahead of her, his scarlet coat radiant and vibrating against the oversaturated verdancy of the surrounding hills. She spurred her black stallion, determined to pass him and race to the lead.

Still in her twenties, Susanna was beautiful, even by the standards of the aristocracy. She was also shy, but impetuous. Her ancestors included Simon de St. Croix, a Norman knight who had fought alongside Richard the Lionheart in the third crusade; and his descendent, Henry de St. Croix, who supported the Lancastrians in the War of the Roses, and for his services, was created Earl of Dorset. The title was one of the oldest in the English peerage—her father being the eighteenth Earl. The only surviving child of an only child, he was the last of the male line. Other than her father, Susanna had no close relatives.

The countryside echoed to the cry of hounds and the pounding of hooves as the hunt stormed into thick woodlands. Susanna saw a dry-stone wall in her path. It was high but not too high. She cracked the horse's flanks with her crop, urging it on. At the last instant it balked. Susanna was thrown through the air and splattered into the mud. She found herself in a deep puddle and tried to get to her feet. 'Damn!' she swore in frustration.

A hand reached down to help her up.

'Thank you,' she said. 'Blast it all, I seem to have...' Susanna recognised that her gallant rescuer was the king.

'Your Majesty, I'm sorry, I really am.' She tried to curtsey but almost lost her balance. Other members of the hunt rode up, the fox forgotten.

David laughed. 'No need for all that. Are you alright?'

'Ah, yes, I appear to be.'

Unnoticed, a news photographer crept out of the woodlands undergrowth.

'I think you might need a bit of a wash,' David observed.

Susanna took a step forward and slipped again in the mud. He grabbed her before she fell. At that instant a flash bulb snapped.

The photo of David and Susanna appeared a week later on the

front cover of Paris Match. It carried the headline: 'OOH-LA-LA'. A copy of the magazine sat on Wallis's coffee table in her Paris hotel suite. She flipped it face down and rose from the sofa. Before a gilt-framed mirror that hung above the fireplace, she executed a flurry of catwalk half turns, scrutinizing her evening gown, annoyingly unsure if its revealing cut flattered the contours of her figure. Rear to the mirror, twisting her torso to keep her eyes fixed on her reflection, she ran both hands over her buttocks, smoothing her palms against the gown's shimmering red silk. Despite the back being cut provocatively low, the fabric adhered to her sinews as shamelessly as latex. Satisfied, she swung around to her footman. He was a young man of rustic appearance, with unruly hair. 'Marcel, avez vous du champagne sur la glace?'

'Oui, Madam,' he answered with a well-tutored bow.

There was a knock on the door. Marcel went to answer it. Wallis retreated to the bedroom. A few seconds later, the footman led in the German ambassador. He took the minister's hat and coat. Wallis's gentleman caller was dressed in white tie and tails and shone like a newly minted Reichsmark.

Marcel tapped lightly on the bedroom door before opening it. 'Madam, Monsieur von Ribbentrop.'

Wallis appeared.

Joachim von Ribbentrop clicked his heals, swept up her hand and kissed her fingers with his wet lips. 'Wallis, you are as radiant as ever.'

'And you as dashing,' she replied.

'You flatter me too much,' he protested as he thrust

forward a bouquet of seventeen roses. 'White for the purity of my love,' he declared unabashedly.

Wallis took the flowers and savoured their perfume. 'Why, Ribbie, they're beautiful.' She handed the flowers to Marcel. 'Give these to the maid and have her arrange them in the Boucher vase.'

The footman scurried away as Wallis led her guest to the sofa. They sat down. With his back erect, Ribbentrop crossed his legs and rested one hand on his upper knee; the high-ranking German diplomat had pretensions to the aristocracy and behaved accordingly. Not born into the nobility, he was only allowed to add the nobiliary particle 'von' to his name after his aunt Gertrude adopted him. His Fuhrer didn't mind, he was fond of Ribbentrop; he represented the wealthier business class of Germany that the Nazi Party had, at first, struggled to attract.

Having returned from Canada to enlist in the German army at the start of the First World War, Ribbentrop's frontline service saw him awarded the Iron Cross first class and he was soon promoted to the rank of 1st lieutenant. After the war he married into the wealthy Henkell family and became a successful wine merchant. He didn't see any advantage in joining the Nazi Party until 1932. However, having done so, he made up for lost time with impressive shows of entrepreneurial skill, notable in his efforts to facilitate Hitler's grab for power. Ribbentrop had worked with Franz von Papen in Istanbul in 1918 and they had become friends. By the time Ribbentrop joined the Nazi Party, von Papen had risen to become chancellor of Germany. Utilising this relationship, Ribbentrop had organised a series of meetings to negotiate Hitler's takeover of the government, even using his home as the venue for the talks between President Hindenburg's and Hitler's emissaries. The negotiations had been a great success and Hitler was soon the new chancellor. Ribbentrop had helped to achieve what many had thought impossible, making himself a firm favourite with the Fuhrer. Since then, Ribbentrop had further solidified his position through the simple mechanism of always telling his leader what he wanted to hear. His political career never looked back. He was appointed Ambassador-Plenipotentiary at Large, and in that capacity had visited London frequently. It was in Belgravia he was first introduced to Wallis, their meeting quickly blossoming into a fleeting romance. The German recalled their romps with pleasure, but all that was a long time ago, and the two had not beheld each other since. Though in his forties, Wallis was impressed by Ribbentrop's youthful good looks—a quality he shared with David.

Marcel returned and uncorked a bottle of champagne.

'The wine isn't German,' Wallis admitted, 'but I recall you like Dom Perignon.'

'Yes, I do,' Ribbentrop said smoothly. 'I have the import license for it in Deutschland, aber Geschaeft ist gut—Heil Hitler.'

Wallis laughed nervously, glancing at Marcel who hovered beside her.

Ribbentrop noticed her reticence and decided to show off at the footman's expense. He turned to the young man and demanded: 'Allez-vous verser le champagne ou vous asseour la comme une statue?'

Marcel jumped into action and poured the drinks. 'Pardonnez-moi, M-Monsieur.' he sputtered, with all the grace he could muster.

Wallis waited till the shaken footman had finished then nodded for him to leave. 'Really, Ribbie,' she said, after Marcel had left the room, 'you are the limit. Still as mischievous as ever.'

'Like when we first met in London?'

She squirmed ever so slightly. 'Perhaps, but still…'

Ribbentrop smiled and picked up their drinks, handing a glass to Wallis. 'Your footman's Alsatian, he understands.'

'How do you know where he's from?'

'Ah,' he replied smugly, 'as you, no doubt, are aware, I've just become Ambassador to the Court of Saint James; it is my job to know everything.'

Wallis reached toward the coffee table and flipped over the copy of Paris Match, revealing the photo of David and Susanna. 'What do you know about her?'

'Ooh la la! Is this what it seems?'

'It can't be.'

'It looks as though it could be—while the cat's away the mice will…' Ribbentrop straightened his bow tie. 'They'll do what mice do well.'

Wallis inhaled sharply. 'I need to be there.'

'Why? Look at you—a beautiful woman wasting away, locked up, while outside, all of life's pleasures abound.'

'But, Ribbie,' said Wallis, as she segued into her little match girl persona she knew could always be relied upon, 'I feel so helpless here in Paris.'

'You are never helpless when you have old friends,' he countered, taking his cue to display all the qualities that had made him a successful wine salesman. 'I'm back next week. Allow me to show you the sights of the city. I'll be your chaperone.'

He clinked his glass of champagne against hers and they drank.

Since William the Conqueror all English monarchs had been crowned at Westminster Abbey; David's coronation was no exception.

The church's actual name was the Collegiate Church of St. Peter, Westminster. It was a free church of the sovereign, exempt from any ecclesiastical jurisdiction. Until the nineteenth century it was England's third seat of learning after Oxford and Cambridge. Much of the King James Bible was written there.

The Abbey began as a large stone church built by the Saxon king, Saint Edward the Confessor. It was consecrated a week before he died, and two hundred years later, was rebuilt by King Henry III. The architect of the new building, Henry of Reyns, built it in the new style of the cathedrals at Reims, Amiens and Chartres. Known as Gothic, it featured pointed arches, ribbed vaulting, rose windows, flying buttresses and an apse with radiating chapels. When completed, the Abbey's vault was the highest in England.

Henry was buried there in 1272, establishing it for five hundred years as the principal place for the burial of royalty.

Since then many famous commoners had also been interred there, including Chaucer, Handel, Dickens, Darwin, Lord Tennyson and Sir Isaac Newton. Following the great fire of London, large amounts of money meant for the Abbey (dedicated to St. Peter) were diverted to the reconstruction of St. Paul's Cathedral, thus coining the phrase: 'Robbing Peter to pay Paul.'

It was now the day of David's coronation as King Edward VIII: 12th May 1937; one year, three months, three weeks and one day after the death of his father, King George V. Being unwed, he rode alone to the Abbey, seated in the Gold State Coach, a vehicle so heavy it required a train of eight horses. On his procession he was preceded by squadrons of the Life Guards and the Blues and Royals, then by Yeomen Warders and senior officers of the three services; following his coach were the massed bands and serried ranks of Grenadier, Coldstream, Scots, Irish and Welsh Foot Guard regiments.

He was the focus of a multitude, yet felt completely alone, the roar of the people no different to the roar of the waves that pounded Robinson Crusoe's island. He looked out the window and waved to the crowd that pressed against the wall of police lining the roadside, and at that moment, heard another noise. Not the clip-clop of the horses' hooves, not the creaking of the timbers that supported all that gold, but a high pitched buzzing sound. There was a wasp inside the coach! But how, with all the elaborate preparation, the spit and polish and centuries-old ritual, how could an insect have penetrated this sanctus sanctorum? David could not escape his unwanted guest, and it quickly made for his ear. He waved it away, and the crowd, thinking he waved at them, responded with even louder cheering. The pest circled around and flew again toward him, swinging behind his head and landing on the back of his neck. Then, for no apparent reason, it bit him. A burning pain dug into him like a drop of molten lead. A second later, the damage done, the wasp flew out the window and was gone.

Thousands waited at the Abbey. As their king alighted from his coach, many were bemused by the expression on his face; David was starting to feel ill, his countenance anguished, his lips flexed over gritted teeth.

With all possible solemnity, David entered the Abbey. The congregation was already standing. Greeted by the first anthem, Psalm 122, the king and his procession passed down the nave and choir to the chancel. Winston Churchill had a seat in the lower row of the oak choir stalls and was close enough to wonder what had happened to the king's neck. After completing his long march down the aisle, David wobbled slightly before ascending the steps of the sacrarium. At the Chair of Estate he caught his breath. The wasp bite began to itch.

The Garter King of Arms, the Archbishop of Canterbury, the Lord Chancellor, the Lord Great Chamberlain, the Lord High Constable and the Earl Marshal walked to the west of the chancel. David turned to face in that direction, and would have given all the crown jewels sitting on the high altar just for the chance to scratch his bite, or have Wallis scratch it for him.

The archbishop asked if those present were willing to pay homage to the new king. The people responded with loud and repeated acclamations of 'God save King Edward.' This was then repeated to the other three points of the compass.

The ceremony proceeded with the administering of the coronation oath by the archbishop, the presenting and kissing of the bible and the communion service. David then had to remove his crimson robe. As he did so, he took the opportunity to give his neck a quick scratch. This only made things worse, the bite becoming itchier still. Stoically, David crossed to Saint Edward's Chair for his anointing.

Created by order of King Edward I and used as the coronation thrown at the crowning of his son and heir, King Edward II, Saint Edward's Chair was designed, among other things, to house the Stone of Scone. Sometimes called the Stone of Destiny, it was said to be the stone upon which Jacob had rested his head at Bethel, the pillow on which he dreamt that God had given him and his descendants the land on which he lay. It was believed the stone had somehow found its way to Britain, and being much venerated, became the object upon which the kings of Ireland, and then Scotland, sat during their coronations. King Edward I seized it and brought it to Westminster in 1296. Since that time the stone had been lodged, like a chamber pot, under the seat of the chair.

As soon as David sat down, a canopy of cloth of gold was placed above his head and the choir sang out the heavenly strains of Handel's 'Zardoc the Priest'. The archbishop anointed him with holy oil on the hands, chest and head, and then, returning to the altar, took up the Sword of State. Placing it in David's hands he said: 'Receive this kingly Sword, brought now from the Altar of God, and delivered to you by the hands of us, the Bishops and servants of God. With this sword do justice and stop the growth of iniquity.'

Still feeling a little woozy, David lifted up the sword, and as instructed, returned it to the altar. Turning to walk back to King Edward's Chair, his head began to spin at the sight before him. Across the chancel, his mother, Queen Mary, sat in the royal box; beside her, the Royal Dukes and Duchesses of York, Gloucester and Kent, the Princess Royal and the Earl of Harewood; behind them, rows of peers, dressed in robes of ermine and seated in order of creation—the dukes of Norfolk, Somerset, Hamilton, Buccleugh, Richmond, Grafton, Beaufort, St. Albans, Bedford, Devonshire, Argyll and Marlborough. On the other side of the chancel were the kings and queens of Norway and Denmark, King George of Greece, King Gustaf of Sweden; David's cousins, the old Duke of Connaught and the Earl and Countess of Southesk; behind them, the kings and queens of Romania, Italy, Bulgaria, The Netherlands, and Spain; and at the extreme right of the second row, the thirteen year old king of Yugoslavia; in the ranks of seats beyond the European royalty, seated in order of precedence, were squeezed the dukes of Athol, Montrose, Roxburghe, Manchester, Northumberland, Leinster, Abercorn, Wellington, Sutherland and Westminster; further to the rear, a selection of marquises, earls and a couple of lucky barons. Among these, David caught a glimpse of a distinguished looking gentleman with snow-white hair—the Earl of Dorset. David looked down the central aisle and glimpsed the choir of thirty boys and twelve lay vicars; and above them, the orchestra of the Royal Academy of Music. Beyond the choir screen, the aisle was lined with troopers from the household cavalry, the narthex with guardsmen and yeomen warders. To either side of the nave, and largely invisible behind the screen, were several hundred lesser members of the aristocracy, as well as ambassadors, bishops, judges and old friends.

A deathly hush filled the great vault of the Abbey. It was broken seconds later by a worried cough. Every eye was on David. With a look of shock he realised he hadn't moved in some time.

The Dean of Westminster stepped up to him and whispered: 'Your Majesty, are you alright?'

'Yes,' he said, 'I'm sorry,' and turned to face the altar. The relief was palpable, as if the entire congregation had been holding its breath and now exhaled.

The archbishop continued: 'Receive the Imperial Robe and the Lord God endue you with knowledge and wisdom.' The dean and the Groom of Robes wrapped David in the Robe Royal and then, to his great relief, he was able to sit down again.

The archbishop stepped forward and presented David with the Orb, given as a reminder that the whole world is subject to the power and empire of Christ. The dean returned the Orb to the altar as the archbishop placed on the fourth finger of David's right hand the King's Ring with its ruby cross set in a sapphire.

Mercifully, the itch was starting to subside, but David still felt slightly faint. When the dean handed to the archbishop the Sceptre with the Cross, he knew his ordeal would soon be over. The archbishop put the sceptre in David's right hand, signifying power and justice, and then the Rod with the Dove in his left hand, signifying equity and mercy.

Finally, the people rose as the archbishop, standing before the alter, lifted the five pounds of solid gold and precious stones that was Saint Edward's Crown and very reverently, very carefully placed it on David's head.

With the crown safely in place, the people shouted: 'God Save the King! God Save the King! God Save the King!' The princes and peers put on their crowns, the trumpets sounded the fanfare and the great guns of the Tower shot off.

David, the eighth king since the Norman Conquest to be named Edward, had finally been crowned. If the three Saxons: Edward the Elder, Edward the Martyr and Saint Edward the Confessor had been included, he would have been the eleventh. Edward was the name chosen from a selection available on his birth certificate. It was a thoroughly English name for a genetically German king. He was now sovereign of Britain, her dominions and empire.

Two hours later, David stood on the balcony of Buckingham Palace to receive the ovation of the people. Beside him stood his mother, Queen Mary, and his siblings— Georgie, Bertie, Henry and the Princess Royal—but no Queen Wallis.

That evening a coronation banquet was held in the ballroom at Buckingham Palace. Although it was the largest room in the Palace, it could not accommodate all who had attended the coronation. Additional seating was created in the adjoining Cross Gallery and in the State Dining Room, but even then, of the over seven thousand guests that were present at the Abbey, only three hundred received invitations to the banquet. A delicate and elaborate system of protocols and precedents had been exercised. While the governors general and prime minister of the dominions attended, presidents of republics did not. While European kings were present, their prime ministers were not. The archbishops of Canterbury and York were there but no other Anglican clergy nor representatives of the other denominations or religions. The Royal Family, the Great Officers of State and some of the dukes were invited, but only a handful of lesser peers. The Cabinet ministers were present, but few other members of the Commons or the Lords, nor the mandarins of the civil service. And so it went on. The Lord Chief Justice but no other judges. Some captains of industry, but the selection was far from exhaustive. The only exceptions to the ruthless process were those individuals invited on David's specific instructions. So it was, this one room contained the cream of the cream of the establishment and the very essence of king and empire, an invitation to attend, the hottest ticket in town.

The meal had been sumptuous. Prepared by a battalion of chefs, the six-course dinner started with Puree Madeleine, then filets of whiting in anchovy sauce, quenelles with Regency sauce, roast leg of lamb, chocolate profiteroles, nuts and fruit.

With the end of the feasting and after the loyal toast, the guests got up and mingled. Churchill walked toward the king who sat at the High Table, beside his mother. David noticed his approach, and ignoring protocol, rose to greet him.

The old politician shook his hand warmly. 'A wonderful

evening after a glorious day, Your Majesty.'

He blushed at being addressed so formally by his friend. 'No need for all that, I'm still David, you know.'

Churchill turned to Mary and bowed. 'Your Majesty.'

The queen's nose rose in the air just slightly. 'Mr Churchill, how nice to see you again.'

David removed a cigarette from his gold cigarette case.

'Allow me,' said Churchill, offering him a light. 'I do love a good coronation.'

'How many have you attended?' asked Mary.

'This will be my third and I'm sure my last. God save the King.' Churchill gulped a mouthful of his brandy. 'A truly splendid occasion.'

'If you like this sort of thing,' David demurred.

Churchill took a puff on his cigar. 'The pageantry of the coronation is based on centuries of tradition. It is a display of our glory that leaves an envious world to swoon at what it means to be British.'

The king was having none of it. 'There's more to the monarchy than pomp.'

Georgie approached. 'David, look who I've just run into.' At his side stood the Earl of Dorset and the earl's daughter, Lady Susanna.

'Why, Lord Dorset, how are you?' asked Mary.

Dorset bowed as deeply as his bad back would allow. 'Still in the realm of rude health, Your Majesty,' he rasped. The earl was ageing quickly. Presenting a figure of forlorn dignity, his eyes drooped above a white moustache that all but completely overpowered his cadaverous face.

Without waiting for the ossified earl to continue their conversation, the queen addressed his daughter. 'And Lady Susanna, how nice to see you again.'

Susanna curtsied. 'Your Majesty.' Turning, she repeated the same to the king.

David found himself struck by the young woman's beauty; her eyes shone, Chartres blue, below a crown of silver blonde hair. Dressed in diamonds and white satin Susanna radiated an aura of dazzling light.

At the other end of the ballroom, Baldwin shared a port with Chamberlain, and stared across at David and Churchill.

'Churchill's ingratiating himself with the royals again. Go on Winston have another slurp of brandy. Untrustworthy souse.'

Chamberlain adjusted his pince-nez. 'The king seems rather taken with old Dorset's daughter.'

Baldwin grunted. 'I hope she's a virgin. I don't think we could cope with more scandal.'

Chamberlain removed his glasses and polished them with his handkerchief. 'I believe the lass is still intact.'

'Good, maybe he'll marry her.'

'Rumour has it that Queen Mary is manoeuvring with that intent.'

Baldwin sipped his port with incongruous daintiness. 'I hope it happens soon. Seal the gates for good against that Simpson woman.'

'Oh, I doubt she'll be back.'

'Excellent! A fitting legacy with which to end my term in office.'

Chamberlain reaffixed his pince-nez. 'You intend to retire?'

'Yes, I'm done with it, be gone within the fortnight. I shall recommend you to the king as my successor.'

Chamberlain adjusted his tie.

The orchestra in the gallery began to play a Strauss waltz. Mary looked at David and nodded her head toward Susanna. He glanced at the young beauty before turning back to his mother, deeply suspicious of her motives. To acquiesce to her suggestion was risky, but he knew not a soul would dare step onto the dance floor before him. Reluctantly he took the hint and stubbed out his cigarette. 'Lady Susanna, may I have the honour of this dance?'

She smiled. 'It is I who would be honoured, Sir.'

'Please,' he whispered in her ear, 'no need for all that, just call me David.' He placed her hand on his and led her to the centre of the ballroom. The crowd looked on, whispering to one another.

'Now hold on tight; I'd hate to see you slip over again.'

Susanna looked down, trying to hide her embarrassment.

'I'm only joking,' David reassured.

She raised her head and gazed into his eyes as they twirled across the floor. Other couples joined them, transforming the room into a glittering, moving arabesque.

Black clouds weighed down on Dowlais. From the Victorian era through to the Great War, the town of ten thousand souls had been a thriving community based on ironworking, but the ructions of the Great Depression had laid to waste the factories, the workers and their families.

The townsfolk lined both sides of a cobblestone road that led to the shut down ironworks. With their bodies bent against a damp and spiteful wind, they stood three deep and clutched little flags of red, white and blue; the Union Jack the only brightness to be seen on a pallet of greys. A Rolls Royce drove up the road. The crowd shook their flags, the colours fluttering, as the car came to a halt. David climbed out, doffed his bowler hat and waved. To the sound of cheering, he took in a view of stone rowhouses, treeless hills and mountains of rusting slag. It was but the latest in a series of bleak landscapes he had beheld, having decided to tour Britain's industrial heartland within days of his coronation.

The town's choir began to sing the Welsh hymn, Crugybar: 'Guide me, O thou great Redeemer, Pilgrim through this barren land…'

His path eased by half a dozen bobbies, David made his way through the crowd, the men and boys removing their cloth caps as he passed. Watching their king, the people gradually joined the choir in song. 'I am weak, but thou art mighty, hold me with thy powerful hand.'

David entered the ironworks and approached the wreck of a huge blast furnace. He stared in silence as the hymn continued: 'Bread of heaven, bread of heaven, feed me till I want no more—want no more. Feed me till I want no more.'

The singing stopped and there was nothing but the sound of water dripping from the leaking roof. David made his way along a rotting catwalk to the centre of the cavernous building. He faced the crowd and saw beleaguered hope in every face.

He was in their town, he was in their mill, and he was determined they should know he was the one man in Britain who might end their plight.

David had thought long and hard about this day. He had thought on the Earl of Salisbury who had rescued children from being forced to work long hours in the mines, and William Wilberforce who had ended the scourge of the British empire's trade in slavery; he thought on Robert Owen, Titus Salt, Josephine Butler and the chartists; he thought on those and several others, and he thought, if the king's subjects could achieve so much, why not the king?

David looked across his makeshift auditorium, taking in as many pairs of eyes as time might buy, making intimate the instant of that glance, leaving each recognised as a long lost friend, the tension in the room growing palpable as the time for this played out. They were individuals, not a mob, and like a brother, he understood their pain. After a long moment, unbroken by the merest whisper or muffled cough, the silence straining like a floodgate holding back a lake, he stepped forward and closed the space between himself and them: a man amongst men. There was no microphone, but when he spoke, the walls echoed and amplified his plangent voice, his words a deafening cascade against the rock of time.

'I know what it is to feel the terror of the battlefield. To huddle in the filthy trenches beneath a fire of exploding shells, a report that might rend the earth and all beneath to pulp. I stood among you then and heard you swear, that this would be "the war to end all wars". And you were promised by Lloyd George that if you survived such hell you would return to "a land fit for heroes".'

The crowd clapped but sensed that greater things were yet to come.

David's voice rode over the applause. 'The brutality of that war has made our generation long for something better, a new kind of society, free of the old injustice. These dark ages are of the past, these horrors, must be dragged from out the shadows for all the world to see and rightly be condemned.'

The crowd again applauded, this time with cheers. David felt the tide of emotion rise up through his body—euphoric for him as much as for his audience. 'These ironworks brought men hope, a faith in a better tomorrow. As your crowned king, anointed by God, I pledge to you the return of your jobs, the return of hope, the return of the free-flowing abundance of that future that was promised. I pledge to you a land fit for heroes!'

The crowd exploded. The men waved their caps in the air and the women wept with pride. David waited for the roar to die down, taking his time before continuing, again allowing the tension of silent expectation to mount. Then he spoke more softly. 'We must see you once again in work; something must be done. And as God is my witness, something will be done.'

Once more the crowd erupted, the applause deafening. David nodded, acknowledging the support, and went to leave. He stopped when the crowd began to sing again. This time it was the national anthem: 'God save the King.'

For the first time in his life, the plodding notes of the old tune made goose bumps rise on the back of his neck. It was almost overwhelming.

To the tick-tock of the clock on the mantle piece, Chamberlain pondered upon a pile of newspapers that lay on the table before him. The headlines read: KING'S PLEA FOR ACTION, KING SAYS SOMETHING MUST BE DONE, KING CONDEMNS GOVERNMENT and more. Not a masthead failed to mention the king's address.

Horace Wilson sat opposite. He was now Chamberlain's key aid, with his own section and staff, and much in favour with the new prime minister.

Chamberlain shuffled the newspapers into a neat pile on the Cabinet table. 'God, what have we unleashed?'

'I shudder to think Prime Minister,' said Wilson with an already well-honed deference.

'We should have let him abdicate, we should have let him marry, we should have let things take their natural course. It's all that interfering Churchill's fault. So long as I live I will insure he never returns from the backbenches. Wilson!'

'Yes, Prime Minister.'

'Wilson, I've kept you here at Number Ten because you get things done. The king has thrown down the gauntlet and the government will need to respond to the challenge. I want you and the staff to liaise with Treasury, prepare a number of options to submit to Cabinet. Nothing too extravagant mind you.'

'Yes, Prime Minister.'

Chamberlain pushed the newspapers aside and muttered: 'Churchill!'

Their name was an abbreviation of the American word, nickelodeon. Almost overnight they appeared across Britain like a new species of mushroom, fed by the damp of the Great Depression. Every town had an Odeon Cinema. The cities had many. The middle classes filed at the box office in numbers only slightly less than the impoverished who filed at the soup kitchens; the movies were an escape.

The marquee above the Odeon, Guildford read: THE CHARGE OF THE LIGHT BRIGADE.

Before the main feature, the audience watched a Fox Movietone newsreel of David visiting a blighted industrial estate. The plummy-voiced narrator spoke over discordantly upbeat music.

'His Majesty's tour serves to highlight the continued effect of the depression on our industrial heartland. The king's visit to Yorkshire has cheered the people of Leeds as nothing else could.'

David was filmed, speaking behind a BBC microphone. 'Let no one belittle the work of the social services but their travails are not enough. New industries must be brought to the stricken areas of Britain. These men want work.' The cinema audience applauded.

David and Georgie walked toward the airport hanger. They had been joyriding over Buckinghamshire, the king in his Gipsy Moth, the duke in a Hornet Moth. Georgie recommenced a conversation they had begun before taking off.

'So, you seem to be making some headway on the

unemployment issue. I'm sorry for referring to it as your crusade.'

His brother sighed. 'It's fine. In point of fact, a crusade may not be such a bad way to term it; I certainly feel, at times, like I'm dragging my way about in a heavy coat of chain mail.' He sniffed before getting to the point. 'It's important these people know I know their plight. If I fight for them, they will fight for me.'

Georgie laughed as he took off his gloves. 'A new Cavalier army?'

David smiled at the dig, but was quickly serious again. 'The government, Cabinet, they got the better of me last year, they bullied me, but it will not happen again. I will get what I want. Whether it be Chamberlain or any other, I will get my way.'

'Job creation?'

'Yes,' David acknowledged, 'jobs, and other things.'

'Wallis?'

'Georgie, do not underestimate my determination. Wallis will be my queen.'

'You'll get no argument about that from me, nor Marina.'

David slapped his leather flying helmet against his leg and scanned the horizon. 'This is my realm and I shall protect it. Who better than I?'

Georgie squinted at his brother, not quite sure what he meant, but hoping the king's intentions were as his own ambitions for the nation. 'Indeed,' he nodded, 'who better than you?'

David continued to stare at the surrounding hills and

tapped his clenched fist on his chin. 'With just a little patience, I believe I should be the strong leader Britain needs—a king with the power to take on the strong men emerging across Europe.'

'Stalin?'

Lost in thought, David ignored the question, addressing no one but himself. 'The only thing missing is a queen.' Walking again, he confessed: 'Georgie, do you know Wallis is always in my thoughts? I imagine her by my side at every ceremony, every cutting of a ribbon or unveiling of a plaque. I feel her there in spirit every time I give a speech. She's there in all my negotiations with…' He hesitated as his eyes shot about, as though pursued as the quarry of some voracious carnivore. 'Well, Georgie, you can imagine how it is. Taking on, again and again, an increasingly hostile Cabinet. I need her; she is my strength. We've been apart too long.'

Most of the state and private apartments were on the piano nobile and the second floor, but when David moved into Buckingham Palace he chose to live in the Belgian suite. Located on the ground floor, it was less imposing and enjoyed relaxing views of the garden.

The Palace was originally built as his London home by the Tory politician, John Sheffield, later created Duke of Buckingham. Half a century later, King George III bought Buckingham House for his wife, and it became known as the Queen's House. Fourteen of their children were born there. Rebuilt by the architect John Nash in the early 19th century, it became known as Buckingham Palace. Queen Victoria was the first to make it the monarch's main London home, although St James's Palace remained the official address of the sovereign.

The Royal Standard now flew above the east wing, indicating the king was in residence. It was late at night and David was stuck at his bedroom desk, poring over a Home Office report. Illuminated by the glow of a French lamp, he sat in a little gully of red boxes, each box stuffed with government documents. He stopped working to take a sip of coffee. The cup was empty. He poured another and noticed the small, framed photo of Wallis. It looked up at him from the bottom of a canyon in his mountain range of paperwork. He picked up the phone. It rang in her suite at the Hotel Ritz and was answered by the maid. She was still dressed for work, but had been asleep in her room.

'Allo?' she said, a little groggily.

'J'ai un appel telephonique pour Madame Simpson,' said the operator.

'Madame n'est pas ici a l'heure actuelle,' the maid replied.

Across the English Channel, David waited. 'I'm sorry Sir,' said the operator at the British end. 'Mrs. Simpson still isn't in yet. Would you like to leave a message?'

David looked at his watch. It read five past one. 'No, that will be all. Thank you.' He hung up and stared at Wallis's photo, worried she was out so late. 'What could you be doing?' he whispered. 'Are you safe?' He got up and poured himself a nightcap. 'You idiot! Did you not tell her to enjoy Paris? "Oh, it's not London; there's plenty to do after the pubs close!"' He put down his glass and wondered if there was too much to do.

Might others recognise that ethereal flame so blindingly apparent to him? He rubbed his eyes, tormented by his conjectures. Would some interloper seek to take advantage of his absence? Could Wallis be trusted to resist such overtures? The flesh was weak, of that he could well concede. Was his pragmatic request for her to remain abroad, even if only for a short while, a test that might push her to breaking point? Was he putting too much trust in the love of his life? No, he reassured himself, how many men had he met on the front during the War? How many had sweethearts who kept the home fires burning? These women waited faithfully for months, sometimes years, dreading each knock on the door, fretting upon the welfare of those they loved and praying constantly for their safe return. Wallis was surely forged of that same metal. David sipped his coffee and returned to his papers.

At eleven thirty the next morning, the new guard marched into the palace forecourt. The captain barked out the drill. 'Guards… Halt! Slow march!' The regimental band played Men of Harlech as the new guard approached the old guard. The guns snapped into a perfect line, the bayonets reflecting the headlights of the passing traffic. The weather was fowl so nobody had stopped to watch.

At the northwest corner of the Palace, within the King's Audience Chamber, David sat with Chamberlain for their weekly meeting. Although it was comfortable enough inside, outside, swathes of rain whipped the windows. With water sliding down the panes, distorting a soft-focused view of the exterior world, the two men had faced each other and taken tea. The now empty cups sat on the coffee table that formed a barricade between them.

The prime minister unsheathed a handful of documents from his briefcase. 'Our plans for introducing the Factories Act are well advanced,' he announced with pride. 'These are aimed at bettering working conditions—placing limits on the working hours of women and children. We also have plans for a Holidays Act that would recommend employers give workers a week off each year… with pay.'

David was less than impressed and said facetiously: 'Oh, jolly good.' He then became deadly serious. 'But in order to have a paid holiday you first need a job! You've cut public spending, cut wages, raised taxes; nobody has any money to spend, so nothing gets sold, so nothing gets made. No wonder we have unemployment.'

Chamberlain was crestfallen. 'There is simply not the money available for new spending. We need to wait till the financial situation improves.'

'No,' said David, 'people are suffering as we speak. We must break this Gordian knot. We must do it now. Have you considered a special purpose loan or a new government bond issue?'

'That, Sir, would lead us down the broad road to destruction.'

'Much of the country is already down that road.'

Chamberlain closed his eyes as if receiving a tetanus shot. 'The national economy must be allowed time to recuperate from the Wall Street crash.'

'And when will that be, Prime Minister? What would the destitute think of your call for patience? Starve a little longer till things get better. Some of your children may die but surely not all of them.'

'Sir, you forget yourself,' Chamberlain protested. 'You must abide by the advice of your government.'

David bridled. 'That is a convention, it is not the law.'

The prime minister was not finished. 'And you must cease seeking the people's support against the government in pursuit of your agenda. You threaten the political neutrality of the crown.'

'A crown you are ever ready to take from me.' David strode to the drinks table and poured himself a scotch. 'I'm leaving for my summer holidays at Balmoral. If the need arises, I can be contacted there. Good day, Mr Chamberlain.'

The prime minister got up to go, offering a conciliatory note. 'I will commend your views to committee.'

In accordance with the medieval English laws of aristocratic primogeniture, David, as the first-born son, was upon the death of King George V, bequeathed the vast bulk of his father's estate; this included Balmoral Castle. Located in Aberdeenshire in the Scottish highlands, the castle sat in the midst of a sixty-four thousand acre estate of mountains, forest and farmland. Like his father, grandfather and great-grandmother before him, David chose to spend his late summer and early autumn holidays in its remote vastness. During this time it was a tradition for other members of the royal family to drop in and stay for a week or so. In light of which, the king had invited most of them up for the bank holiday weekend. It was Queen Mary's suggestion that they be joined by a couple of special guests.

Late afternoon, on the Friday of the weekend, Lady Susanna de St. Croix found herself riding in the back seat of the king's Rolls Royce. Mouth agape, she had marvelled at the splendid scenery to be observed during the sixty-minute drive from Aberdeen station. Her father, the Earl, journeyed beside her, and between slack-jawed naps, likewise had enjoyed the passing highlands landscape. Now, at last, they were through the gates and on the final approach to the castle, the car gliding down a drive that led through a wood of sycamore and oak. At the end of this leaf-drenched arcade of overhanging boughs, Susanna took her first glimpse of the castle. It was the battlement of the clock tower with its four turrets, its balcony and arrow loops. Upon sight of the black clock face, she instinctively checked her watch. Yes, they both read four o'clock—she and her father were arriving on time. Looking further she noticed, fluttering from the highest of the clock tower turrets, the Royal Standard used in Scotland, a flag emblazoned with four quadrants: the first and third being the Royal Arms of Scotland—a red lion rampant on a gold background. As with the Palace of Holyroodhouse, this flag unfurled meant the king was in residence. The sight of it sent Susanna's heart racing.

As the car moved along the curving drive toward the carriage porch, the entire building shifted into view. It was a fantasy cast in granite, an exuberance of crenulations, conical corbelled turrets and crow-stepped gables. Excitement drove her to poke her head a little out the window. She looked skyward and caught a glimpse of the enormous, rooster weathervane. It swung around, perched high on a copper, pepper-pot tourelle that jutted from within the depths of a larger octagonal tower. Like the prow of an ancient galleon this corner tower passed by, revealing in its wake the ivy clad, south façade of the castle's west wing.

'For God's sake, Susanna, what do you think you're doing?' said her father. 'You look like a child at a circus. Pull your head in and try to maintain some sort of decorum.'

'But aren't you excited to be here, its all so beautiful?'

'Don't begin your sentences with "but",' growled the old Earl as he pulled out a handkerchief to remove a little drool that had collected on his chin during his nap. Somewhat deflated by the reprimand, Susanna sat back in her seat and fixed her gaze straight ahead. However, this allowed her to see over the chauffeur's shoulder and through the windscreen to the castle's backdrop. The view made her gasp.

'What now?' demanded Dorset.

Susanna smiled at him but said nothing; she knew her father wasn't usually this crabby. She suspected he was just as nervous as she, but so what? It was a breathtaking location. All around were Caledonian woodlands, heather covered hills, Lochnager, the towering Cairngorms and something completely out of place: a small plane that banked around the scenery and flew past them, directly overhead.

The car slipped into the porch. The chauffeur and a waiting footman opened the back doors for Dorset and Susanna. No sooner had they stepped out than David emerged from within the building.

That evening, in the castle's main dining room, the king sat down to dinner with his family and friends. As well as Lord Dorset, Susanna and several members of the royal family, David had decided to add a little spice to the occasion by inviting Churchill. On short notice, the redoubtable, sixty-two year old politician had chartered a small plane and flown himself up, landing at the same time the Dorsets had arrived. Churchill was now tucking into his dinner with gusto.

'Enjoying the venison?' David asked.

'Very tender,' he said, his mouth still full. He swallowed and wiped his mouth with his napkin. 'Best I've eaten since I was the local member, down the road at Dundee.'

'That was during the war?' Mary asked.

'Yes, Ma'am, sad days.'

The Earl of Dorset slid his knife and fork together on his plate, appetite gone and his eyes becoming watery. 'Winston, I lost both my sons on the Western Front.'

'I know,' said Churchill, 'my heart goes out to you.'

Dorset took a deep breath and regained his composure. 'Life has never been the same since. Do you think there will be another dreadful war with Germany?'

'Not if we can get rid of Hitler. We should have stood up to him when he remilitarized the Rhineland. Then he was still weak.'

'And what of Stalin?' asked Georgie. 'Nobody seems to talk about him, but he's murdered millions, executed or starved to death.'

Churchill stabbed his fork into another hunk of meat. 'They are both ruthless men. Don't be surprised if they align for mutual profit.' He shovelled his venison into his mouth, and it bulged under his cheek as he continued, 'Either way, we must be ready, we must rearm.'

David rested his elbows on the arms of his carver and slid his forefinger down his cheek. 'If more spending on weapons means more jobs then I'm all for it.'

Georgie was eager for a debate. He leaned toward Churchill. 'Yes, but if we were clever—'

Mary interrupted him. 'David, perhaps a toast?'

'Of course,' he agreed, raising his glass. 'A toast to our guests, the Honourable Mr Winston Churchill, the Right Honourable, the Earl of Dorset and his beautiful daughter, Lady Susanna.'

Susanna coyly lowered her gaze then glanced up, her luminescent eyes riveting the king. The royals drank to their guests. Henry, his face even more ruddy than usual, drained his glass. He had not uttered a word during the entire meal, but now chose to speak. 'Jolly good show,' he said, indicating for a footman to refresh his drink.

David had tried to get to bed earlier, but the conversation around the snooker table had been entertaining and the cognac mellow. He hoped he wouldn't be too shabby in the morning as it would be an early start, up to the high tops, deer stalking. He took off his robe and climbed under the blankets. After some minutes of tossing and turning, he concluded slumber had no priority in his thoughts. Getting up, he walked to his bedroom desk, picked up the phone and dialed the operator; Balmoral had a direct line to the exchange in Dundee. His call was put through to Paris. The phone rang in Wallis's hotel suite. It went unanswered.

David thanked the operator, hung up and returned to bed. His watch lay on the nightstand. Checking the time, he noted it was almost midnight.

David and Georgie quickly retraced the almond-shaped hoof prints they'd earlier so closely followed. They passed the gillie, the pony boys and the boys' horse on the way home.

'He's four hundred yards back,' yelled the duke, the wind carrying away his voice, 'just below the ridgeline.'

'What did you bag, sir?' the gillie yelled back.

'A big old stag, twelve pointer,' he replied, beaming. 'Took him down in one, dropped on the spot.

'A fine morning's shooting, sir!' The gillie gave the duke an informal salute as the collection team disappeared over the hill.

Georgie's smile stayed on his lips as he sauntered along. He felt invigourated by the brisk highland air and was thoroughly enjoying his start to the day. 'Another fine brace of antlers for the wall,' he boasted.

David didn't reply, his jaw set.

'I say,' Georgie asked, 'did last night get the better of you? One too many Hennessies, what?'

'No,' the king answered curtly, keeping up a cracking pace, advancing like a scythe through the wind and waves of purple heather, 'not too many drinks at all. I feel fine...

physically.'

'And mentally?'

David stopped and faced his brother. 'On the phone to Paris, I advised Wallis to enjoy the delights of Paris. I'm somewhat concerned she may have taken my suggestion to extremes.'

'Have you spoken to her?'

'No, I haven't been able to get in touch. I tried ringing her hotel last night. It was late and she wasn't in. She's been out late quite a lot these days.'

The duke pulled down his cap against the stiff breeze. 'There's plenty to do in gay Paris.'

'Yes,' the king agreed, adjusting his rifle sling and recommencing his march back down to the valley, 'I, myself, said as much to her.'

'Maybe she's been seduced by some lascivious Frenchman?'

'I know Wallis as well as I know myself!' David snapped, not appreciating his brother's jest.

'Well,' Georgie replied, the smile now wiped from his lips, 'it would seem you are in something of a pickle. Perhaps you should try ringing again, but this time at a different time? Perhaps after tea?'

'Perhaps,' David grunted between puffs. 'I really must cut back on my smoking.'

The wind had died down and the afternoon was warm and sunny, perfect for drinks on the lawn and croquet. Marina was enjoying a singles match against Susanna. Everyone else sat watching on lawn chairs. All except for Henry who was snoring under his fedora, and Churchill who was inside proofreading the second draft of the third volume of his latest book, a biography of his ancestor, 'Marlborough: His Life and Times'.

David sipped lemonade as he watched Susanna strike her second ball. It rolled through the red hoop. She jumped with delight, yelling: 'Yes!'

Everyone applauded and Henry woke with a snort, coughed and mumbled again, 'Jolly good show.'

Marina played her shot. It missed. Her audience moaned in sympathy. Then it was Susanna's turn. She lined up her mallet and struck. It was a confident stroke and it hit the peg. There was generous applause to which she grinned winsomely.

Mary noticed how David was watching Susanna. 'David,' she said, 'why don't you show Susanna the gardens?'

He looked askance at his mother, knowing how close she was to Elizabeth. He suspected the women were plotting, but considered that might be helpful to his ends, toying with the thought of what Wallis might make of the Earl's young daughter? David accepted the suggestion. He put down his drink, walked over to Susanna and complimented her on her game. 'Well played.'

'Thank you, Sir,'

'Please, as I said before, just call me David.'

'Oh, sorry, Sir… I mean David.'

'Would you like me to take you on a guided tour of the place?'

Susanna's nervousness evaporated and her face broke

into a broad smile. There was no need for her to say yes.

The pair strolled around to the west and up the stone steps that led to the formal gardens. Surrounded by a wall of manicured hedges, the gardens were laid out in a pattern of square and curved flowerbeds. They gushed in an effervescent profusion of perennials and annuals in full bloom: fuchsias, zinnias, dahlias and lavender roses, intoxicating in colour and bouquet.

The king walked slowly, his hands behind his back, as he would on a public occasion. 'My great-grandparents, Victoria and Albert, bought Balmoral as a summer holiday home. Like Sandringham, it's private property, not part of the crown estate. The money to build the castle was bequeathed by a wealthy and eccentric old miser named John Camden Nield. His will stipulated that the money be used for Queen Victoria's sole use and benefit, believing she was the only person who wouldn't squander it. The man was so mean, not only could he not stand to see his money spent in his own lifetime, he couldn't bear the thought of its being spent when he was gone. But as you can see, it has been spent and rather well, wouldn't you say?'

'Yes, I would,' Susanna agreed.

'Do you like it here?'

'Yes, it's so beautiful and quiet, so far removed from all the troubles of the world.'

'Your family has made a great sacrifice in the name of all those troubles.'

Susanna showed no surprise that David knew so much about her family. She realised such intimate knowledge was common within the rarefied salons of the aristocracy. 'Yes, both my brothers,' she said softly. 'And my mother. Their loss killed her. She took to her bed and quietly died… But I don't want to talk about the war.'

David looked at her closely. 'You're all your father has.'

Susanna shrugged. 'I know, a vast estate and no son to inherit the title.'

They walked up to the fountain. She sat at its edge and looked into the water. 'He's terrified that I'll be seduced by a bounder. He can be very protective.'

David sat down beside her. 'Many a girl would rebel.'

Susanna noticed the multi coloured carp in the water. 'Oh, look!' She pulled back her hair and leaned closer 'Your fish are very pretty.'

'Yes, I seem to own a lot of pretty things.' David watched as Susanna trailed her fingertips through the sparkling water, her hair shining in the summer sun. 'Are you fond of the theatre?' he asked.

A hard-faced man in a trench coat walked down a dark, narrow street in Soho and entered a corner pub. The front of the pub was crowded with patrons. The man ploughed through the smoke and the clumps of drinkers, and on reaching the bar, ordered two double scotches. He warily cased the room while the drinks were poured neat. The man in the trench coat told the bartender to keep the change as he paid up and carried his drinks to the back of the room, sliding into a dark booth near the entrance to the gents. A younger man sat opposite, dishevelled and bleary.

The hard-faced man pushed one of the double scotches across the table. The younger man grabbed the drink and gulped it down. Though he seemed well bred, he was obviously a dissolute wreck, unshaven, his Savile Row suit looking like he had slept in it. He handed over a large envelope.

The man in the trench coat looked over his shoulder. Nobody was watching. He put on a pair of reading glasses, opened the envelope and inspected its contents. 'Good,' he assessed in a low growl, and in return, handed over a smaller envelope. The dishevelled man opened it and saw a wad of five-pound notes. The man in the overcoat got up and left. The dishevelled man threw back the second double scotch.

The first Royal Command Performance was in 1912. King George and Queen Mary were invited. The king enjoyed it so much he agreed to attend such a show every year, provided the proceeds went to charity. It would be seven years till the next time the event was staged, but since then it had taken place almost every year. In July 1937 the show was staged at the London Palladium. It was a gala event. A large crowd waited around the main entrance to catch a glimpse of the arriving celebrities. One of the last to appear was the king.

Moments before the curtain rose, a Rolls Royce pulled up under the marquee. An attendant opened the back door and David got out. He turned to take the hand of his companion for the evening. Susanna alighted from the car and the crowd went crazy. The press closed in, blinding her in an explosion of flash bulbs. There was pandemonium, the reporters and photographers jostling for position. The spent bulbs fell in an avalanche onto the pavement. They cracked under David's shoes as the couple was escorted through the crush to the theatre's foyer. Once inside, they were greeted by applause from the other guests. Their king waved as they ascended the stairs to the Royal Box.

The show opened with a big production number: a medley of hit tunes from *Porgy and Bess*; followed by George Formby, strumming his ukulele and warbling, through a buck-tooth smile, *Chinese Laundry Blues*. The third act on the program was the latest sensation, Vera Lynn. Standing alone, under a single spotlight, the orchestra barely visible in the pit, she performed her latest hit.

In the Royal Box, behind Susanna and David, sat the American Ambassador to the Court of Saint James, Joseph Kennedy, and his wife, Rose.

Vera Lynn's voice drifted up to the gods as dozens of people in the audience glanced at Susanna.

In the box opposite sat Chamberlain. He was with his wife, Anne. She watched the Royal Box intently and saw Kennedy speak in Susanna's ear. He seemed to be flirting. Susanna giggled.

Vera Lynn's voice melted like honey into the final bar of the song. '…A nightingale sang in Berkeley Square.' She took her bows to rapturous applause, but the audience was not looking at her.

Anne fiddled with her pearl necklace and whispered to her husband, interrupting his genteel clapping: 'I don't see why Ambassador Kennedy should be in the royal box and not us.'

'It's of no consequence,' Chamberlain assured. 'All eyes

are on Lady Susanna.'

David watched Susanna give a shy little wave to the crowd. He turned away and gazed at an inner place, his expression melancholic. Word of this evening, and Susanna, would get back to Wallis. Speculations on her reaction were uppermost in his mind. He was fretting as to whether or not she would care, again wondering what Wallis was getting up to in Paris. He began to have second thoughts about the game he was playing.

The next morning there was a knock on the office door of the German Ambassador. Ribbentrop looked up from his work and barked: 'Geben Sie.'

The man in the trench coat entered, gave the Nazi salute and rasped: 'Heil Hitler!' He handed the ambassador a folder. 'Das Dossierddas sie bestellt haben Herr Botschafter.'

Ribbentrop carefully placed the folder on his leather desk mat. It was a dossier; the subject's name, *Lady Susanna de St Croix*, was typed on the front cover. His lips pursed when he opened it. Arranged in chronological order, lay dozens of hand written letters. 'Ja, sehr gut. Ausgezeichnete arbeit, Dorfman,' he muttered, dismissing his agent with a wave of his hand.

Despite the ambassador's brusque manner, Dorfman knew he had done well. He adjusted his trench coat and acknowledged the compliment: 'Vielen Dank, Herr Botschafter.' With that, he saluted, cried: 'Heil Hitler!' and departed.

Ribbentrop leaned back and put his feet on his desk. From his office he could see the equestrian statue of King

Edward VII; it stood just metres away up Waterloo Place. The former wine merchant had gone out of his way to choose Carlton Street Terrace as the location for the German Embassy; it was the most fashionable address in London. Designed by John Nash, the same architect responsible for Buckingham Palace, the structure consisted of 18 large buildings, formed into two terraces that overlooked St. James Park. Three former prime ministers had lived there: Lord Palmerston in number five, Earl Grey in number thirteen, and Gladstone in four and eleven. In 1937 the German Embassy was in numbers eight and nine.

The ambassador picked up the dossier and flicked through the letters. He allowed himself a small and satisfied grunt before turning back to look out at the statue of King Edward, the present king's grandfather. The monument led him to recall how much the former Edward and the Kaiser had disliked each other; how much the older king had done to disrupt German foreign policy; conspiring to isolate his country; causing Germany to fight a war on two fronts, against the French in the west and the Russians in the east. He believed it an unforgivable betrayal of a long-time ally, thinking to himself: where would the British have been without Frederick the Great? Where would The Duke of Wellington have been, when facing annihilation at the Battle of Waterloo, without the heroic intervention of Blucher's Prussians? Blucher had saved the day, yet the British had never shown his people the slightest gratitude. He nodded, certain the Anglo-Saxons had always been deceitful manipulators of European politics, hiding behind their mote with their Royal Navy.

Ribbentrop bit off a sliver of his thumbnail and spat it out.

Fleet Street had been the centre of British publishing since an apprentice of William Caxton started a printing shop in Shoe Lane, around the year 1500. Now, the Evening Standard, the Daily Telegraph and the Daily Mail were located there. Fleet street was synonymous with the press, and its beating heart was at 120 Fleet Street—ironically, on the corner of Shoe Lane. Here was the biggest circulation and most powerful newspaper of them all, the Daily Express. When Beaverbrook bought it in 1918 it was dull and losing money, but now it was witty and bright, the first paper to carry sports, women's features and gossip.

It was another busy day at the paper. Reporters typed stories, editors argued on the phone, cigarette smoke filled the air; and on the top floor, a cadet reporter raced past a door with a brass plaque that read: 'Lord Beaverbrook'. Within this oak-panelled office, and behind a cluttered desk, sat the baron. He stared at a small pile of hand written letters. They were all addressed to 'My dearest Harry,' the personalized stationery embossed with the de St. Croix family coat of arms, each billet-doux signed by Susanna. Beaverbrook flicked through the letters and smelt them. 'Yardley, English Lavender—very much the country girl.'

A grubby looking reporter sat opposite. 'I got them from a contact in Soho,' he said eagerly. 'I've made some inquiries, it all seems kosher.'

Beaverbrook whistled softly. 'It might be authentic but it certainly isn't kosher.'

'Strange though,' said the reporter. 'Anyone on the street could see what this is worth, but he didn't want no sausage, not a penny.'

Beaverbrook gave a knowing smile. 'Of course not, politics is a game played mostly by amateurs—can't even cover their tracks.'

'It's hot,' warned the reporter.

'Maybe too hot,' the Baron acknowledged.

'You want to run it?'

Beaverbrook gave the letters another sniff.

The next morning the newsstand vendors held up the Daily Express. 'Read all about it: Lady Susanna's secret past.'

People rushed to buy a copy. The other papers lay untouched.

Wallis sat at her desk, reciting the infinitives and conjugations of the principal French irregular verbs, in the present, past and future tenses; as well as their past and present participles. She was determined to know them so well she could say them in her sleep.

Her roomies, Renee du Pont and Mary Kirk, grabbed their ice skates. 'Come on Bessie,' said Renee. 'The Cockeysville bus leaves in five minutes.'

Wallis looked up from her textbooks. 'Please don't call me Bessie!'

'Okay, okay,' whined Mary. 'Renee didn't mean anything by it, but you still ought to come along; there'll be boys at the rink.'

Renee made for the dorm door. 'Don't bother with

Bessie—Oops, sorry, Wallis—She isn't interested in meeting a boy. Not unless his name is Mr Summa cum Laude.'

The roomies rushed out giggling, leaving the door wide open. Feeling a draft and desperate for some privacy, Wallis was forced to get up to close it. Returning to her desk, she gazed out at the surrounding countryside. Snowflakes fluttered beyond the frost-edged glass of her window, and though falling ever so softly, they blanketed the hedges and trees. The woodland surrounding Oldfields School was as silent and magically white as a Christmas card. Snug in the warmth of her room, Wallis could look forward to a peaceful Saturday afternoon. She returned to her mantra of verbs.

Suddenly, there was a knock on the door. Wallis sat up in bed, woken from a dream-laden sleep. Schoolgirl memories of Maryland spiralled into a vortex and disappeared as the maid entered with a pot of coffee and the morning paper.

'Bonjour, Madam,' she said as she placed the tray on Wallis's bedside table. Walking to the window, she opened the curtains, revealing a crisp and sunny day. The bluish haze of summer had departed from the Place Vendome; it was autumn in Paris and the light was as tawny as the falling leaves.

The maid poured the coffee and bowed out. Wallis leafed through the paper, breezing past stories on the war in Spain, and the Nationalist advance on Gijon; Charles Lindbergh's visit to Germany, inspecting Dorniers and Messerschmitts; the deterioration in the health of Maurice Ravel; even an item on Oswald Mosley being knocked unconscious by a rock while addressing a Fascist rally in Liverpool; but on page seven she froze, her eyes immediately riveted to a story headed: 'Susanna de St. Croix, une dame avec une histoire!' Filled with foreboding, she read the article till the very end, and mortified, tossed it aside. Hands shaking, she struggled to sip her coffee.

The phone rang in the living room. Wallis heard the maid take the call. A moment later she entered and announced: 'Le telephone—c'est Monsieur von Ribbentrop.'

Beaverbrook sat with the prime minister in the Cabinet Room, the midmorning light bouncing off the newspaper baron's tightly skinned pate.

'Sorry, old sport,' he said, 'but it's best the story comes out before it's too late.'

Chamberlain put down his copy of the Daily Express and sniffed. 'A subaltern in the Coldstream Guards?'

'Yes,' said Beaverbrook, nodding sagely, as if the tragedy had nothing to do with him. 'The lad was cashiered two years ago.'

'Damn shame,' said Chamberlain mournfully. 'I thought Susanna was enchanting.'

Beaverbrook got up to go. 'I guess, for the king, it's back to scratch.'

Blandford Castle was in Dorset. It had been the home of the de St. Croix family for four hundred and fifty years. Though added to and remodelled extensively, the oldest part of the building still remained, the outer part of the north wing being the original stone fortification, the dungeons now used as wine cellars.

The Earl stood by the fireplace in one of the drawing

rooms. He was a long way from the dungeons, but on this grim morning, he wished he could have thrown his daughter into one or them, and tossed away the key.

'Bloody Beaverbrook—that Canadian upstart! Our family, an illustrious dynasty going back centuries, is now providing scandalous fodder for his filthy, salacious gossip sheet. How could you, Susanna?'

Susanna sat on the sofa, tears pouring from her eyes.

Dorset threw down the paper. 'The de St. Croix family could have married into royalty!'

Susanna took her hanky from her face. 'No, Daddy, that's just not true. David never looked at me that way.'

'What way?'

'The way a man can look at a woman.'

Her father was having none of it. 'Don't bore me with girlish trifles. You could have been queen! Now you're ruined.'

Susanna got up and rushed out of the room. She ran from the house and down to the stables. Her black stallion was in the last stall. She led the horse to the tack room and saddled up. A moment later, Susanna was galloping away from the castle and into the surrounding fields. She whipped the stallion's flanks with her riding crop as they jumped a hedgerow and entered a large meadow. Beyond the meadow lay the woodlands.

Susanna's dynasty was at an end and she would be a social outcast, snubbed and ridiculed: one of those pitiful old spinsters, living out her years in her lonely tower; or worse, marrying beneath her station; perhaps, even less forgivably, buying love from a parade of slippery, ever younger fops, or even the occasional old rogue. Their words would be pretty, but their aim would always be theft—not only of her money, but also the remnants of her reputation. She would be a laughing stock until the day she died.

Since the deaths of her brothers, Susanna had been imprisoned by the extinction of the earldom, her father smothering her with his ambitions for her bridal cot. Only twice had she ventured beyond that portcullis, only twice had she allowed herself to fall in love. Now, the Gods had contrived for those two loves to face each other in a deadly duel. The first had killed the latter, and she had furnished his ammunition. 'Damn you, Harry,' she cursed, 'but damn me too.'

Steam gushed from the horse's nostrils as Susanna entered the woods. The trees rushed past. A dry-stone wall appeared in the distance. She spurred the stallion forward. The wall was just a leap away. She dug her heals into the stallion's belly. Rider and mount were in the air. One of the horse's hooves clipped the wall. Half a ton of beast fell sideways and rolled over. The stallion staggered upright, its leg broken and hanging loose. Susanna lay on the ground, blood trickling from her mouth and her blue eyes drained pale, staring skyward.

'I blame you, Mama.'

Mary sat in her favourite chair. 'Take a hold of yourself. Remember who you are.'

David got up from the sofa, walked to the drinks table and refreshed his scotch. 'You were behind this from the start—you and your scheming. If you had not encouraged me to such a ridiculous flirtation, if you had left me alone, that poor girl would still be alive.'

Mary crossed her legs. 'The de St. Croix name is in tatters.'

'And Susanna…' David slammed down the whisky decanter. 'Susanna is dead, Mama, dead!'

'She had a past. She should have been honest about that.'

'She was just a child,' David moaned. 'A sweet, lovely, innocent child, with more on her poor shoulders than anyone should be expected to bear.'

'Sweet and lovely,' Mary repeated, 'but not innocent.'

'Oh, I see, is that the way it is? Susanna was a blood sacrifice to duty!' David downed his scotch and left. He would never visit his mother again.

Chapter Three, the Deals

The Times of London noted that not since the days of Barbarossa had so many German-speaking people been united under the one flag. It was late 1937 and the British sat in their Odeon cinemas, watching newsreels of German troops marching through the streets of Vienna. Massed crowds of Austrians threw flowers from the sidewalks and raised their hands in the Nazi salute. Standing tall in an open Mercedes convertible, Hitler responded with his own custom-designed salute, the palm of his right hand thrust up to the clouds. After 20 years away he was coming home in triumph, the conquering hero; but, unlike a Roman general, no slave stood behind him, tasked with the duty of whispering in his ear, 'Hominem te esse memento.' Remember that you are but a man. And, 'Memento mori.' Remember that you are mortal. Hitler had annexed Austria. Anschluss. From the Ballhausplatz to every local rathaus the Swastika was run up the flagpole.

The Odeon newsreel crossed to London with footage of David greeting well-dressed people who were alighting a plane. The narrator spoke in a matter-of-fact tone. 'The king meets those lucky enough to be able to make a last minute escape from Vienna.' The movie theatre audiences watched David shake the hand of a dapper man with thinning grey hair and a trim moustache. The narration continued. 'His Majesty greets his old friend, Louis Rothschild. I'm sure they both wish it were under better circumstances.'

Outside, the rain again fell heavily as Chamberlain met with the king in the Audience Chamber. It was their regular Tuesday meeting.

'We registered a protest through our ambassador in Berlin,' Chamberlain said.

David read a copy of the protest letter. 'At least the annexation was bloodless.'

'Yes,' the prime minister agreed, 'the Germans appear to have been welcomed by the general population.'

'Why not? The Austrians are Germans too. It's like England annexing Yorkshire.' David lifted up the teapot. 'Another cup?'

Chamberlain packed his papers into his briefcase. 'No, thank you, I have to get back to Number Ten.'

David put down the pot. 'The government has a budget surplus of twenty eight million pounds. Could you not see your way clear to spending some of it on rearmament?'

Chamberlain froze. 'Have you been listening to Churchill?'

'Hitler is on the march. Who knows where it will all end. An expansion of war production would leave him in no doubt that we're prepared to make a stand. Plus, think of the thousands of jobs it would create.'

Chamberlain got up. 'I really must be going.'

'What good is the money doing, just sitting in the bank?'

'With the greatest respect, Sir, it doesn't grow mouldy in a vault; it is used to pay off government debt.' Picking up his briefcase, the prime minister enunciated peevishly: 'Good day, Sir.' Once outside, he was met by a page of the backstairs, and via the minister's staircase, escorted from the building.

His guest now gone, David also left the Audience Chamber, but by a different door to that taken by Chamberlain. This door gave private access via the Royal Closet to the lobby, avoiding the minister's route. Traversing the lobby, the king entered the Picture Gallery and strolled past a Rembrandt, a Rubens, a Vermeer, a van Dyke and a maid who was changing the flowers. She respectfully turned away to face the wall as he wheeled into one of the palace's most beautiful reception rooms.

The White Drawing Room was a symphony in gold and vanilla cream, the walls sumptuously panelled and punctuated by massive, gilt-framed mirrors. A magnificent portrait of Queen Alexandra graced the north wall and an enormous chandelier hung from the ornately patterned ceiling.

Upon entering, David turned to face a silk lounge suite that lay to his left; it seemed strangely small and insignificant within the immensity of the chamber. The suite clustered around a fireplace, warmed and brightened by the glow from its hearth. He approached the farther of the two sofas. 'Where have you been?'

Wallis reclined before him. 'I've been enjoying the gaiety of Paris,' she said, 'and waiting for my divorce to become absolute, both, as per your instructions.'

'Do you know how often I've tried to call?'

'You never left a message.'

'Why didn't you call me?'

'I didn't think you'd want that.'

'Not want to hear your voice?'

'I thought you'd found someone new… Susanna.'

'Just because I'm seen with someone doesn't mean I'm in love.' David picked up the poker and tended the fire. 'I was trying to make you jealous.'

Wallis suddenly sat up. 'Why would you do such a cruel thing?'

'You were out every time I called.'

'You told me to enjoy myself.'

'I know,' said David, throwing down the poker. 'I know I did.' He walked back to the sofa and stood before her. 'Distance is a tyrant and silence worse.'

She stared at him impassively, teasing as a cat high on a bough, impervious to the threat of a barking dog.

David recognized that look, felt it tingle in his groin. A sensation akin to being in a diving plane, painfully delicious and greatly missed. 'You are the most extraordinary woman I've ever known,' he whispered. 'I've been lost without you.'

Wallis rose to her feet. 'Oh, Boysie, have you?'

'Yes.'

'Yes?'

'Yes.' David kissed her passionately and unfastened the clips on the back of her dress.

'Boysie?'

'Yes?'

'I want to be loud.'

'How loud?'

'Very.'

David pressed against her. 'I'm all ears.'

'Hmm,' Wallis purred, 'I wouldn't say that.' She pressed as hard against him as he to her. 'No, I wouldn't say that at all.' Then she moaned, 'Encourage me.'

David spoke softly. 'You're the place where I dwell.'

'Yes.'

'My shelter from the storm,'

Wallis fell backwards, dragging them both onto the sofa. 'Am I?'

David's tone became more earnest. 'Without you I am naked.'

'Oh, goody,' Wallis kicked off her shoes.

David's hand slipped up her dress and he found she wasn't wearing knickers.

Wallis broke away. 'Do you need me?'

'Do I need you?' he asked back.

'Yes, do you?'

David removed his jacket. 'You're the air I breathe.' He tore away his tie. 'You turn my water into wine.' He undid his collar button. 'My loaves into fishes.' He fiddled with the next button down but it wouldn't budge. Losing patience he ripped open his shirt. The buttons sprayed all over Wallis. David took her in his arms. 'Blessed is the ground on which you walk, even the water you walk on is blessed.'

Wallis laughed ecstatically. 'I'm being beatified.'

David stood to loosen his braces and pull down his pants, using the distracted moment to assert: 'A saint trumps a queen!'

'Oh, Boysie, yes, it does.' Wallis pulled the king back down onto the couch and straddled him. 'It does, it does.' She continued without respite. 'It does. It most assuredly does!'

A spark flew from the fireplace.

Out in the Picture Gallery the maid was still arranging the flowers. She whispered: 'She's back,' and snipped off a dead leaf.

Wallis lay in bed with David. This was the first time she'd been in the Belgian suite and she liked it; the rooms were smaller, cosier, not as overpowering as the other state apartments. She looked up at a small painting of Queen Victoria that hung from the opposite wall. 'You need to redecorate.'

David lay on his stomach, drifting off to sleep. He sighed with an interrogative inflection.

Wallis elaborated: 'She gives me the creeps.'

'Who?' David moaned. He rolled over to locate the source of annoyance. 'Oh, Great Grand Mama.'

The painting surveyed them with disapproval. Wallis instinctively pulled the bedcovers over her naked breasts. 'She looks so stern.'

'That's just her German thing,' David whispered conspiratorially, 'designed to scare the French.'

'Did she ever smile?'

'I can't recall.' David leaned on his elbow and appraised the painting. 'Maybe she had bad teeth. I should take her down, put up someone more appealing—someone with a better dentist. I'll commission a portrait of you, immortalized in oils.'

'Would you?' Wallis asked, failing to disguise her surprise.

'Of course, I've been tardy. I should have done it earlier, while you were in Paris.'

Wallis grew serious. 'I don't want to see myself watching me.'

'You're a funny one. Maybe I should put up a portrait of Mr Chamberlain.'

'Yes, that's a great idea. He could watch us at play.' David pretended to shiver as she asked: 'What's he like?'

'Stingy,' David opined, without hesitation. He poured a glass of champagne from a bottle that sat on the bedside table. 'Been too many years in the exchequer. He's sitting on his hands, not touching millions of pounds that could be put to good use.' He passed the glass to Wallis.

She sat up to take a sip. 'Can't you order him to spend the money?'

'If only it were that simple.' David dropped the empty bottle on the floor and lit a cigarette. 'I have more power than most people realize. For example,' he sniffed, 'I don't have to have a driver's license, stick to the speed limit or pay tax. If Parliament wants to declare war they need my ascent, but it doesn't cut both ways. I can declare war on whomever I wish, and to hell with the lot of them. I could even declare war on America.'

Wallis smiled and put aside her glass. '*Would* you declare war on the States?'

David considered the point. 'No,' he adjudged with eyebrows raised, 'I rather like the place… Anyway,' he smiled, 'might be dashed risky.'

'Good,' said Wallis, 'I'll leave my gasmask in the attic.'

'No,' David continued, unperturbed, 'my power lies in not using it. Use a power and I risk parliament legislating to remove it. All about timing, really—who gets in first. Besides, one power I definitely do not have is the power to get my hands on the national piggy bank. Country had a civil war over that one. I might chop off a few heads, but leave that coin alone.' He sucked on his cigarette and exhaled slowly. 'Oh, dear, almost makes one nostalgic, but such are the slings and arrows of kingly fortune. Bottom line: I don't have any *real* power over the exchequer's spending.'

'Or power over who you can marry?'

David blushed. 'It would seem not.'

Wallis whistled and shook her head. 'Amazing.'

David coughed a little at that. 'I should rather call it idiosyncratic.'

'You need a strong voice in the Parliament.'

David frowned, taken aback, and scratched his chin, drifting into deep thought. 'Yes, you're right,' he slowly observed, 'that's a very good point: I need a voice.' His frown disappeared and he stubbed out his cigarette. 'I need an ally! An ally on the floor of The Commons.'

The king's throat pulsated with a growl. It burst forth as an exuberant kiss, planted firmly on Wallis's lips.

'What's that for?'

'Your beautiful, wrinkly grey matter.' David leapt from the bed to grab the telephone on his desk. 'Has anyone ever told you that you have a very sexy brain?'

Wallis sat up. 'What are you doing?'

'Giving Winston a call—invite him to lunch for a chat.'

'At this hour?'

'Don't worry,' David assured, flicking through his address card file, 'he'll still be awake—his most creative time of day. Does all his writing in the wee small hours.'

Wallis suppressed a satisfied smile as she took a quick sip of champagne. 'While you're at it, phone Louis.'

'Which Louis?'

'Your pal, Louis.'

'Rothschild?'

'Yeah, I mean the Germans stole his castle, his artworks, it cost him a fortune to get out of Vienna.'

David blinked. 'So?'

'So, he's a banker.'

Wallis threw herself back on the bed, arms outstretched in mock exasperation. 'He's a banker who's been robbed. You don't see how that could be useful?' She rolled sideways to drain the dregs of her drink. 'Invite him to your lunch with Churchill.'

Two days later, footmen removed dirty coffee cups from the king's private dining table. One hundred and fifty feet from the crockery's clatter, standing at the bow window of the music room, Wallis gazed out at David. He was taking a postprandial walk amidst the west gardens, accompanied by Churchill and Rothschild.

'I have always loved this beautiful park,' said Rothschild, snapping shots with his Brownie box camera. He looked up from the viewfinder and raised his eyebrows toward David. 'Photographic record for my albums, you see. I hope you don't mind?'

'No, of course not,' David chuckled. 'Fire away, and if you find *this* impressive, you should visit the botanic gardens at Kew.'

'I already have,' Rothschild replied with a knowing smile. Then, suddenly changing the subject, he announced: 'I'm selling Vitkovitz.'

The cigar almost fell from Churchill's mouth; Vitkovitz was the largest steel mill in central Europe. 'To whom?' he asked, his voice uncharacteristically panicky.

'To a consortium in Prague.'

Churchill was impressed. 'You kept it out of the clutches of the Nazis?'

'Winston, as I have told you, I got out of Vienna by the skin of my teeth. What I have not told you is just how thin was that skin; I saw the SS trucks arrive at the airport, saw them through my window, saw them as our plane left the ground. It may have only been the morning of the Anschluss, but they made straight for me. And I tell you this—these NSDVP, they might call themselves socialists but they outdo the acquisitive proclivities of this capitalist that stands before you today; Goering and Himler wasted no time in divvying up the loot.' Rothschild sighed like a man whose daughter had just eloped. 'The Palais Rothschild has been taken, my priceless art collection broken up and flung to the four corners of this new "Reich". Oh dear, I really should have shipped out my favourite pieces.' He shook his head slowly. 'But there would have been talk if I had done that; it would have looked bad. God knows, it doesn't take much for a banker to be seen in an unflattering light—a rat deserting the ship!'

'And the castle at Enzesfield?' asked David.

'Gone, all gone. Everything that wasn't nailed down, everything that *was*.' Rothschild took another photo.

David became wistful, reflecting: 'I loved my times spent at Enzesfielf,'

'I know, it had a wonderful golf course, but at least I am out. Not rotting away under house arrest.'

'Or in a prison cell,' Churchill observed.

'Prison cell? No, the National Socialists are not stupid. At worst they would have set me up in a plush hotel till their account had been settled. Much more plunder in that. More than the ransom you paid for your King Richard the Lionheart. My ransom would have cost me a fortune!' Rothschild laughed at the irony.

David shoved his hands deep into his pockets as if the weather had suddenly turned cold. 'You seemed to have endured the pillaging with remarkable sangfroid.'

'I've lost much, but I have a little tucked away and—as I said—there's Vitkovits. They couldn't take that, and do you know why?'

Rothschild drew a blank from both David and Churchill.

The banker laughed again, leaving his companions yet more baffled. 'It's officially British property, I own the stock, but the factory is a subsidiary of Alliance Insurance.'

The men continued walking as Rothschild explained his thinking. 'I've had my eyes on Hitler's Nazis since the putsch.

They seemed at the time like little more than a street gang rolling dice against the German establishment, but when I read of their leader's tirades, willingly allowed by the judge during his trial, and the light sentence he received for his beer hall uprising; well, it was then that I realised the true nature of the threat he posed. Though seemingly a nobody, it was obvious to me that he spoke for a great swath of the German speaking peoples. He articulated their frustration over the loss of the war, the great "stab in the back," as some have quite incorrectly called it. However, Versailles really was too much.'

Churchill harrumphed.

'I know, Winston,' Rothschild continued, 'the winner takes the spoils, but if you punch a man when he's down, might he not return another day? I know the pent up power, wounded pride and anger that Hitler represents. The Germans will follow him till he has become death to all they know. Nothing will ever stop Hitler except a bullet or a bomb, and I'm not in the armaments business.' The banker slapped his hand against his thigh as if checking all was well in his pocket. 'So, in short, I decided to take out some protection. What better way to insure an asset than to make it part of your family's London based insurance company.'

David and Churchill nodded, acknowledging the banker's wisdom. Louis was part of an extensive clan. It was a dynasty that went back to Louis's great great-grandfather, Amschel Rothschild. He was born in the Judengasse ghetto of Frankfort in 1744. The son of a money lender, he created an extremely prosperous banking business in the German Rhineland states, and facilitated the growth of the family's interests by sending four of his five sons to different European cities to start up branches of their growing financial empire; the Viennese branch of the family was founded by Amschel's second oldest son, Salomon. In Vienna he founded the S.M. von Rothschild Bank. It funded many government enterprises and played an integral role in the development of the Austrian economy. In honour of his services, the Emperor made him a baron. Salomon's great-grandson was Louis. As head of the Rothschild family's Austrian operation he had been one of the Nazi's major targets, with Goering, Himler and their cohorts determined to ransack his estate.

The three men continued their walk. 'At the risk of seeming impolite,' Churchill asked, 'how much will you get for Vitkovitz?'

'Three million pounds.'

Churchill looked at David. 'A tidy sum—I hope it'll be safely tucked away.'

'Yes and no,' the banker shrugged, 'tidy sums do little good when safely tucked away. As you British would say— faint heart never won fair lady.'

'Yes,' said David, 'I'm familiar with the saying.'

The Austrian peered again into his camera. 'It was a smart move to invite me here to lunch.'

Churchill raised an eyebrow. 'Then there is only one problem.'

'And what is that?'

'Chamberlain,' David answered, 'he still has the first penny he ever made. He is resistant to any thought of borrowing money. The terms would have to be very tempting, if not for the prime minister, for a majority of his Cabinet.'

Rothschild looked across the Palace gardens. 'Do you see gentlemen?' he said, pointing with excitement. 'What species of plant do you think that might be?'

'I've not the slightest idea,' David declared before looking at Churchill. 'Winston, you're something of a gardener, what do you think it is?'

'I should say that it's a tree,' he answered, annoyed at being distracted from his plotting. 'More detail than that I cannot furnish.'

'Ah, well, it is a mulberry,' said Louis with a sense of triumph. 'It is the last survivor from a plantation installed by King James the First. He tried to make a killing in the silk business by growing his own silk worms, but the only thing he killed was the worm farm. It was the wrong species of mulberry, but here it still stands, long after King James, long after all its sibling mulberries have fallen.' He took another photograph.

'So, Louis,' David asked, 'can you arrange the money on the right terms?

'Yes, of course I can,' he said matter-of-factly; and, as if to underline the point, he added: 'Roosevelt's "New Deal" hasn't even made a dent in the world's line of credit. Even when people cry poor, there is always an appetite for bonds.' Rothschild took a second snap of the mulberry. 'But will Chamberlain accept a deal?'

Churchill glared at the gnarled old tree, jealous of the attention lavished on it by the banker. Biting down on his cigar, he braced his legs wide like a dance hall bouncer and growled: 'He will once I'm finished with him.'

Minster or Mynster is old English for a large church. Westminster first referred to the palace built by the same king who was responsible for Westminster Abbey, Saint Edward the Confessor. It was located at a place then known as Thorney Island, just west of London. Fifty years later, the son of King William the Conqueror, King William Rufus, added Westminster Hall.

Located on the north bank of the River Thames, Westminster was the principal place of residence of the medieval Norman and Plantagenet kings, with the Royal Council meeting in Westminster Hall. The first official parliament gathered there in 1295. It was divided into two groups: the Lords, composed of the bishops and the aristocracy; and the Commons, composed of the knights, the priests and the merchants.

After King Henry VIII moved out, acquiring a palace in Whitehall from Cardinal Wolsey, Westminster became the official home of the houses of parliament and the royal courts. The House of Commons gained a permanent meeting place in St. Stephens Chapel, during the reign of Edward VI.

Most of Westminster was destroyed by fire in 1834. Reconstruction began six years later, with the House of Lords completed in 1847 and the House of Commons in 1852. The Commons chamber was at the north end of the building and was decorated in shades of green. It measured 47 feet by 68 feet and could only accommodate two thirds of its members. During question time and important debates, junior backbenchers didn't actually sit in parliament but stood at the ends of the room.

As a member of the governing party, Churchill sat to the right of the speaker. Though no longer a member of the Cabinet, his seniority was such that he still took a seat on the front bench, albeit, a good distance from the despatch box.

Churchill had already been speaking for a few minutes. As part of his role in the plot hatched with David and Louis, he was lambasting the government for their lack of insight or resolve. Eyes glaring and jowls aquiver, he pronounced: 'Now Austria is devoured as a tasty appetizer and we do naught but wait for Germany to belch.'

Chamberlain glared at him from the middle of the front bench but Churchill continued unfazed.

'Every day Hitler's Third Reich grows stronger as we grow weaker. We need more guns, more artillery, more tanks. In the air our squadrons of aircraft are obsolete. We must modernise. We must rebuild our armoury. We must harness the reserves of this great nation. We must be ready for the fight. We must build and build now or be destroyed.'

The Labour benches applauded as did many Conservatives but the ministers were unimpressed. Churchill bowed and sat down. The up and coming, young MP, Brendan Bracken, sat on the bench beside him.

'They'll never spend the money,' he muttered.

'Don't speak too soon,' Churchill shot back. 'The king has very useful friends.'

'So, in short, allow me to offer my congratulations,'

Chamberlain conceded. 'With the Cabinet's backing of this new rearmaments program, you'll have the spending you've been fighting for. Though I can assure you, I left my colleagues in no doubt at to my views on the matter.'

David sipped his tea. For the first time he was enjoying his Tuesday meeting with the prime minister.

Chamberlain gave him a long look and smoothed down his moustache. 'Don't think I don't know what's been going on: the maneuvering, the meetings in the city, etc.'

David smiled. 'I might reign over the nation but I also serve it.'

It had taken a lot of arm-twisting, threats and inducements; it had taken a lot of politics, but the king's plotting had been successful. Heralded by a cloud of moths, funds were released from the exchequer's wallet, the prime minister arguing till blue in the face that such an excessively Keynesian reaction to the unemployment situation was unnecessary, pure folly; but to no avail, king had taken rook, round one to the Palace.

The meeting ended, Chamberlain shook hands with David and left. As he was escorted down the Minister's Staircase, he saw Wallis lurking in the upper lobby. He looked directly at her but said nothing.

'Hey, presto,' Wallis pronounced as she entered the Audience Chamber. 'All of a sudden, they've got the dough.'

David was still sitting in his armchair. 'Were you listening in?'

'Can I help it if you leave the door open?' Wallis sat down on the sofa, in the very same spot where the prime minister had only just been. 'Hmm, the seat's still hot. Neville must have been nervous.'

'You'd think it was his money, from his personal safety deposit box.' David pointed to the teapot. Wallis nodded and he rose to pour a cup.

'Was it Churchill's speech?' she asked.

'Yes, in part, it created the demand for action that Louis's offer made irresistible.'

With the aid of a little pair of tongs David picked up a slice of lemon and raised his eyebrows to Wallis. She nodded again and he plopped the lemon into her tea.

'I've trained you well.'

David smiled, amused by the impertinence. Nobody in his world spoke to him the way Wallis did. She could treat him like a servant, like a slave, like a dog, and leave him aroused by the experience. He was mystified as to why this was so, but accepted it; in fact, revelled in it. He handed her the cup of tea. 'Hope it's still hot.'

'I feel sure it will be hot enough,' she parried. 'At home we usually drink it iced.' Wallis made a show of sipping her tea, alluding to an absent heat. 'Okay,' she continued, 'so Winston gave a holler, Louis wheeled in a truckload of money and Neville coughed up, but who'll get the credit?'

David's eyes filled with unalloyed determination. '*We'll* get the credit.'

Britain began to rearm. War or the prospect of war had always magically drawn credit from a money well, earlier professed to be dry. Louis had proved true to his word: his terms more generous than many in the world of high finance could have imagined, drilling where the water table of liquidity was higher than anyone could have dreamed. The borrowed millions were thrown into a national cupboard so bare that the money was gobbled up without the slightest fart of inflation. The orders went out for the design and manufacture of modern tanks and howitzers, royal ordinance factories began the large-scale production of munitions and shadow factories were created to supplement the effort. The Royal Navy began modernising the fleet with such innovations as horizontal armour and large command towers. But far and away the biggest effort was put into air power. The front-line fighters of the Royal Air Force were still biplanes, little improved since the Great War. Now, the nation began to design and develop monoplanes, unleashing the full potential of British energy and ingenuity, creating modern fighters and bombers and prepared to manufacture them in quantities unheard of. All these efforts and more created jobs in the tens of thousands, the once-full soup kitchens losing much custom, the nation going back to work.

It was a beautiful sunny day when David got up to address the hundreds of workers gathered at the new Hawker factory in Langley, Berkshire. In front of an enormous airplane hanger a stage had been erected. It was covered in red, white and blue bunting, and supported a swarm of local dignitaries. Success has a thousand fathers, but only one mother, thought David as he stood, centre stage, and winked at Wallis. She was there, immediately to his right. This was the first time since her return she had accompanied the king to an official function.

The press had noted her presence, but the heat had gone out of the marriage story; it was yesterday's news. The government didn't like Wallis being seen so publicly. In fact, they had advised against her attending, but David ignored them; if it hadn't been for her the Hawker factory would still be sitting on the drawing board. Besides, the king's popularity had grown so great that Chamberlain and others in the Cabinet dared not take him on. Many people even spoke of the king as the strong man that Britain would need to counter the challenge of German expansionism, and to hell with the finer points of constitutional democracy.

David positioned himself precisely two feet behind his two imported Neumann microphones. Customised by the Berlin manufacturers for British amplification technology, he took the bottle shaped instruments with him everywhere. He had even hired a German-trained electrician to travel ahead of him and oversee the sound design for public address systems ranging in size from town halls and factories to opera theatres and football stadiums.

Head held high, David stared out over his audience, and without reference to notes, he addressed them. 'The nation is embarked upon a bold new enterprise. This factory like others around the country will create much-needed jobs. Your work will bring fresh hope to you, your families and your city.'

The workers applauded and cheered. David turned and smiled at Wallis before continuing. 'Here you will build a bold new fighter plane, the Hawker Hurricane. A weapon that will inspire awe and envy in less happier lands, a mighty part of a mightier program, creating jobs for many others just like you.

We will insure the peace by keeping you and Britain strong. This will be a nation fit for heroes!'

As had happened so many times before, the crowd went wild.

That evening, at Number 10 Downing Street, Chamberlain and his wife, Anne, had the American Ambassador, Joseph Kennedy, and his wife, Rose, over for dinner. They sat under the vaulted ceiling of the wood-panelled State Dining Room, the two couples clustered on opposite sides of the table, halfway along its thirty-foot length.

Kennedy munched on his roast beef. 'How's it feel to have Wallis Simpson back in town?'

Chamberlain adjusted his napkin. 'Not pleasant, but the situation is tolerable, so long as she remains Mrs Simpson.'

'Ah, yeah,' said Kennedy, 'but single again, foot loose and fancy free.' He wiped his mouth with his napkin and took a sip of wine. The grandson of Irish immigrants, Joseph Patrick Kennedy was a native of Boston, Massachusetts. After graduating from Harvard, he started his career on the government payroll as a bank examiner, and through some judicious borrowing, was a bank president 18 months later. He went on to make his fortune on Wall Street, trading stock in the bull market of the 1920s, and making even more money selling short after it crashed. He said he knew it was time to get out after receiving stock tips from a shoeshine boy.

During the depression Kennedy increased his fortune from four million to 180 million dollars. He invested in liquor importation, real estate and the movies; he owned the

American import licenses for Gordon's Gin and Dewer's Scotch, and was the founder of RKO Pictures; but through all of this, he was ever the passionate New Dealer, and for his support, appointed by President Franklin Roosevelt as the first chairman of the Securities and Exchange Commission.

Kennedy had realised early in life that the key to business success was knowledge. He owed his astounding good fortune, not so such much to any particular gifts, but to a love of facts and the energy he put into ingratiating himself with a diversity of lucrative social and political contacts. It was no surprise that Rose, his wife, was the daughter of a former Boston Mayor. Apart from other considerations, this was a good career move. Plus, as a wife and mother, Rose had proved to be yet another profitable investment, bearing him nine children. In 1937 Roosevelt appointed Kennedy as United States Ambassador to the Court of St. James.

'Yes, Mr Ambassador, Wallis is now irrevocably single,' sniffed the prime minister. 'Her divorce is absolute. We can only hope that it doesn't mean another matrimonial crisis.'

'Such a tragedy that he never married Lady Susanna,' said Anne.

Kennedy nodded sagely. 'A very pretty girl, I liked her a lot.'

Rose looked askance at her philandering husband, but diplomatically chose to ignore the lust she recognised as implicit in his worldly observation. 'Certainly an improvement on the Warfield woman,' she quietly added.

'Simpson woman,' Chamberlain corrected.

'Warfield, Simpson, Spencer,' said Kennedy, losing

patience, 'the label might change but it's still wrapped around a can of worms.'

Chamberlain was taken aback. 'I'm given to believe that Wallis is very popular in America.'

Anne added: 'Time Magazine named her woman of the year.'

'Perhaps,' said Rose, 'but Joe and I refuse to have anything to do with her.'

Kennedy took another sip of wine. 'Woman's a tart.'

Rose shook her head slowly. 'I've heard appalling stories from Baltimore where she grew up.'

Neither of the Chamberlains dared ask her to elaborate.

Kennedy looked the prime minister square-in-the-eye. 'She could still become a real pain in the neck.'

Chamberlain could see that Kennedy knew more than he was letting on.

That same evening David and Wallis invited Georgie and Marina to dinner at the Palace. The couple had become regular guests. Many in the royal family disliked Wallis, seeing her influence as akin to Eve with her shiny apple, but Georgie and Marina were not of that opinion; they saw the strength and resourcefulness Wallis inspired in David.

Marina was David and Georgie's second cousin, and a great-granddaughter of Tsar Alexander of Russia. The murder of the Russian royal family had left her scarred for life, her fear of communism almost pathological, and her loathing for its adherents exceeded only by her loyalty to her husband and her brother-in-law, the king. These passions were impossible to perceive as she smiled serenely at David from across the table. 'I see you've been busy of late,' she observed, an oyster quivering from the end of her fork, 'the press are singing your praises.'

David watched as a footman refreshed her glass of wine. 'These are heady times. Arms manufacture has the capacity to employ thousands.'

'To fight the Germans?' Georgie asked.

'Heaven forbid!' said David. 'No, to discourage them.'

Georgie turned and clicked his fingers to his footman. 'I have something for you.'

The footman walked across to the king and handed him a book. He looked at the cover. '"Mein Kampf"—My Struggle. Yes, I've heard about this.'

Georgie put his elbows on the table and rested his chin on the back of his hands. 'It's available in quite a few bookstores. Read it. Bit heavy going in places but you'll soon discover that Hitler has no quarrel with us. Not even with the French.'

Marina put down her fork. 'His eyes are focused east.'

David handed the book to Watson. 'I wonder if his eyes were on the thugs who plundered Louis?'

'You're the king,' said Georgie. 'Does that make you responsible for each and every excess that might be committed by our police or armed forces?'

Marina chimed in. 'If left alone, Hitler could bring down the Bolsheviks, the thugs who killed my family, your cousins. The thugs who'd kill us if we don't kill them first.'

David turned to Wallis. 'What do you think?'

'About Hitler?'

'Yes.'

Wallis had heard David the first time, but she was loathe to talk openly on political issues for fear word might get out to her many detractors. She solved her dilemma in an instant by speaking not from her own point of view, but from that of the Germans. Shrugging nonchalantly, she said: 'He's a big hit.'

Georgie saw the need for a more enthusiastic response. He leaned back and spoke with clear-eyed excitement and moral certainty. 'The man has been extraordinary. He's put the German people back to work. Zero unemployment.'

David sighed and looked into his wine glass. 'I wish I could make such a boast.'

Later that night David lay in bed smoking. He looked at Wallis who was leafing through the copy of Mein Kampf. 'It's been over a year since your divorce. Do you think we should try—'

'No way,' said Wallis, her nose still in the book, 'I'm not going to be the centre of another crisis.'

'But time has elapsed, the Cabinet and Chamberlain—'

'Would love a reason to get rid of you. Sorry, but this girl's already seen enough pain in her life.'

'I'm sorry, I should have—'

'No, not you, sweetheart, you're a pussycat. I'm talking about real pain.'

David frowned, perplexed. 'Physical pain?'

Wallis looked closely at him and ran her tongue over her teeth. 'Let me show you something.' She lowered her head and carefully parted the hair on the side of her scalp. 'Can you see?'

'Shift closer to the light.' David pulled back. 'Oh my God, I can't believe I've never noticed this before.'

'I keep it well hidden.'

'It looks like a shrapnel wound.' David gingerly touched the scar. 'What caused it?'

Wallis reached for a cigarette. 'Not what, who.'

'Alright, who?'

'My husband.'

'Simpson?'

'No, the first one, Spencer.'

David lit Wallis's cigarette as she continued. 'We were in Shanghai, he was drunk, I must have said the wrong thing and kablooey! I wake up in hospital. Bastard nearly killed me. And that wasn't the first time either, but it was certainly the last.'

'How did you get mixed up with such an animal?'

'He was rich. Mother was determined that I'd get hitched to money. I was her retirement fund.'

'That's terrible. What sort of man would do such a thing? I mean, Chamberlain may not like you, but he'd never hit you on the head.'

'But what would he do to his king?'

Wallis sat up and put her cigarette in the ashtray. 'Boysie, you are the most loved monarch since Victoria, maybe since forever. Can't you see? The politicians hate you for that. Your popularity makes you a threat.'

'Good,' said David defiantly, 'but you know who has the real power?' With his fingertip he touched Wallis on the end of her nose and answered his own question. 'You, you're the power behind the throne.'

'You bet your sweet ass,' said Wallis. She took his finger and sucked it.

The night outside was clear, the stars twinkling brightly. The German agent, Dorfman, stood by a street lamp on Constitution Hill. The cold light carving deep shadows into the fissures of his face, he stared up at the Palace and threw down the butt of his cigarette, grinding it under his heel.

That same evening there was blood and fire on the streets of Czechoslovakia. The Sudetenland was in open revolt.

Horace Wilson passed his report across the cabinet table. 'He devoured Austria with ease. Now Herr Hitler feels secure enough to turn to the next course on his menu.'

Chamberlain was horrified. He leafed through the pages of Wilson's exhaustive background paper. The senior civil servant had rewarded the prime minister's faith in him. It was a superb effort considering he'd only been briefed 24 hours earlier. 'Please, take a seat, Horace, and give me a quick outline of your findings.'

Wilson sat down on the opposite side of the Cabinet table. Chamberlain had not needed to use his favourite advisor, he could have turned to the foreign office for a report, but he wanted to take charge of the Czechoslovakian issue personally, and keep Lord Halifax, at a distance; the foreign secretary had been making too many noises about taking a stronger line against further concessions to Germany. Chamberlain meant to use Wilson as a de facto plenipotentiary and circumvent Halifax.

The civil servant brimmed with barely constrained enthusiasm for the task ahead. He spoke with clarity and confidence. 'As you would of course know, prime minister, following the Great War armistice, the treaty of Versailles called for the break up of the Austro Hungarian Empire into several parts. These included the new nation of Czechoslovakia. However, the basis for this revised map of Europe was the right to national self-determination for the many ethnic groups within it. However, the three million German-speaking people of the Sudeten region were denied this right. They have been ignored—left stuck within the borders of a Slavic Czechoslovakia these last twenty years. They are an ethnic minority. The German Chancellor considers this to be unfair, arguing that it is inconsistent with the aims and intentions of Versailles. As you will find, expressed in greater detail in my report, it is my view that this is a situation that Germany will no longer tolerate and which their leader is determined to exploit. Herr Hitler is prepared to do whatever he considers necessary to bring the Sudetenland into the fold of what he now calls the Third Reich.'

'I see,' sniffed Chamberlain. 'How much support has he amongst these Suden people?'

'Sudetenlanders,' Wilson politely corrected. 'Hitler has enlisted the support of the region's leader. His name is Konrad Henlein. Intelligence reports suggest that he privately endorses the slogan of "ein Volk, ein Reich, ein Fuhrer," but in front of the public he has pragmatically campaigned for the lesser ambition of self-determination for his community, who he argues, could still be part of a greater Czech state. Henlein demands a plebiscite on the question of semi-autonomy for the Sudetenland, but I suspect he is secretly planning its full incorporation into Germany.'

Chamberlain perused the contents page of the report. 'I suppose we should have made more noise about Austria.'

'But still, Prime Minister, he has a point. It is the same one used to support the Anschluss, the union with Austria. That is to say that he is simply acting within the aims and aspirations of the Versailles treaty. If it is good enough for all the Poles to live in Poland, all the southern Slavs in Yugoslavia, Latvians in Latvia, why not all the Germans in Germany?'

'Whether his position is right or wrong, defensible or otherwise, we can't be seen to be submissive,' the prime minister asserted, employing all the statesmanship his weary bearing could muster. 'We must negotiate and negotiate hard. Any concessions that Herr Hitler may gain from us must come at a cost that will leave the international situation in balance. Any victory must be pyrrhic, or at the very least, be seen to be so.'

Chamberlain rose from the Cabinet table and walked to the window. He took out his fob watch, checking the hour as if to reference the urgency of the situation. 'Horace, I'm appointing you as a special emissary to Czechoslovakia. Persuade the Czech prime minister—what was his name again?'

'Edvard Benes.'

'Yes, have a talk with this Benes chap. Get him to accede to Henlein's request. It seems reasonable enough: a vote by the Sudeten Germans that might lead to a greater recognition of their rights, language and culture. That sort of thing.'

'And if he should prove recalcitrant?'

'Then we face the prospect of a war between Germany and Czechoslovakia, a war the Czechs could never win. Benes must agree to Hitler's demand, otherwise he would put Great Britain into a very difficult situation.'

Wilson flew to Prague the next day, but it was too little too late. Henlein had already broken off from his negotiations with the Czech government and had ordered his people onto the streets. The fight had begun. The Sudeten Germans were forcefully demanding not just recognition of their language and culture, but instead, the region's full unification with Germany. Their campaign of violence and disruption reverberated all the way to Chamberlain's desk at Westminster.

Churchill was appalled by the turn of events. Over breakfast he complained to his ever-patient wife, Clementine, of his frustration at his lack of influence in Whitehall. He was locked out and incapable of doing anything to bolster Britain's position. Clemmie watched her poor 'Pug' with large, doleful eyes. After thirty years of marriage she well knew his mood swings: from breathtaking ebullience to the depths of despair. She could think of nothing to say that might improve his temper except to mention that their guest, arriving later in the morning, might go some way to helping address the issues that so concerned him. 'I've heard something of Major Kleist,' she said as she sipped her tea.

'Oh,' enquired Churchill, taking a mouthful of soft-boiled egg. 'Are you in possession of information that Sir Robert

Vansittart has kept from me?'

'Winston, you should never forget that the old boy's network has a subtext.'

'Please tell me more, my dearest. Are you hinting at subversion within the Foreign Office.'

'I'm not hinting at anything. I'm telling you what should be obvious: Bobby might be the Permanent Under Secretary, but he is also a husband.'

Churchill put down his spoon. 'What has Susan told you?'

Clementine lifted his napkin from his lap and wiped egg from his chin. 'Our guest, Mr Kleist, is no friend of Mr Hitler. Susan heard from a little bird that the major refuses to fly the new German swastika flag from his castle. He's sticking with the old imperial flag.'

'Clemmie,' Churchill conceded, 'I would be nothing without your talent for espionage.'

'And my enduring optimism,' she added, pouring herself more tea.

An hour later Churchill greeted Major Ewalt von Kleist-Schmenzin. His visitor was dressed in civilian clothes but still appeared stiff and formal. Churchill suggested a walk in the garden in the hope that it might get him to relax.

As they wandered through the grounds, Churchill pointed out items of interest, as if dictating to one of his many amanuenses the text for a tour guide. 'We have a flat near Victoria Station, but this is where the family is at its happiest. We have over eighty acres here. The place is named after Chart Well which is located nearby.' Churchill pointed across the hills. 'The word chart is Old English. It means rough terrain.'

Kleist nodded. 'The area *is* hilly.'

'Good for defence,' Churchill chuckled. 'The house is located on high ground, positioned to offer a spectacular outlook over there, across the Weald of Kent. You might call it my redoubt. It was this view that convinced us to buy the house some 15 years ago.'

'Do you get lonely out here?'

'Oh, no, never, Clementine and I love to entertain. Every weekend, and sometimes on weekdays too, we have at least a couple of people over for dinner.'

Churchill wasn't lying. The sparkling conversation at the Chartwell dining table attracted a wide circle of friends and colleagues, but all that was now far from Churchill's mind. On this otherwise sunny day, he was still pinioned by the weight of his depression, the battle to be a good host only made successful by his curiosity as to why Kleist had come calling.

Beyond the orchard they arrived at a winding brick wall. 'Built that terrace myself,' said Churchill.

'You are a bricklayer?' the German asked.

'Paid up member of the guild.'

'You could help the French with their Maginot Line.'

'Better that than the Siegfried Line.'

Von Kleist enjoyed the quip and finally relaxed enough to smile. 'I have been sent to Britain by certain elements of the German General Staff to assess where the British government stands with its policy on Europe.'

'I see,' said Churchill as he pulled two Havana cigars from his jacket pocket. He offered one of the Cubans to his guest.

'No, thank you,' said Kleist, shaking his head as he leaned over to inspect the pointing on Churchill's brickwork.

'Major, I am loath to reveal anything without knowing a little more about the people for whom you speak. Are you a National Socialist?'

Kleist's immediately stood up, his posture again stiffening. 'Not all Germans are mad, and certainly not I.'

'My dear Major Kleist, please forgive me, I didn't mean to give offence.'

'Good, then none is taken.' The two men returned to their ramble as Kleist continued. 'The senior officers of the Wehrmacht supported Hitler when he first came to power, seeing him as a steady hand to bring strong government, the means to a national revival of Germany and the only solution against the threat of communism. But now, many fear that Hitler's policies are leading our country to disaster.'

'Who are these leaders?' asked Churchill, disguising the eagerness of his curiosity by going through his pockets to find a light.

Kleist was wary, but realised that if he wished to be taken seriously he had no choice but to answer. 'Please understand, this information I give you is strictly confidential.'

'Anything you say will be treated with the utmost discretion,' Churchill reassured, still looking for his matches.

Kleist gave him a long, steady look before continuing. 'The leaders of the antiwar movement within the General Staff are Chief of Staff, Colonel General Ludwig Beck and Rear Admiral Wilhelm Canaris, head of the Abwehr, which as you would be aware is our chief military intelligence agency. It is under their direct orders that I have travelled to see you.'

Churchill was impressed; he realised that he was effectively talking to the apex of the German military command. After further investigative conversation, Kleist revealed that he was a Conservative Monarchist and a devout Christian. Unlike most of his fellow officers, he had opposed Nazism from the very start. His assignment meant talking to Sir Robert Vansittart, Permanent Under-Secretary of the Foreign Office, and to his host, Winston Churchill, whom he now informed was seen by many in the German General Staff as a force that might be useful to their cause.

The major and the politician walked past the pond and looked at the ducks. Kleist thrust his hands behind his back. 'Where does Britain stand exactly?'

Though flattered at being asked for the commentary, Churchill feigned modesty. 'Major von Kleist, I find that question strange. Why would Admiral Canaris and General Beck send a secret emissary to see me?'

'We wish to influence British foreign policy.'

'But I'm not a minister in the Government. I'm not even a parliamentary secretary.'

'Let me assure you that we are in no doubt as to the power you wield…' The German looked out across the meadows and wooded hills of Kent. 'You and the king.'

Fascinated by what he was hearing, Churchill had forgotten all about finding his matches. 'Would you like a light?' asked Kleist, handing him a box of his own.

'Thank you,' said Churchill, and took the matches. 'I would never be so bold as to speak for the king,' he continued, finally lighting his cigar, 'however, I believe that the spectacle of an armed attack by Germany upon a small neighbour, such as Czechoslovakia, and the bloody fighting that should surely follow, would rouse the whole British Empire and compel the gravest decisions.'

'I see,' said Kleist, 'that is good.'

Churchill chewed pensively on his cigar as he mulled over this seemingly contrarian response. He offered back the matches.

'No, you keep them. I don't smoke,' said Kleist.

'Thank you,' said Churchill, pocketing the matchbox, 'always forgetting the blasted things.'

'So I've been told. That's why I decided to come prepared.'

Churchill laughed, though he was secretly alarmed that Kleist had been so thoroughly briefed. 'Major, I have been frank with you. I expect you to be frank with me.'

Kleist became very still as he considered his response. Again he stared into the distance, looking for-all-the-world as if he thought he might catch a glimpse of the English Channel. 'How I wish Germany could be so protected by geography,' he bemoaned. 'You may not know it, few British do, but my beloved Prussia stands in the midst of a vast plain, flat as a potato pancake, stretching from the North Sea all the way to Moscow. The borders of the intervening nations are as changeable as the alluvium on which they stand. It irks me that people called Prussia, not a state with an army, but an army with a state. What would the British do if their ramparts were as difficult to defend?' Churchill shrugged. 'Yes,' the major interpreted from the gesture, 'things would be different. Like us, you would have to invest far more in your army and far less in your navy. You certainly wouldn't have enough money left over to create the Royal Navy, a force big enough to project British interests to every corner of the globe and thereby control the world's sea-lanes. He who owns the ocean controls its trade, and therein sits the source of British power. You, Mr Churchill, as with all of your citizens, enjoy the benefit of controlling a vast empire, while Prussia is now just one of several German states.' He looked away and tried to think of other things. 'There is a great deal of suppressed opposition to Hitler in my country,' he admitted after a prolonged hesitation. 'Britain must stand up to him and reject its policy of appeasement. This would encourage Hitler's opposition in the High Command. He could not stand up to the weight of the Wehrmacht. He is a house of cards. Deny him success, break the spell and we will topple him.'

Churchill smiled, his dark mood forgotten. 'Do you like pork sausages?'

'I am German,' Kleist replied.

'Then you must come and take a look at my prize-winning pigs.

Chamberlain leaned over the Cabinet table and placed his palms together in front of his bowed head. After a second's pause for silent meditation, he looked skyward and spoke emphatically.

'The Czechoslovakian Sudetenland is of no strategic importance to Britain.' He turned and sipped his tea. 'I mean, to begin with, anyway you look at it, the region is ethnically German.'

Horace Wilson again sat opposite, having only just returned from Czechoslovakia. 'Yes, that's true, Prime Minister, but I've just been speaking to Mr Churchill.'

'Oh, no,' groaned Chamberlain.

Wilson pulled from his folder a transcript of his meetings with Benes and passed it across the table. 'Churchill's keen to know everything of our negotiations. He's demanding that we send the Germans an ultimatum, that any violation of Czech territory will mean immediate war.'

'Churchill!' said Chamberlain, spitting out the word.

Wilson continued, warming to his task. 'He says that both the French and the Russians are ready for an offensive against Germany.'

In disbelief the prime minister put aside Wilson's transcript. 'What could Churchill possibly know of Stalin's thoughts, or for that matter, the French. Is the man insane?'

As an ex-serviceman David took a keen interest in the welfare of the veterans. After the Great War he constantly visited hospitals for the treatment of the wounded, and following the formation of the British Legion, visited many ex-servicemen's clubs and associations. After becoming king he invited six thousand Canadian war veterans to a garden party at Buckingham Palace, and soon the function was repeated for other units. Dressed in lounge suits and wearing their medals, these men strolling through the Bow Room to be served tea and cakes al fresco, formed an alien sight for the conservative officials of the royal court. They were used to seeing top hats and morning coats on Palace guests.

In early September David hosted a garden party for veterans of the 18th division, an elite unit that spent the duration of the Great War on the Western Front and saw distinguished service at the Battle of the Somme and at Ypres. The men were mostly raised from the south east of England and many were able to attend.

David met them on the main lawn with an informality not seen before in a British monarch. Most of the ex-servicemen were still in their late thirties and forties. A large number were amputees. They all smiled warmly when their turn came to greet their king.

David, like his guests, wore a lounge suit, his medals pinned to his jacket. A new generation had grown up, the children of his fellow veterans. In conversations with Wallis, and with Georgie, David had expressed the view that he was the person who was ultimately responsible for the welfare of this coming generation. As the king he was the commander in chief of the British military. He felt it to be within his gift to give these children peace and life, or war and death.

He approached a former infantry private. The man wore the crimson and bronze of the Victoria Cross, and two craters lay where once his eyes had witnessed a world gone mad. David shook his left hand because the right hand was gone.

In the spring of 1918 Private Jenkins was on duty in a forward trench when his unit was suddenly faced with a German massed assault. The young private held his ground while all those around him fell. Some ten minutes into the battle, Jenkins saw an enemy grenade fly toward his trench. It landed between two wounded comrades who lay beside him. Showing total disregard for his own safety, he leapt over his mates and seized the grenade, throwing it back to its original owner. The grenade exploded before it had carried any distance, the shrapnel blowing away his right hand, leaving him deaf in one ear and totally blind. Jenkins caught his breath when he felt the king shake his other hand.

'Don't grip it too firm, Your Majesty. It's the only one I got left.' He smiled into the darkness and everyone laughed in support.'

David compensated by gently cupping the ex-serviceman's remaining hand in both of his. 'Are you being looked after?'

'Oh, too right, Sir,' he answered, quite gleefully, and raised the retractable hook at the end of his arm. 'The Missus keeps it nicely oiled for me.' Another broad smile appeared on the veteran's scarred face.

'Good luck, Mr Jenkins, and give your wonderful wife my best regards.' David turned to move down the line.

'Sir?' said Jenkins.

David turned back to see the man saluting, his hook pressed against his forehead. 'With respect, Sir, please look after my two sons. They're young men now. I don't want them to see what my lost eyes once saw.'

David was taken aback, causing him to hesitate for an instant before returning the salute. 'Rest assured,' he said, empathising with the mutilated but proud old soldier, 'I will use all the power that God might grant me to keep your children safe.'

'Thank you, Sir.'

With that, David continued on his way, but the power of Jenkins's humbly phrased request would never be forgotten.

After personally greeting many more men, David walked up to the West Balcony and his Neumann microphones. His voice carried with crystal clarity.

'Former brothers in arms, ladies and gentlemen, nobody believes more than I that a strong and well defended Britain is vital…'

Behind the balcony, through the French doors of the Blue Drawing Room, Wallis and Georgie watched as David continued.

'But nobody knows better than we that war is a terrible thing.' The king looked across a sea of trusting faces. 'Our sons and daughters deserve better than our generation experienced. The British people should not be expected to sacrifice themselves to another bloody war.'

From then on, between stops, waiting for the interruption of applause to pass, David spoke of the strength of Britain's growing industries and the bright future that lay ahead beyond the present troubles. When he had finished he left the balcony and entered the palace. Wallis was able to give him a quick kiss before Georgie stepped forward to whisper in his ear. 'We need to talk in private.'

Minutes later they were sitting in the Audience Chamber. 'Chamberlain has just made an announcement in the Commons,' said Georgie, his voice hushed. 'Hitler's invited him to a conference in Munich to negotiate an agreement over Czechoslovakia. He flies out tomorrow morning.'

Wallis looked concerned. 'What about the Czechs?'

Georgie lit a cigarette. 'The Czechs can suit themselves.'

For the first time in his life, Neville Chamberlain entered an aeroplane, and together with Horace Wilson, flew to Germany. There was a lot of air turbulence and it proved to be a bumpy ride. Whether through bad nerves or airsickness, the prime minister was compelled to procure from the flight crew a receptacle in which to lose his breakfast. That afternoon at the conference things were no less bumpy, the talks held in the cold and echoing marble hall of the Fuhrerbrau. Hitler sat before an enormous swastika that hung down between two brutally large columns. All around were dozens of his henchmen. He glared across a conference table the size of a paddock, and spoke harshly, his voice churning with a throaty vibrato. 'Das Reich wird die Beklemmung der dreieinhalb Millionen Deutschen im Sudetenland nicht dulden.'

Ribbentrop sat beside him, elegantly translating the words and honeying the tone. 'The Reich will not tolerate the oppression of the three and a half million Germans in the Sudetenland.'

'Das Beruaben dieser Leute ihrer Rechte muss ablaufen.'

'The depriving of these people of their rights must come to an end.'

Chamberlain smiled, exposing his teeth like a country parson. 'Great Britain is not opposed in principle to the self-determination of these people.'

Ribbentrop translated the British prime minister's words. 'Grosbritannien ist night grundsatzlich an die.'

And so it went on for hours, until all but Hitler were exhausted. Chamberlain and Wilson rose from their seats as a short recess was called. They walked out into the lobby and conferred. The prime minister was exasperated. 'We should not be talking of going to war over a quarrel in a far-away country between people of whom we know nothing.'

'The Czechs have been calling,' said Wilson. 'They're desperate to know what's going on.'

Chamberlain inhaled sharply, his irritation amplifying his confidential remarks to the broadcast level of a stage whisper. 'They must leave this matter to us. If they do not, we will wash our hands of them.'

'Tell the Czechs, they need not worry.'

Chamberlain turned around in surprise. 'Herr von Ribbentrop!'

The ambassador spoke in a voice that soothed, sympathetic to the prime minister's anxiety. 'The Fuhrer has no wish to include any Slavs in the Reich. Why would we want them? We only desire the German speaking lands, dishonestly held by Czechoslovakia.'

Chamberlain was feeling each of his sixty-nine years. Broken by the torture of Hitler's haranguing and intransigence, his voice was reduced to a rasp. 'All we want is a fair and peaceful settlement.'

Ribbentrop's arms opened wide. 'And that you shall have.'

Churchill had spent several hours with his two friends and supporters, Leslie Hore-Belisha, the Secretary of State for War, and Sir Robert Vansittart, the permanent head of the Foreign Office. They discussed in detail the implications of Kleist's visit and how they might make the most use of his information. All agreed that Kleist must be legitimate because none could see how the Nazi cause could possibly benefit from his entreaty. Following his visit to Vansittart's Whitehall office, Churchill took a cab to the Palace.

David was surprised by Churchill's mood. The normally outspoken old politician seemed strangely reticent, deeply troubled by the situation in Czechoslovakia. If not for a politeness elicited by the fact he was king, David suspected his guest would otherwise have been far less subdued, descending into irascibility with outbursts of unabashed rhetoric.

Seeing the weather was warm and sunny, David suggested they take a stroll in the garden. In the past they had found the ploy useful, both agreeing that fresh air and pleasant scenery could elicit inspired thinking not possible indoors. If there was anything important to discuss, the garden was the place to do it.

Churchill waddled at a surprisingly fast pace. 'Your garden party for the veterans was well attended.'

'Thank you, Winston, it's a pity you weren't there.'

'But, Sir, your party was for the Eighteenth Division. I was a Lieutenant-Colonel in the ninth.'

'Oh, Winston, I know that, but you could have come as my special guest, maybe said a few words.' David paused and smiled. 'You're a busy man—you've not dropped in simply to pass the time. Why are you here?'

Churchill stopped and leaned both hands on his cane. 'I feel I must warn you that your call for appeasement may be popular right now but you risk encouraging Hitler to make greater demands.'

The smile dropped from David's face.

Churchill knew that his argument could never be advanced if he should irritate the king. He quickly switched to a lighter topic, indicating with the end of his cane a new flowerbed. 'Beautiful chrysanthemums.'

'Thank you, they were planted at Wallis's suggestion.'

Churchill nodded, 'Very nice,' and they continued their walk.

David's mood brightened again and he returned to their earlier topic of conversation. 'Hitler simply wishes to restore German pride.'

'Does he?' asked Churchill portentously. 'We must make a stand even if it means war. Why rearm if not for war?'

'We rearm for peace,' David protested, 'to discourage adventurism not only by Hitler but also Stalin.'

'If that is our aim then we shall fail.'

'So nothing is settled except by war? Forgive me if I disagree.'

'No matter how beautiful your strategy, you should sometimes look at the result. No war was ever won by rattling a sabre.'

David smiled and took the liberty of giving his friend a gentle dig. 'And none but you, Winston, would draw that sabre with more glee.' He looked up and saw Wallis on the West

Balcony and gave her a small wave. 'Listen to the people, Winston,' he warned. 'The people want peace.'

After a quick drink with David and Wallis, Churchill bid them farewell and took a cab to the Savoy Hotel. There he met Anthony Eden and a handful of other politicians, most of whom were not his fellow Conservatives but members of the Liberal and Labour parties. In one of the hotel's conference rooms, Churchill asked Eden and the senior Labour politician, Clement Atlee, to sign with him a telegram to Chamberlain, saying that if he were to impose further onerous terms on the Czechs, they would fight him in the House. Both refused.

'How can you, both honourable men, give consent through your silence to a policy so cowardly?' he asked, enraged.

Eden was the first to leap to his own defence. 'I understand your concern, Winston, but—'

'Concern?' Churchill asked, his voice rumbling like a pent up volcano.

'Here me out,' Eden pleaded. 'I will not be seen to be party to a vendetta against the prime minister. Now is a time for unity. Our strength is in presenting a united front.'

Atlee was more conciliatory. 'I wish I could agree to sign, Winston, but I cannot without the approval of my Party Room.'

Churchill rose to leave and said: 'The sequel to this sacrifice of honour will be the sacrifice of lives, our people's lives.' With that he left. In a deepening gloom, he passed by the entrance to one of the hotel's restaurants and heard the sound of laughter. He stopped, looked in and backed away. 'Those poor people,' he murmured, 'they little know what they will have to face.'

That night Hitler and Chamberlain arrived at an agreement. Areas of the Sudetenland with a majority German-speaking population would become sovereign territory of the Reich.

At the signing Ribbentrop and Wilson stood behind their respective leaders. The German ambassador whispered into the civil servant's ear. 'Have you informed the Czechs?'

'Don't worry,' said Wilson, his mood buoyant. 'I'll make those Czechos sensible.'

Ribbentrop snickered and rested his hand on the Englishman's shoulder. 'Good.'

Wilson flinched. 'Yes, indeed,' he coughed, somewhat startled by the gesture. Clearing his throat, he was quick to add: 'Before we leave, the prime minister would like a private meeting with Herr Hitler.'

Fifteen minutes later, after the commemorative photos had been taken and he was alone with Hitler and his foreign minister, the prime minister produced a sheet of paper. On it was typed three short paragraphs. 'I have here an Anglo-German agreement.'

'Ich habe hier eine anglo-detsch Abmachung,' Ribbentrop translated.

'Symbolic of the desire of our two peoples never to go to war again.'

'Ein Simbol des Wunsches das unsere zwei Volker nie wieder gegeneinander Krieg fuhren werden.'

'Ja, Ja,' said Hitler, grabbing the document and quickly signing it. 'Das is gut.'

A moment later, Chamberlain came out to the lobby. As he met Horace Wilson he patted his breast pocket and smiled. 'I've got it. He signed.'

The next day a plane landed on the main runway at Heston Aerodrome. It came to a halt at the terminal and Chamberlain disembarked. He was met with cheers from the huge crowd that had gathered to greet him. Walking down the tarmac, brushing his windblown hair from his face, he stepped behind the waiting microphone, and in the midst of the throng, announced: 'The Czechoslovakian problem is now settled.' Despite the strength of the gusts whistling around his straining voice, the hush that fell upon the crowd was almost tangible. The prime minister continued, his tone becoming one of modest triumph. 'Last night, I had a talk with Herr Hitler, and here is the agreement which bears his and my name.' Chamberlain took the written agreement from the breast pocket of his jacket, unfolded it and waved the document in the air. The thin sheet of paper flapped loosely in the wind. 'I believe it is peace in our time.'

Chamberlain drove to Buckingham Palace to personally deliver the good news to the king. David and Wallis, together with Georgie, Marina and many others from court were there to greet him.

'Damn fine work,' said David as he led the prime minister to the doors of the east balcony. 'Come, the people await.'

Chamberlain had never seen anything like it. The cheering

crowd extended for as far as the eye could see. Not a patch of the Mall's pavement was visible. The crowd covered everything, people even clinging to the Victoria Memorial and hanging from the fences and trees like a swarm of locust. Tears welled in Chamberlain's eyes as David made a point of shaking his hand.

That night Churchill rose to speak in the House of Commons, the chamber almost empty. 'Herr Hitler will not be satisfied with his latest winnings in the Sudetenland. He will not be happy until he has gobbled up the rest of what is left of little Czechoslovakia. Owing to our mishandling of the German problem, we seem to be very near the bleak choice between war and shame. My feeling is that we will choose shame, and then have war thrown in later.'

Chapter Four, the Infiltration

An uneasy calm settled over the nation as it went back to its day-to-day business. Nobody noticed anything unusual about the black cab as it drove from the borough of Westminster, past Hyde Park and up Kensington Church Street to Notting Hill. Wearing a scarf and dark glasses, Wallis sat in the back, smoking nervously, terrified lest she be recognised by the driver or someone on the crowded sidewalks.

The cab turned west into Notting Hill Gate and continued toward Holland Park Avenue. Wallis leaned forward, and with an English accent, spoke to the driver. 'Take the next on your left.' The cabbie turned into a side street with a small row of shops. She ordered him to stop outside a corner grocery store.'

Wallis paid the fare with a tip that seemed appropriate, not noticeably small or large, and before alighting, took a moment to surreptitiously check nobody was around. Once on the footpath, she put her head down and walked up to the store's display window. In the reflection of the glass, she watched the cab as it turned and drove away, not daring to move until it had completely disappeared down the street. As soon as it was gone, she walked to a small antique shop three doors on. When she entered, the shopkeeper nodded, acknowledging her arrival. He was talking to a shady looking character in a trench coat. She would soon know him as the agent, Dorfman. He leered at her as the shopkeeper pointed to a door that led to the rear of the store and its rickety staircase. Wallis could feel their eyes upon her as she entered the semidarkness of the back room, and from the floor above, she heard the distinctive pop of a champagne cork. Slowly she made her way up the stairs and there he was.

'Come in, Leibchen,' said Ribbentrop with a charming smile. He looked as smooth as ever, elegant and holding a bottle of Dom Perignon in one hand and two glasses in the other.

Wallis stepped back and gripped the staircase banister. She had considered ignoring Ribbentrop's invitation, but instinct told her to be wary. He was a connection with the past that could prove embarrassing if not quickly and quietly severed. It would have to be a clean cut, with sufficient anaesthetic to avoid rancour, but the sight of the ugly flat suggested that might be difficult.

Wallis looked around and beheld a frilly standard lamp, garish cushions smothering a brocade upholstered settee, walls covered in cheap reproductions of famous nudes by Ingres and Rubens, a Persian rug that screamed at the paisley wallpaper, a titanic chandelier, ponderous velvet curtains and tidal waves of roses in fat vases, their sweet perfume assaulting the air. 'Why have you asked me to this place?' she asked nervously.

Ribbentrop lifted the bottle of champagne as if it were liberty's torch. 'I have returned to Britain, the conquering hero, and thought you should be the first to know.'

Wallis suppressed a backwash of nausea. Ribbentrop's manner brought back memories of Paris, the city where he had offered to be her chaperone. An offer she had declined for fear that tongues might wag if they were ever seen together. Wallis recalled that it was for this reason that she had at first refused his solicitations, not yielding until he offered to remedy her concerns. His inducements consisted of the most expensive wig he could procure, a pair of false, gold-framed eyeglasses and lots of cash to grease the palms of nosy hotel staff. Discovering that her identity could be so well disguised, she acquiesced and accompanied the German ambassador on a grand tour of the city's delights. It proved to be that nobody really cared about the strangely bookish-looking but decidedly Aryan blond at Ribbentrop's side: she was thought to be yet another new mistress; it was Paris after all. Liberated from recognition Wallis was free to join Ribbie for evenings at the opera, the ballet and the Comedie Francaise; dinners at Maximes and La Tour d'Argent; and the intimacy of late night cabarets in Montmartre, sipping cognac while listening to Damia Frehel or Edith Piaf. It was with the sweet reverberations of 'La Vie en Rose' still ringing in her ears and a liver full of Grand Marnier, that she succumbed to him— and immediately regretted it. The woman was too strong to cry over a predicament she had assayed so many times before, but this betrayal had proved a constant companion, like the ache of a decaying tooth unable to be pulled. Wallis remained at the top of the staircase, silently cursing her libido.

'The Fuhrer has made me foreign minister.' Ribbentrop announced, beaming with joy. The former ambassador had won again, his victory in matters of state as certain as in the bedchamber. Looking into Wallis's turquoise eyes, he recalled how difficult it was to prise her from her gilded cage at the Ritz. Achieving his goal had exercised a talent for patience he had hitherto not found apparent. But, like any good salesman, he knew well the marketplace he had to trawl, and trawled it neatly.

Still fixed at the top of the stairs, Wallis longed to run away but suppressed the urge. She knew how the powerful behaved if they were crossed; she'd bedded enough of them. Taking off her sunglasses and scarf, she prepared for trouble, but was no less determined to set the henchman adrift.

Her expression betrayed her thoughts and Ribbentrop was taken aback. 'Why the long face?' He moved in on his old pal. 'I think congratulations are in order.'

He tried to kiss Wallis but she turned away. 'No, Ribbie, I can't.'

'What, don't need me anymore?' Ribbentrop suddenly looked glum, dangerous. All his plans would come to naught if she outfoxed him. 'Not even a little kiss?'

'It wouldn't be right,' she said. 'Not now.'

'I see,' he sighed as he poured the champagne, annoyed that morals and manners were suddenly at issue. The foreign minister continued, still satin smooth: 'I'm afraid it's not as easy as that. You owe the Reich for your good fortune.'

Wallis felt the nausea return. 'How? And what could you possibly mean by my "good fortune"? My circumstances, good or bad, are my own affair. What have you to do with anything?'

Ribbentrop dropped the bottle into a silver ice bucket.

'Let us say—I met your request and cleared from your way an impediment, a pretty and eligible young lady who caught the king's eye.' He smiled as he offered her a glass. 'Imagine what he would think if he knew you were responsible, even if indirectly, for her death.'

Wallis waved away the drink. 'I only asked you to find out what you could about her. I didn't ask you to ruin her.'

'That is not my understanding of the matter,' he demurred, casually sipping the champagne. 'I believed I was acting under your specific instructions. As I said, how would David react if he knew it was you who soiled Susanna's reputation? You who caused the tragedy of her untimely passing, hmm?' He took another sip. 'This really is very good. Are you sure you don't want some?'

'I never asked for—'

'Can you be certain how he would react?' Ribbentrop was implacable. 'No, of course you can't.'

Considering attack to be the best form of defence, Wallis played the brave heroine. She flicked back her hair defiantly and took a sharp breath. 'You underestimate the power of love.'

Ribbentrop smiled like a small boy tormenting an insect. 'Like your love for our child?'

The moisture drained from Wallis's mouth. Her tongue felt wrapped in cotton. 'We both agreed—you, me, both of us—agreed to never mention… You promised…' She became breathless. 'Promised to never again utter a word of the… of the…'

'Adoption?' Ribbentrop ran his hand down his face,

attempting to drag away a smirk. Wallis's pregnancy had put her exactly where he wanted her: imprisoned within the walls from which he had earlier contrived to set her free. At first she had railed against her condition, her disposition far from compliant to his needs. She even mentioned something about the back alleys of Pigalle, but with a few words in the right ears and a few francs in the right pockets, Ribbentrop had ensured she never got the chance to avail herself of such an option. Whether she liked it or not, Wallis had found herself in confinement and under his thumb. 'I'm sorry,' he said, 'but I feel I may be forced to break our promise. Though I know it to be sacred, I must.'

'Why?' she whispered, frowning and wild-eyed.

'There are some things in this world greater than our reputations,' he declared. 'Our tiny needs are as nothing when compared to the cause of world peace.'

'World peace?' Wallis staggered. Ribbentrop came to her aid, leading her to the settee. 'Please, Liebchen, you need to sit down.'

Wallis slumped onto the pile of cushions. 'You gave your word, your word as a gentleman.' Her eyes glistened with tears. She picked up one of the cushions and held it tight to her breast. 'You took my child from my arms, and I let you. I let you!'

'Liebchen, please,' Ribbentrop implored, sitting beside her, thinking her show of emotion overstated, and feeling frankly embarrassed; he didn't think himself that bad.

Wallis began to sob. 'I let you take my child, my baby, because I had no choice. Now, I find I made that sacrifice, suffered that loss, for nothing?' Her body convulsed until she began to retch. Ribbentrop put his hand gently on her arm and she brushed it aside. 'Get away from me, you son of a bitch!'

Her pursuer was not to be deterred. 'Here, my Darling,' Ribbentrop soothed, again offering the champagne, 'this will settle your nerves. Don't let the bubbles get up your nose.' Ribbentrop's insouciance was unflagging. He knew, all he need do was tap Wallis's instinct for survival: a vulpine intelligence born of an insecure childhood spent clinging to the oily margins of Baltimore high society.

Wallis surveyed the champagne with disdain and knocked it out of his hand. The glass flew across the room and shattered on the floor.

Ribbentrop recoiled. He was losing control of the situation. She wasn't listening to him. 'Nobody wants another bloody war!' he shouted.

Wallis stared at him; never before had she heard him raise his voice.

Ribbentrop collected himself and whispered in her ear: 'Hard decisions must be made.' He took his handkerchief and wiped away her tears. 'I know you to be a strong and intelligent woman. You have the wisdom to realise this feeble world will soon need people of great courage. You are to be counted in their ranks.' He leaned back and tucked his handkerchief back into his breast pocket. 'Civilization sits at a crossroads and your hands are on the wheel. Throughout history peace has never come from hegemony. A pax Britannica cannot endure. It can only breed resentment in the vanquished. That is the road to war. Peace can only be maintained by compromise, the great powers knowing that any attempt to destroy their opposite risks the destruction of them both. Yet this peace resides cocooned inside a balance strangely seen as undesirable by either side. If Britain thinks herself strong enough, she'll go to war; but if she feels threatened by an equilibrium that would lead to blood-drenched stalemate, she'll opt for peace. A stronger Germany is the key to peace. Not to make Britain weaker but to secure peace through equilibrium.' His tone again became irritated. 'Britain must get out of the way. She has her empire, isn't that enough? Why must she always meddle in the affairs of continental Europe? She is a fly in the ointment!' He smoothed down his tie and took a deep breath. 'The Fuhrer's intentions can only prove useful to Britain… in the long term. Britain must leave the Reich at full strength, our military power undiluted by any threat from the west. She must leave the Fatherland strong enough to pursue a sacred destiny—victory over the Slavic hoards, Stalin and the threat of communism. That is the way to equilibrium. You must help us to acquire it. Help us create a lasting peace between the two giants of the civilised world: the mighty British Empire and the Third Reich.'

Wallis began to chew her fingernails: a habit developed long ago in boarding school. Ribbentrop gently slipped her hand from her mouth. 'No need for that; we wouldn't want the king to think you hold dark secrets.'

'It's just a nervous habit.'

'Of course, of course it is. And it's a habit that we share. Remember?' He patted her hand. 'I well know bad nails can make a man look ill-kempt, but in a woman it is entirely unacceptable.' Ribbentrop inspected Wallis's fingers and showed her a nail she'd just snapped off. 'If he says anything, tell him you broke it on the clip on your handbag. Who knows, it may even provoke him into buying you some new accessories. A girl can never have too many accessories.' Feeling more confident, he reached for his glass and poured more champagne. 'World peace,' he continued, 'can never be assured until Germany reclaims her rightful place, German pride restored. I ask you simply to help correct the scales in the name of peace. You could be a vital participant in achieving a great and lasting accord. You have the good fortune to be privy to information that could aid our purpose. I invited you here in order to beg that you might share some small part of that information. That is all my country asks of you.' He sipped his drink before switching from the public to the personal. 'Come on now, there's really no reason for David to know about our child. Let us begin, we have a busy afternoon ahead of us.'

'You bastard,' Wallis sniffed, 'you've got to be kidding.' She went to leave, only to see Dorfman standing at the top of the stairs, her escape blocked.

'It's alright, Eric,' said Ribbentrop, 'she can go, but if she does she will lose everything she ever had and everything she ever hoped to gain.'

Wallis didn't move. She couldn't, and she knew Ribbie knew she couldn't. She loathed him for that. The man, once seen as handsome and refined, now appeared to her reptilian and malignant. 'Very well,' she said, turning back to the ghastly room. 'You have the pleasure of my company for this one afternoon, and that is all.'

Ribbentrop was again all smiles. 'Dorfman, bring up more champagne, and another glass.' The agent marched back downstairs.

Wallis returned to the sofa. 'Don't worry,' Ribbentrop assured, 'I don't want your body, just your eyes and ears.'

Six months later, a newspaper vendor stood outside Charing Cross tube station. He waved in his hand a copy of the Evening Standard and barked: 'Hitler breaks promise! Invades Czechoslovakia! Prague occupied!'

Half a mile down the road, Chamberlain sat at the Cabinet table and stared around at the drawn faces of Eden, Halifax, Sir John Simon, Duff Cooper and the rest of the ministry. 'Who will be next?' he asked.

The war minister, Leslie Hore-Belisha, said the one word the others dared not speak: 'Poland.'

The canker lanced, the rest grunted, nodding their heads.

Chamberlain chewed on an arm of his spectacles, sighed and summed up the collective opinion. 'Poland.'

Churchill sat by the fire in his study at Chartwell. Puffing on his cigar, he too agreed. 'Poland.'

Buried in cabinet papers, David sat at his bedroom desk and grumbled: 'Czechoslovakia.'

Wallis entered, dressed for bed. 'Still not finished?'

'It's never-ending,' he whined. 'All this business with Hitler—every ministry has to be seen to be doing something about it. I've got a blasted headache.'

Wallis walked into the en suite and drew a bath. David looked away from his work. 'What are you doing in there?'

'You're tense,' she answered, returning to rub his shoulders. 'What you need is a bit of pampering.'

He listened to the pouring water. 'One of the footmen could have done that.'

'Maybe,' she said, kissing him on the cheek, 'but you'll find it so much more relaxing knowing I did it for you. I'll add some salts.'

Wallis walked back into the bathroom. David yawned and rubbed his temples.

'Almost ready,' she called out.

He put aside the cabinet papers, and a minute later was sliding into deliciously steaming water. 'Hmm,' he purred, 'this feels good.'

Wallis sat on the edge of the bath. 'Mommy knows what's best for Boysie.'

He rested his head on the rim and let his eyes close. 'Darling, do you think we should take them on again?'

She tensed. 'Who?'

'Oh, my heart, the Cabinet of course—seize the moment, make them agree to our getting married.'

She looked down at him sternly. 'You don't give up, do you?'

'No, I mean it. Hit them while they're down.'

'You're in the bath to relax, not conspire.'

'But, darling, we can't go on like this forever. Do you really think I've worked this hard simply to be popular? It's about taking control. Battles are won before they begin. They are distracted. Now is the time to act.'

Wallis suddenly realised the water was almost full to overflowing. 'You make me sound like the spoils of war,' she said, quickly turning off the tap. 'I don't want to push my luck. I've got you and that's enough.'

'But we have them where we want—'

'No!' she scolded. 'And no means no.'

David turned away. It was like he'd been slapped in the face. Over the past few months he had noticed Wallis's behaviour slowly changing. On the surface she seemed the same, but he would often catch her out, her thoughts drifting, her mind elsewhere, somehow detached. Missing was her quick wit and the playful repartee he'd once enjoyed. Now she had snapped at him.

Wallis looked down at his averted face. She had spoken harshly and wished there had been some other way to change the subject, but the last thing she wanted to hear was the old chestnut of the marriage plan. 'Oh, Boysie,' she begged, 'please don't sulk.'

He looked back dejectedly. 'I'm worried, I feel we're drifting apart, that I don't know you as I once did.'

She handed him the soap and sighed. 'Surely you must know by now—I've never truly wanted to be feted as a queen.' He didn't answer. Frustrated, she shook her head. 'I refuse to hear anything more about marriage!' And then, more softly: 'I don't want to end up dead like Susanna.'

David frowned, his expression filled with righteous indignation. 'I never made any commitment to Susanna and her death was an accident.'

Wallis leaned down, her face inches from his. 'We both know her death was anything but an accident.'

Disinterred guilt reconfigured David's anatomy, his eyes dilated while everything else collapsed. Wallis had finally cut through. Grateful to have found the inspiration to kill off further debate, she suddenly smiled and changed the subject. 'Now, I've run you a bath. I'll be hurt if you don't appreciate it.' Tweaking his nipple, she flirtatiously reiterated her earlier request: 'And stop sulking.'

'I'm not sulking,' he mumbled, recalling his insipid resistance to his mother's ruthless plotting.

'Okay, then prove it by giving me a kiss and a big smile.'

David's mood improved. This was a taste of the Wallis that he loved. He lifted his head to receive her kiss.

'And the smile,' she added.

His face broke into a bashful grin.

'Good boy,' she said, relieved, 'and don't forget to wash behind your ears.'

Wallis returned to the bedroom and immediately concentrated her attention on the desk. She crept toward it, not knowing where to start; there were mounds of documents, files and letters.

Something creaked. Wallis turned around and looked about the room. She always found it unnerving how servants could suddenly appear out of the woodwork. There was nobody there. She returned to the desk, riffled through the piles of papers and paused when she found the object of her search. It was labelled: 'Government Code and Cipher School, Bletchley Park'

Guilt and fear drove her to turn and check the room again. She could hear David washing. That was all. She was still alone.

Wallis put the document down in front of her and turned the first page. It was the Enigma Warsaw Codes Bureau report. Well briefed on what to seek out, she leafed through the chapters till she reached a section full of numerical tables. Putting the report directly under the desk lamp, she pressed it flat and pulled a small camera from the pocket of her dressing gown.

There was a knock at the door.

David called from the bathroom, 'Could you answer that, darling?'

Wallis slipped the camera back into her pocket, closed the report and rushed across the room to sit on the bed. 'Come.'

The door opened and Watson entered. On a silver tray he carried a bottle of pills and a glass of water. 'Madam, aspirin for His Majesty.'

'You took your time getting here,' yelled David.

Wallis took the tray of medicine. 'Thank you, and please don't disturb us again.'

Watson bowed and left. She put down the medicine and crossed the room to lock the door. It swung back, almost knocking her over. Watson's head appeared from behind. 'Oh, I'm so sorry, Ma'am. Are you alright?'

'Yes I'm fine,' she assured, rubbing her hand. 'What do you want now?'

'Would His Majesty like his shoes polished?'

Wallis saw David's shoes lying by the bed. She darted

across the room, grabbed them and shoved them out into the hall before the butler had a chance to enter. 'Don't come back,' she ordered as she closed the door behind him, locking it tight. There was the sound of splashing in the bathroom. 'You okay in there?' she asked.

'Fine,' answered David, none the wiser.

'Good. And make sure you have a good soak. I want you to emerge relaxed.'

'Yes, dear,' came the facetious reply.

Wallis walked back to the desk, pulled the camera from her pocket and photographed the first page of tables.

David sang out: 'Darling, can you bring me that aspirin?'

'Won't be a second,' she replied as she turned the page to the next set of numbers. The bulky report knocked a pile of documents from the edge of the desk. Papers flew everywhere. Wallis froze in terror—there was now no turning back—she had to retrieve and somehow collate them all. She fell to her knees and scrambled across the floor, checking paper stocks and page numbers, desperate to keep everything in the right order.

'Darling,' David asked, 'what are you doing?' Wallis's heart sank. Slowly she turned to face the music. There was nobody there. David was still in the tub. 'Darling, you promised that aspirin.'

Even though it was the middle of the day, the window shutters above the antique shop were closed tight. Inside the upstairs flat, the velvet drapes were drawn. Wallis sat in an armchair, illuminated only by the light of the standard lamp. A man in a grey suit lurked behind her, his face obscured by shadow.

Wallis placed a small roll of film on the coffee table. 'I hope this concludes our business.'

A second man sat opposite. It was Dorfman. The lamplight reflected in his round reading glasses, making them seem to hover, disembodied in a sea of black. Unlike Ribbentrop, the timbre of this man's voice was gravelly, his accent coarse. 'Unfortunately,' he said with a precision that could be measured by a micrometer, 'we require a little more.'

The only colour perceptible in the room drained from Wallis's face. The grey suited man placed his hand on her shoulder, as much to menace as reassure.

Dorfman scooped up the film as deftly as David's butler scooped up ice some six hours later.

Watson stood at the drinks table in the drawing room of the Belgian suite and poured gin and a splash of vermouth into the shaker. Behind him, Georgie, David, Marina and Wallis sipped their martinis: the men in dinner suits, the women in evening gowns.

'How was Chamberlain today?' asked Georgie.

'Depressed,' said David. 'It seems the Government is determined to take a stand if Hitler makes any further territorial demands.'

'And he will,' nodded Marina.

David took a cigarette from the box on the coffee table. 'I find it amazing that we are prepared to go to war over a country that twenty years ago didn't even exist. Has the world lost its mind?'

Wallis gazed listlessly into her drink. 'Hitler doesn't want to fight Britain.'

'Of course he doesn't,' said David as Watson lit his cigarette. 'Why would he? I read that book of his, by the way. You're right, Georgie, it's a bit of a slog. I must admit I skipped through most of it, but I did look at the bit about us, and you're right, he's looking east.'

'It's as Marina and I have always maintained: the only means by which Hitler can attack Stalin is through Poland. The place must be traversed, so let's not get in his way.'

Watson proffered the drinks tray and David took a second martini. 'I doubt that even Chamberlain will accept that argument and as for Churchill—'

'Oh, to hell with Churchill,' Georgie interrupted, 'he's yesterday's man.'

The Duke of Kent's aggressive tone scared Wallis. She wanted to run away but couldn't. Her hands felt clammy. She was living a double life and it ate away at her nerves, never left her thoughts, made sleep near impossible. Her mind drifting, she accidentally knocked over her drink. 'Oh, sorry, how clumsy of me.'

Watson was there in an instant, the table wiped and a fresh martini set down in its place. Georgie coughed and surreptitiously pointed to the butler.

'Watson,' said David, 'you can leave us now.'

The butler bowed and departed, closing the doors behind him.

Georgie put down his drink. 'David, you've always believed in a strong defence as a deterrent to war, but Hitler is a risk taker; he doesn't believe Britain will act. He suspects we're too weak, but what if he were to see what we have achieved these last two years.'

David bit down on his lower lip, and made a slight sucking sound as he inhaled through his teeth. 'It would give Hitler pause to think.'

Georgie moved across and sat down beside him. 'It would give us all pause to think. We need time for things to cool down. Who knows what might happen in such an interlude? Perhaps the Soviets might invade Poland. Pre-empt the Germans in the name of defence. Then Germany could enter Poland, coming to her aid against communist aggression.'

David twirled the olive in his martini. 'I think you're drawing a long bow there; the Russians would never invade Poland.'

'Perhaps, but we must have time if we are to avert a catastrophe.'

Wallis reached over and took a cigarette from the box. David lit it and noticed her hands were trembling. 'Wallis, are you alright?'

'Yes,' she said, 'I'm okay.'

'Are you sure? You look unwell.'

'I'm fine, really.'

'You don't have to worry about the drink. I mean if I had a pound for every drink I've spilt—'

'You'd be even richer,' she countered before he could finish.

David looked at her closely then turned back to his brother. 'Georgie, are you thinking there might be a way we could demonstrate to Hitler the strength of our rearmament, the extent of our technical advances?'

'Yes, definitely. Why not invite him to Britain for peace talks? He would be negotiating on our turf, not his. We would be in a position of strength on British soil. And we could take him to Hendon or Farnborough for an air show.'

'Air show?' asked Wallis incredulously.

'Why not?' Georgie enthused. 'The Hurricane is an amazing aircraft—I've flown one.' Suddenly he found himself talking to Wallis's back as she rose and wandered over to the window. He raised his voice to get her attention. 'And as for the Spitties… I mean the Spitfires are—'

David interrupted. 'Chamberlain would never agree.'

'You're the king,' Georgie pronounced, his hands held wide apart.

David was insistent. 'The prime minister has come to regard me in a most unfavourable light. He wouldn't so much as begin to listen to my argument.'

Georgie looked at Marina; it was her cue. 'But what if such a suggestion were to come from the Germans?' she asked.

David raised an eyebrow. 'Go on.'

Impatience getting the better of him, Georgie butted in. 'I have a friend in Germany. His name is Albrecht Haushofer.'

Wallis stepped closer to the window and stared intently. She could see fog outside. It wafted across the lawn and seemed to take human form.

Georgie continued, racing headlong to his point. 'Albrecht's father is Karl Haushofer, he's a Professor at Munich University.'

Wallis's eyes grew wide as she gazed into the hypnotic, roiling fog.

'The Professor,' said Georgie, his excitement mounting. 'The Professor taught, and is a mentor to, Rudolf Hess.'

'Hitler's deputy?' David asked.

Georgie tilted his head and winked. 'None other.'

But Georgie had been upstaged. David was again distracted by Wallis's strange behavior; she remained transfixed at the window. In the mist she saw an apparition of Susanna, and dropped her drink. The glass broke on the parquet flooring.

David rushed to her side. 'Darling, whatever is the matter?'

Wallis stepped back from the window and whispered: 'Someone just walked over my grave.' She moved toward the door. 'I'm sorry, I have to excuse myself for a minute.'

David and the others were left watching her, nonplussed, as she threw open the doors and wandered out into the hall, stumbling in the direction of the powder room.

Georgie scratched his head. 'What was that all about?'

'I don't know,' said David, equally in the dark. He called in Watson to sweep up the broken glass.

Marina picked up her clutch bag. 'I'll just go and powder my nose.'

'No,' said David. 'Leave her be. I'm not certain what's wrong with Wallis lately, but if I know her as well as I think, it will be something best left for her to deal with on her own.'

As soon as she got to the powder room Wallis grabbed a hand

towel, ran it under the cold tap and dabbed her forehead. Looking at the mirror, she stared into the black depths of her pupils until everything around them swirled into a blur. Suddenly dizzy, she clasped the washbasin and concentrated on breathing deeply, letting the pulsing blood in her temples subside. 'It's nothing,' she told her reflection. 'Your mind is playing tricks on you, that's all. Susanna's dead, six feet under in the graveyard of her parish church. Her ghost is not in the Palace gardens.' With eyes squeezed shut, trying to blot out a scalding thought, she whispered: 'Her ghost is in me. I'm the only place she'll ever haunt.'

Georgie had done well. He left Heston Aerodrome in Middlesex before dawn, and with a slight southwesterly tailwind, did the trip in five hours. The young prince had used his German contacts to obtain a top secret special clearance to fly over German air space, but took the precaution of wearing his royal air force uniform should he be forced down and accused of being a spy. He had also decided to take his de Havilland Hornet Moth because it had a range of 620 miles. The flight route was 510 miles so when he arrived in the mid morning, there was still plenty of fuel in the tank. Georgie landed at a small private airfield outside the German village of Sonthofen. It had been recommended by fellow pilot, Rudolf Hess, and was located in the extreme south of Bavarian Swabia where the German border took a bite out of Austria.

There had been snow a few days earlier, but milder weather and rain had washed clean the runway. After landing, Georgie taxied his plane to a small hut. He climbed out of the cockpit and was met by a solitary SS scharfurer. The young man jumped to attention and gave the Nazi salute. He couldn't speak English, but that was of no concern. Like David, the Duke of Kent's German was better than most Germans. Georgie followed as the SS man marched to the car and opened the back door of a silver Mercedes Benz.

The airstrip was in picture postcard farmland with cowbells and farmhouses that looked like cuckoo clocks. As the road led them into the mountains, the Heidi landscape disappeared and they entered a dark forest of towering fir trees. Halfway up the mountain, the car stopped at a checkpoint with more SS guards. The young scharfurer was waved through and they set off to higher altitudes and breathtaking scenery. Three minutes later the car entered a bank of low-lying cloud and it began to rain. As they drove along the precipitous and narrow road the downpour increased, making the surface shiny and slippery. It was a great relief to Georgie when the car turned a corner and the dark forest opened up to reveal Glatzelberg. Set in a one thousand acre estate, the building looked like a medieval castle but was actually a large, eighteenth century hunting lodge. Turreted and grey, it was built from the local stone and seemed to have grown like a tumour out of the precipice to which it clung. The rain cascaded down as the Mercedes arrived at the front entrance. From within the castle yet another SS guard appeared. He held an open umbrella and escorted Georgie inside.

Beneath a soaring vaulted ceiling, the main hall was a cathedral to blood sport. The guard shook the water out of the umbrella and stuck it into a large bronze bucket. After marching past rows of deer antlers that crowded the high walls, they ascended a broad staircase to a gallery. Georgie glanced out the windows but could see nothing but mist. He imagined the view extended all the way down the valley, as far as and beyond the airstrip where he had landed 20 minutes earlier. At the end of the gallery, the guard knocked on a heavy oak door.

A second later the door was opened by an SS adjutant, revealing the castle's library. Sitting around a tapestry-covered table were three men. One of them was his old friend Albrecht Haushofer, the second he recognised as Rudolf Hess and the third was elderly, and no doubt, Albrecht's father, Karl. They all stood to greet him.

'Guten Abend Albrecht,' the Duke said, shaking hands with his old friend.

'Georgie,' said Albrecht, 'it is good to see you again. Allow me to introduce my father, Professor Karl Haushofer, and the Deputy Fuhrer, Herr Rudolf Hess.'

Georgie turned to his host. 'Ein Vegnugen, stellvertretender Fuhrer.'

Hess had a handshake like a steel trap. 'Your Grace, this is indeed a pleasure.'

Struggling to extricate his hand from Hess's firm grip, Georgie looked back in the direction from which he had arrived. 'I see from the hall that the hunting here is rather good.'

'Those sad trophies,' Hess sighed, 'are the responsibility of the former owner. They remain for reasons that are purely cultural. It would be a desecration to remove them.'

Hess finally released Georgie's hand and admired a framed portrait of Hitler that hung from above the fireplace. 'For my own part, I detest hunting, I am strictly vegetarian.'

Karl Haushofer spoke for the first time. 'The whole estate has been declared a nature reserve, no hunters' guns, a place of peace.'

Georgie allowed himself a wry smile. 'It's a great pity Europe is not a nature reserve.' They all laughed, even Hess.

That night, Michael drove the Rolls Royce through the English rain to a secluded airstrip. David sat in the back, worried about the weather; it wasn't good for flying. He produced a silver flask from his coat pocket, unscrewed the cap and took a nip.

The king's car passed an unmanned gate and pulled up on the tarmac. David wound down his window and looked into a wet sky. To the east he saw a light. Moments later the Hornet Moth landed safely on the runway. David left his car and walked up to the plane. Georgie stepped out onto the wing. David found it impossible to speak. All he could do was stare in expectation.

Georgie jumped to the ground and smiled broadly. 'Hitler says yes.'

David still couldn't find words to utter. Tears dampened his eyes as he hugged his brother in silence.

Back in London, Wallis sat again in the dark flat, illuminated only by the standard lamp and accompanied by the two German agents.

Dorfman spoke again with sibilant precision. 'Are the king's motives sincere?'

Wallis shrugged. 'He isn't the government, but he speaks for the people who matter.'

'How can you be sure?'

Wallis glanced at the agent who stood behind her. The grey-suited man aggravated her frayed nerves. These Germans were like Rotweilers, always coming at her from opposing directions. She turned back to the spectacled agent. 'I can be sure because sie sind meine freunde.'

Dorfman smiled. 'You are fortunate to enjoy such confidence in your friends. Foreign Minister von Ribbentrop sends his regards.'

David and Georgie sat in the back seat of the Rolls Royce as they were driven back to London. 'You should have arrived alone in the Rover,' grumbled Georgie. 'It would have been less conspicuous.'

David checked to make sure that the window separating Michael from the back seat was firmly shut. 'Sorry, I'm not used to all this cloak and dagger stuff.' He offered his hip flask to his brother.

Georgie took a nip. 'They don't intend to take Poland. They just want a corridor to East Prussia.'

'What about the Soviets?'

'Hess assures me that the destruction of communism is still their ultimate goal. Of that they're determined.'

'And the air fighter displays?'

'They gave one at the Berlin Olympics for the whole

world to see. They're not shy. Ribbentrop will suggest reciprocal displays as part of the ongoing talks. They'll show us theirs if we show them ours.'

'Bloody marvellous,' said David. 'I could kiss them.'

'Of course, Cabinet has to agree.'

'How can they not; Germany has opened the door to serious negotiation. To walk away from such an opportunity would demonstrate cowardice on Great Britain's behalf, and goad Hitler on to further acts of brinksmanship.'

Georgie handed back the flask. 'Perhaps, but we must be prepared for all eventualities. Hitler may still renege on his side of the bargain.'

'No,' said David, his face aglow, 'not after we show him what we've got. It'll be too much for his competitive nature.'

His brother became pensive. 'I hope you're right.'

'Georgie, it doesn't matter what he shows us. The whole aim of the exercise is to impress upon him that we are serious about the prospect of war and are prepared to fight.'

'I thought you were against war.'

'I am, but we want him to think we are following Teddy Roosevelt's dictum.'

'What's that?'

'Walk softly and carry a big stick.'

Georgie laughed. 'I think I'll have some more of that flask.'

David passed back the whisky. 'You should feel very proud. This is a very clever ruse and it was all your idea, Georgie.'

'Mine and Marina's.'

'Yours and Marina's,' David agreed. 'We are both blessed in our partnerships.

Georgie took a sip from the flask. 'How has Wallis been?'

'She's fine. She assured me it was just a woman's thing.'

'Good,' said Georgie, 'It would be handy if men had "things" to use as an excuse.'

'But we do, Georgie. We're just not quite as clever when it comes to making our things seem mysterious.'

Georgie laughed. 'Maybe we're just too lazy.'

David took back the hip flask and drained it. 'You know what? I think it's time to throw a little party.'

Two days later, Chamberlain and Wilson invited ambassador Kennedy to Number 10. The prime minister opened the proceedings.

'Your Excellency, I have—'

'Neville, forget the formality, just call me Joe.'

'Yes, well, Joe, the British government thinks it wise to forewarn you of an important development.'

Kennedy's mood became serious. 'I'm listening.'

Chamberlain's eyes shifted from Kennedy to Wilson and then back again. 'We've decided to invite Herr Hitler to Britain for peace talks. As a prelude, there'll be a display by the Royal Air Force.'

Kennedy raised his eyebrows. 'Trying on some war paint?'

Chamberlain nervously fiddled with his cufflinks then continued. 'The might of the Royal Navy protects this island, but any new war will be dominated by air power, to which the English Channel is no barrier. We know that the Luftwaffe development chief, Ernst Udet, has caused major advances to be made. Their dive bombers are of particular interest, being based—I might add—on technology learnt from the Helldivers that America sold them.'

'And Kestrel engines which you British sold them.'

Chamberlain blushed. 'Be that as it may, we want to shock the pants off them.'

'Have you asked the French to join you?'

'No, we told them that these talks will be strictly bilateral. If we invite the French, Hitler will want the Italians, perhaps the Spanish and who knows what might happen next?'

Kennedy's mouth formed into a lopsided smile. 'The whole League of Nations.'

Chamberlain's reply came with an equally mirthless smile. 'Exactly.'

'So, why are you alerting the United States?'

The prime minister glanced again at Wilson.

This made Kennedy even more suspicious. 'Have you warned the Russians?'

Chamberlain jolted back in his chair. 'Good God, no!'

Wilson took the liberty of stepping in. 'Though America is strongly isolationist, we thought it important that we make a gesture of good will.'

'Right,' said Kennedy, nodding slowly. 'Okay, I get it. What do you want in return?'

To prepare for his impromptu party David called a meeting in the Bow Saloon with Wallis, Georgie and the senior palace staff. These included his new Lord-in-Waiting, Frederick

Smith, 2nd Earl of Birkenhead, who had, at Wallis's request, replaced Peregrine Cust. Also present were the Private Secretary to the Sovereign, Major Sir Alexander Hardinge; Comptroller of the Lord Chamberlain, Lt Col Sir Terence Nugent; Master of the Household, Brigadier Sir Smith Hill Child; and a small group from the Master of the Household's department that included the assistant master general, the assistant master food, the royal chef de cuisine, the page of chambers, the yeomen of the royal cellars and of the royal pantry, plus the king's ever-reliable butler, Watson. David looked carefully at the guest list before turning to his lord–in–waiting. 'Well done, Freddy, everyone who should be invited appears to be here.' Then David frowned. 'Oh, wait a second. Georgie, should we not invite Winston and Clementine?'

Georgie shook his head. 'No, I think not. Why spoil the mood.'

'I know you don't like him,' said David, 'but he is my very dear friend.'

'What if he wants to say a few words?' asked Wallis.

'Yes,' David sighed, 'I suppose that could strike the wrong note.' He turned back to Georgie. 'What about Noel? Will he grace us with his company? You know, regale us with his wit and play a few tunes?'

'Yes, he said he'd be delighted.'

'I dare say.' David gave Georgie a wink, knowing full well the rumours that surrounded his brother's friendship with Noel Coward.

'With respect, Sir,' said Watson. 'There are over two hundred guests. Should we not be using the ballroom?'

'No, this is a cocktail party, not a state banquet. I want things to be intimate. People can spill out of the Music Room into the Picture Gallery and the drawing rooms.

'Could still prove a bit crammed,' noted Georgie.

'Good!' said David. 'I want it that way. A crowd that would look small in the ballroom will seem huge in the Music Room. I want the effect to be powerful but exclusive. You know what I mean: everybody who's anybody, that sort of thing.'

Georgie glanced at Wallis; he was concerned there might be a repetition of the behavior he'd witnessed the last time they met. 'I hope this doesn't all seem like a bit of a shock,' he inquired, as if in all innocence.

Wallis knew Georgie's playful kid brother routine was anything but playful, his remark bereft of innocence. She shook her head unequivocally. 'No, it's no shock, nothing of the kind.'

David took her hand. 'If you think it will be too stressful—'

'No,' she insisted, and embarrassed they were anxious about her state of mind, she gave a sudden, dazzling smile. 'No, it won't be difficult at all; it will be fun.'

On the piano nobile of the west wing of Buckingham palace were the principal rooms, used only for state and other special occasions. On a Tuesday evening, in late March, a battalion of important guests arrived for the cocktail party.

Following the formal route, they ascended the Grand Staircase up to the Guard Room where they passed statues of

Queen Victoria and Prince Albert. From there they entered the Green Drawing Room, and might have continued forward to the Throne Room, but instead were led left, crossing the Picture Gallery to the Music Room. With its bow window dramatically enhancing the view of the gardens and a domed ceiling that rose almost forty feet above, the Music Room was David's choice for what he saw as an intimate gathering of a select group.

The party had been in progress for some time and everyone was there. David mingled with his guests as Noel Coward sat at the grand piano playing 'April in Paris'. Wallis stood at the other end of the room, talking to Baron Norman, the Director of the Bank of England. The Baron was bearded, and for a banker, strangely arty in appearance. He was also a member of the Anglo-German Fellowship. A few days earlier six million pounds in Czechoslovak gold held by his bank was transferred to the Reichsbank. What, if any, role he played in this, nobody knew.

'Actually,' said Wallis, putting her index finger under her chin, 'my favourite spot is next door. It's the White Drawing Room.'

Baron Norman stroked his beard. 'Really?'

'Yes, wonderful fireplace, so big and yet so cosy.'

Marina appeared with a pretty, young woman in tow. 'Lord Norman, my apologies for interrupting.'

'Quite alright,' said the baron, his eyes settling leisurely on Marina's cleavage.

The Duchess continued, unaware of his admiration: 'Wallis, I thought you'd be interested to meet someone who's just come back from Germany, Lord Redesdale's daughter, Unity Mitford.'

Unity looked at Wallis as if appraising a pallet load of beaver pelts. 'Interesting to finally meet you.'

'And I you,' said Wallis.

'Unity is a great pal of Herr Hitler,' Marina enthused. 'Summers at the Berghof and all that.'

Wallis sipped her champagne. 'You don't say.'

The duchess tugged at Lord Norman's arm. 'We'll leave you two to chat. Come on Montagu, time to mingle.'

Marina and Lord Norman melted into the crowd as Wallis asked: 'What's he like?'

'Who?'

'Hitler?'

'You mean Herr Hitler. You Americans are frightfully informal.'

'It's one of our more engaging qualities. So spill the beans, what's he like?'

Unity inhaled sharply. 'The Fuhrer is the greatest man of our age. He has performed miracles in Deutschland.'

Wallis persisted. 'But the man himself?'

Unity looked around the room, suddenly embarrassed by her present company, but nevertheless persevered. 'He's incisive and a perfect gentleman—doesn't drink, smoke or use bad language. Really, I could not bear to live and see our two countries tearing each other to pieces. If there is a war I shall shoot myself in the head.'

'Wouldn't it be smarter to shoot your sister?' Wallis enquired.

Noel Coward finished playing. Unity became guarded. 'I have several sisters.'

'Yeah, that's right, but I'm talking about Jessica. You know, the communist.'

Watson sounded a small gong.

Georgie had taken position beside the piano. 'Ladies and gentleman, if I could have your attention please?' Henry, the Duke of Gloucester, standing at his younger brother's side, grabbed a fresh glass of champagne from a passing footman. Georgie took no notice. 'Good evening to you all,' he announced. 'His Majesty the King should like to welcome you here to the Palace tonight…' The prince looked around the room for faces worthy of special mention. 'The Duke and Duchess of Wellington and the Duke and Duchess of Westminster, the Earl of Galloway, Baron Redesdale, Baron Norman…' Not wanting to be tedious, he declined to single out anyone else, and without pause, grouped the rest. 'My Lords, Ladies and Gentlemen, I give you my brother, His Majesty the King.'

The guests applauded as David stepped forward, smoothing his hair. 'Let me begin by apologizing for inviting you here tonight on such short notice; we live in exciting times. As Wallis would say, the fate of the world could turn on a dime.'

The guests looked toward Wallis.

'Darling,' David asked, 'what are you doing all the way back there? Come over here.'

Wallis threaded her way self-consciously across the room. The crowd looked on in silence until she was beside the king.

David gave her a warm smile and looked back to his audience. 'In just three days the German Chancellor will visit our shores for vitally important peace talks. I thought it timely that my court, the City, the Lords, the financial and moral backbone of the nation, should join us together for a few drinks. I hope you're enjoying the particularly rare vintage of Dom Perignon that Wallis was able to procure.'

Lord Norman lifted his glass. 'Yes, hear, hear!'

'A few drinks,' David went on to say, 'in celebration of all that we hold dear and share with our cousins, the Germans. Let the peace talks put an end to any further talk of war between the British Empire und das Deutsche Reich.'

David raised his glass. 'To peace!'

They all raised their glasses. 'To peace!'

'And to Wallis,' said Lord Norman, 'for the champers.'

'Jolly good show,' added Henry.

They all drank.

It was a cold night in rural Kent. Churchill sat by the fire in his study, his cheeks rosy from the glowing warmth. Captain Brian Gorton sat in the chair opposite, watching him puff on his cigar and seeing the flames reflected in his old friend's watery eyes.

Churchill took a sip of cognac and recited Shakespeare. 'That England that was wont to conquer others, hath made a shameful conquest of itself. Ah, would the scandal vanish with my life. How happy then were my ensuing death.'

'Don't let the black dog eat you up,' said Gorton.

'How can it not? When we roll out the red carpet for Nazi

jackboots.'

'Yes, quite, but still,' said Gorton, reaching for the half empty bottle of Remy Martin. 'Bit of a dry argument… More brandy?'

'Thank you, Brian.'

Gorton poured them each another drink.

'But still what?' Churchill asked.

'What?'

'You said: "but still." But still what? Something from Section Five, from MI Six? What have you learnt?'

Gorton swirled his cognac, warming it in the palm of his hand and inhaling its aroma. His home was only a short walk away, he and Churchill getting together often to discuss politics and international affairs. 'I have it from Bobby at the Foreign Office that our invitation to Germany came at their suggestion.'

'Why would Hitler want to come here?' Churchill asked, staring at his Cuban as if the answer might be encoded on the cigar band. 'It doesn't make sense. He doesn't travel abroad except at the head of an army.'

'I know, it's very odd,' Gorton agreed, 'and there will be an air display.'

'There'll be a what?' Churchill gasped.

Gorton raised his brow and closed his eyes, collecting his thoughts. Though well used to his friend's temperamental disposition, Gorton's personality was quite the opposite: the epitome of Whitehall—phlegmatic composure. He rested his drink beside the fireplace screen and took a deep breath before answering. 'The feeling seems to be that Hitler may be reined in by a demonstration of British resolve, as made manifest by the technological advances of the Royal Air Force—show him our hand.'

Churchill gnashed the tip of his cigar to pulp. 'It's a good thing Chamberlain doesn't play poker for he'd soon be bankrupt.'

Chapter Five, the Conference

Three days later a Focke-Wulf 200 Condor landed on the runway at Hendon Aerodrome. There was an insignia on the plane's nose: a black eagle's head on a white disc, within a thin, red ring. The all metal, four-engine monoplane was called the Immelmann III. It taxied to a halt in front of the terminal and was immediately surrounded by a guard detail of two companies from the SS-Leibstandarte regiment. The door opened and the air stairs dropped down. Sturmbannfuhrer Bruno Gesche and three other storm troopers from the elite eight-man Begleitkommando rushed down the stairs and took up their positions on the tarmac. A moment later Herman Goering, Field Marshal of the Luftwaffe, appeared from the plane, accompanied by Ernst Udet, the Great War fighter ace, and commander of T-Amt, the Reich Air Ministry development wing. After them followed Rudolf Hess, co-conspirator behind the surprise visit, responsible for the German half of the plan. The guard of honour snapped to attention. All three walked briskly down the stairs and gathered to the right of the bottom step. Then followed a long silence as everyone looked up and waited. Finally, after much anticipation, just as the sun emerged from behind a lingering cloud, he emerged, the Fuhrer and Reich Chancellor, Adolf

Hitler.

It was the climax of 72 hours of frenetic preparation. Chamberlain's visit to Germany had been a simple affair, but the prime minister was only the head of government, while Hitler was the head of state and government, and he knew a lot of people wanted him dead.

The logistics had been a nightmare, but not from the British end. Chamberlain had set up a special committee to co-ordinate security for the German leader's visit under the chairmanship of the Home Secretary, Sir Samuel Hoare. The committee included the London Metropolitan Police Commissioner, Air Vice-Marshal Sir Philip Game, his assistant commissioners for operations and traffic and the chief superintendent of Special Branch; plus, from outside London, the chief constables from Buckinghamshire and Hertfordshire; as well as Vernon Kell, the head of MI5, and representatives from the air and war ministries. Their first decision was easy to make. For security reasons, the German leader had to be kept well away from Westminster and the City. It was therefore decided that the conference would take place at Chequers, in the Chiltern Hills of Buckinghamshire. It was the official country retreat for serving prime ministers and perfect for the task; the location was as remote as could be expected anywhere in the southeast of England. It was situated on a country lane, well away from any major roads, towns or even villages, the nearest neighbour over a quarter of a mile away.

The closest airport to Chequers suitable for the arrival of a head of state was at Hendon. The Department of the

Assistant Commissioner, Traffic, was given the task of preparing the safest and most efficient route. In accordance with their directions, the motorcade would leave the airport in a northwesterly direction via Edgeware Road, then swing around to the south of Watford and north of Mill End. Travelling south of Amersham to Bow Road it would continue on to London Road, before turning into Dunsmore Lane, just north of Wendover Dean. Police and troops would line much of the route. The bobbies would be from the Met and the two affected counties; with back-up from all five foot guards division regiments; the household cavalry armoured units; elements from Fourth Division, based at Horseguards; and several other London and home county regiments. Hitler would fly in at noon on Saturday 1st April, watch a Royal Air Force display at Hendon and stay the night at Chequers. The conference would take place on the Sunday, with Hitler leaving that evening.

While the British planning went smoothly, in Germany things were altogether different, the visit precipitating a feud between Reichsfuhrer Heinrich Himler, head of the SS, and Obergruppenfuhrer Sepp Dietrich, commander of the Leibstandarte SS Adolf Hitler, the regiment charged with Hitler's personal protection—his praetorian guard which formed the second circle of security after the Begleitkommando. There was a great deal of prestige attached to the task of protecting the Fuhrer on his first overseas journey, and the resulting internecine wrangling and backstabbing over who would be in charge created lifelong enemies.

In the end it came down to Hitler making a choice. Himler was a superb manager but in the end he was a uniformed bureaucrat, a vitally important clerk. On the other hand, Dietrich was a former policeman, a war veteran who had won the iron cross second and first class in the Great War; and a man who had proved his worth during the Night of the Long Knives when, on the Fuhrer's orders, he had personally dispatched half a dozen leaders of the SA. In the end the decision had been easy.

Besides this wrangle, Reichsmarschall Herman Goering was also jockeying for position, vociferous in his demands. Principally, he insisted his Luftwaffe supply two squadrons of Messeuschmitt ME 109s as a fighter escort for the Fuhrer's Condor. However, this plan was completely rejected by the British War Office. The Germans could fly over Belgian air space, if the Belgians were amenable to that, but the Royal Air Force would take over the escort at the English Channel. Goering would have to be placated, so Hitler invited him along.

Now, all the preparations had been completed and Hitler was on British soil. He, Hess, Goering and Udet were greeted on the tarmac by David and Chamberlain, and escorted to the raised dais where they were joined by the foreign ministers, Halifax and Ribbentrop.

The German foreign minister looked like the cat that swallowed a flock of canaries. Through Wallis he had been kept up to date on every aspect of the king and Georgie's plotting. Because of this, Hitler knew well in advance all the details of Georgie's overture to Hess at Glatzelberg. As the primary conduit for this intelligence, Ribbentrop received the special gifts of the Fuhrer's gratitude and his colleague's jealousy. In rising an extra rung up the ladder, Ribbentrop had trodden on a lot of fingers. Fingers that would point to him should things not turn out for the best.

The band of the Grenadier Guards played the British and German national anthems, followed by the firing of a 21 gun salute by the 13 pounders of the King's Troop, Royal Horse Artillery. Then Hitler inspected the guard of honour. The German leader took his time, lingering to look closely at the men, eyeing their red and navy blue uniform, the colours chosen to camouflage blood. He had read that the regiment's name was given to them in honour of their defeat of the Grenadiers of the French Imperial Guard at the Battle of Waterloo. The regiment had fought at Blenheim, Salamanca, Inkerman and the Somme; and had served with distinction eleven kings and three queens. At first glance the Grenadier's dress uniform looked the same as the other guards regiments, but he knew there were differences in the details: the buttons down the front of the tunic were equally spaced, not bunched in twos, threes, fours or fives as were, in turn, the buttons of the Coldstream, Scots, Irish and Welsh Guards; the plume on the bearskin cap was white, not red or blue or red, white and green; and the brass collar badge was particular to the regiment, a depiction of a grenade 'fired proper' with 17 flames. Hitler chanced to remember their motto: 'Honi soit qui mal y pense', old French for, 'Evil to him who evil thinks'. He liked that; it was a message of purity. He was firm in his belief that one day soon his Waffen SS would be covered in such glory, steeped in such traditions. He had designed their uniforms with care, in preparation for that destiny. Nevertheless, he was impressed by these young men of Britain, seeing them as Aryans in control of a vast empire. He had faced their fathers on the Western Front, during the Great War, and had learned through hard-won experience that their fight was every bit as impressive as their spit and polish. He nodded, favourably impressed, and all the more convinced it would be as he had foretold: Germany would conquer the vast tracts of Eastern Europe, the two great nations of the master race, as one, achieving world domination. He knew it had to be; this was the Wagnerian land of Tristan and Isolde. Despite what he saw to be their fussy and tedious protests over the Reich's expansion, he could not envisage any means by which Germany could be denied the privileges the British had enjoyed for so long. He was certain they would never be so hypocritical.

Hitler stopped and looked at a young corporal. Obviously moved, he sighed: 'Ja, ein hubscher junger Obergefreiter, genauso wie ich war.'

Ribbentrop spoke into Chamberlain's ear: 'The Fuhrer says: "Yes, a handsome young corporal, just like I was."'

Rat-tat-tat-tat! The .303 blanks burst flame from the wing's gun ports, the four Browning machine guns legitimising the Spitfire's name as it climbed at an astonishing 2,800 feet per minute, its thin cross-section elliptical wings achieving record speed. Hitler adjusted the focus on his binoculars, trying to keep track as the plane banked thousands of feet above him.

In an instant the Spitfire turned and went into a sharp dive. It headed straight for the grandstand and flew past, almost at arm's length. The air turbulence had the VIP audience holding onto their hats—all except Hitler who remained perfectly still; he knew his steel plated cap wasn't going anywhere.

David looked closely at the leader who stood beside him. He saw the Iron Cross and the gold Nazi Party badge, the dreadful haircut and the Charlie Chaplin moustache. The man had sculpted himself to suit the image he'd ordained: he was fast becoming the world's most famous face, a titan to be loved or feared or both, like a master to a dog. But David saw the dark stubble on his chin and smelt the halitosis; he was just a man and he could be manipulated.

To the opposite side of the German leader sat Goering, his uniform a shade of powder blue. David saw Hitler whisper something in the Reichsmarschall's plump ear. David wondered if he was impressed. He hoped so; the display by the Number 19 Squadron had gone perfectly. David pitied any bomber with a Spitfire under its belly and he knew how important it was that the German leadership understand the consequences of such a scenario: the consequences of a war with Great Britain; the Spitfire and the Hurricane had turned England's green and pleasant land into an angry hedgehog.

The grandstand was overflowing with military personnel. Generals Dill, Ironside and Lord Gort were there, as well as dozens of other generals, admirals and air marshals. Chamberlain and the foreign secretary, Lord Halifax, had made sure to remain for the display. Dressed in lounge suits, they stuck out like barn owls in a conference of peacocks.

Conspicuous by his absence was Leslie Hore-Belisha, the secretary of state for war. He had made his position clear a day earlier, saying: 'I'll be damned if I'm going to be caught at Hendon or Chequers, there to parley with Hitler and his gang of strutting thugs!'

David scanned the scene and saw the many pale Germanic eyes squinting in the spring sunshine; heads turning in unison, mouths agape, looking up in awe at the arcing swarm of hornets their policies had unleashed. He was pleased the demonstration was having its desired effect, but also amused by the extent of the German leader's security, and wondered why it was so. This was not France, America or the Balkans; assassination was not a preferred Anglo-Saxon sport. In contrast to the German leadership, there he was with Georgie, and not even a police detective to protect them. His brother turned and said: 'Wonderful show. Should enjoy a good run if the critics are impressed.'

David glanced along the stand, and at that very instant, he saw Goering lean forward, wave at him and nod. He waved back, not sure what else to do, when suddenly, all conversation on the grandstand was drowned out by the whine of the spitfires' supercharged V12 Merlin engines. Now the full squadron climbed and demonstrated a number of manoeuvres: barrel rolls, vertical rolling scissors, inward turnabouts and even the Immelmanm. In unison the full squadron climbed, stalled, spun, dived and pulled out inches from the ground. Like a flock of starlings they flew as one, a single bird. The crowd let out a gasp.

While David was at Hendon, Wallis was at Bruton Street, Mayfair, with the couturier, Norman Hartnell. She had been arranging the fittings for her summer wardrobe and was just leaving the fashion house when met by a stranger. With a flourish he presented her with a bunch of roses. He was gone before she had a chance to ask why. As Wallis was chauffeured home to the Palace, she read the attached card and was reminded there was no such thing as a free rose.

That night David and Georgie attended an official dinner for Hitler at Chequers. It was an all male affair and Wallis didn't get to speak to David until he returned to the Palace, by which time she was in bed.

'How did you read him,' she asked nonchalantly.

David discarded his jacket and was already pouring them a nightcap. 'Hard to say, but Goering looked decidedly uncomfortable. I mean, he was full of laughs and chuckles and actually very amusing, but I wouldn't like to be in his shoes. He'll have his work cut out when he gets home.'

'So your plan was a success?' asked Wallis.

'You mean our plan; we're a team, remember?'

'Okay, coach, so what's the strategy for the second half of the game?'

David stared into his drink. 'Keep my promise to an old, blind soldier.'

The next day, it was obvious to all Hitler had been impressed by Britain's fighter planes; he said as much, caring not if it might embarrass Udet or Goering. At the Chequers conference his mood had been friendly, and despite attempts to bring up the subject, he refused to discuss the possibility he might make further territorial claims against Germany's neighbours. Despite that the conference had still gone on longer than planned. Not because anything of substance had been achieved, but because Hitler would not stop talking. His hosts were not subjected to one of his famous tirades but to an oleaginous embrocation of his charms, peppered with endless questions on aviation technology and air tactics. Goering filled in whenever Hitler took a breath. Playing follow the leader, he was all smiles and cracking jokes. Everybody laughed: Halifax, Ribbentrop, Wilson, Chamberlain; everybody except Hess who remained as taciturn and impenetrable as a sphinx.

Over cups of tea, which he drank with his pinkie erect, Hitler celebrated the shared destiny of the North Sea tribes, much to the embarrassment of his hosts, the more sensitive members of whom felt uncomfortable at having Slavic cultures likened to the many native cultures within their own empire. The conference seemed to have descended into farce, and most were relieved when it came to an end late Sunday afternoon; all the talking had achieved little more than a reiteration of the letter the two leaders had signed after the Munich conference. Halifax now wondered if they had been duped into showing their competitors too much, their efforts merely serving to prompt Hitler into an even greater expansion of Germany's rearmament. Chamberlain saw the matter in a more positive light. He told the worried foreign secretary that their exhibition of military strength had alerted the Germans to Britain's determination. Standing at the front door of Chequers, he insisted: 'Hitler, has been kept in leash, the only way he can be, by our strength. The Poles can sleep soundly in their beds tonight.'

The British negotiation team waved, the press took photographs and the military men saluted as Hitler's motorcade departed.

The Guards swung open the gates on Missendon Road as a Humber Pullman drove out, Sir Philip Game and Sir Samuel Hoare sitting in the back seat; the Pullman was followed by another three government cars, all containing British military and police officers. After these came the Germans: a Humber snipe with Goering and Hess; a Rover 10 with Sepp Dietrich and Ernst Udet; and then Hitler. With his favourite body guards, Bruno Gesche and Gustav Weler, the Fuhrer graced the interior of a Rolls Royce Phantom, the vehicle driven with difficulty by the Fuhrer's personal chauffeur, Obersturmfuhrer Erich Kempka; the SS man found it tiresome to deal with the heavy steering and right-hand drive.

Next came the follow-up cars. The first was packed with members of the Begleitkommando, all armed with brand new MP40s. The second follow-up car contained a squad of hand picked guardsmen: some squeezed inside, others clinging to the running boards, all armed with Bren light machine guns. The third car carried Hitler's adjutants and his personal physician, Dr. Theodor Morell; the fourth and fifth held yet more of the German leader's staff. At the tail end came an ambulance with a busload of press bringing up the rear.

The motorcade crawled along Missendon Road and turned into Dunsmore Lane. On Hitler's instructions, the cars travelled at a sedate 20 miles per hour, as he disliked being driven fast. Sir John Simon's committee knew that it was impossible to completely line the procession route because it extended for more than 30 miles. The police and troops had therefore been concentrated in spots where they thought trouble most likely to arise, such as in villages, in urban areas and their outskirts. Dunsmore Lane was in mostly open countryside and only skirted a handful of country estates. It was considered a lower risk portion of the drive, and the only police along its entire length were stationed at a sharp turn, about half a mile from Missendon Road. The police presence consisted of three constables. They were relaxing around an old horse trough and chatting with a couple of locals who'd made the event an excuse for a picnic. When they noticed the motorcade's approach they broke off the conversation, formed into a line at the roadside and came to attention. The locals were two squires and their wives. They had little German and British flags. These they waved as the motorcade slowed to take the turn. After Dietrich's Rover swung past they were offered a clear line of sight; Hitler's Rolls Royce, swastikas flying from the front fenders, was moving slowly toward them. They dropped their flags. The two women produced Webley revolvers from their handbags. The men opened their picnic baskets and pulled out Thompson submachine guns. The stocks were detached but the receivers, fore-grips and magazines were assembled and ready to fire.

The assassins had chosen well. Standing on the outer edge

of the angle in the road, they would be difficult to outflank, and behind them lay woodland to cover their retreat. They ran up the passenger side of the Rolls Royce and fired point blank into the back seat, churning it into a mass of blood and shattering glass. Hitler's car ran off the road and ploughed into a low wall. One of the women tossed a grenade under the boot, the explosion lifting the vehicle's rear end.

The bobbies, their truncheons useless against bullets, took cover behind the horse trough. Begleitkommandos poured out of the first follow-up car and began firing. The four assassins jumped behind the wall. Blood splattered from the shoulder of one of the women. She staggered and was hauled over by a comrade.

The Germans spread out and moved forward, sending out a hail of bullets. The guards raced up in support. Sepp Dietrich, armed only with his luger, jumped out of the Rover and advanced on his enemy's left, taking cover behind the crashed Rolls Royce. For a few seconds the air was thick with lead and cordite. Seeing that their job was done, the assassins grabbed their wounded comrade, and made a run for the protection of the woods.

The SS-Begleitkommandos and the Grenadier Guards raced up to the wall, and shoulder to shoulder, delivered a blazing sheet of automatic gunfire. Any protecting cover from the woodland undergrowth vaporised and the assassins were cut to shreds.

Dietrich looked into the back of the Rolls Royce and saw Hitler's metal lined cap swamped in an unrecognizable mass of flesh. He swung around to the front passenger seat and forced open the door. From the clearing smoke, Hitler staggered out. He was covered in blood and viscera, but the gore wasn't his. On the back seat, Bruno Gesche and the Fuhrer's look-alike, Gustav Weler, had earned the right to a funeral with full SS honours.

Chamberlain was just about to leave Chequers for Downing Street when the news was radioed through to the communications room. He was at the scene of the crime within minutes, but Hitler was already gone. Dietrich had walked him into his Rover and ordered the motorcade away at high speed. All that was left from the action was the destroyed Rolls Royce, the shaken bobbies, the wounded and the dead. The assassins had killed three of the four occupants of the German leader's car, but Hitler had ducked down and escaped without a scratch. His psychological wounds were another matter.

News of the assassination attempt reached the BBC as soon their reporter could talk his way through the front door of the nearest country home. Ten minutes later the story was on the air.

The king met him in the palace audience chamber. The prime minister came straight there immediately after being briefed by MI5 and Special Branch.

'Communists,' Chamberlain said while trying to sip a sherry. The glass teetered in his bony fingers and missed his lips, the liquor dribbling down onto his starched winged collar.

David had offered him the drink to help calm his nerves.

The prime minister was not an ex-serviceman. He'd spent the Great War in the Birmingham City Council House as head of the town planning committee and later as Mayor. In 1917 he was appointed Director of National Service. He'd ordered thousands to the war and to their death, but he'd only heard and read of the carnage of battle. Never before had he seen it.

'You caught them all?' David assumed.

'It depends on what you mean by caught,' said Chamberlain. 'Three of the assassins are dead. One of the women is still alive. She's being questioned by Scotland Yard.'

At that moment, deep below the Victoria Embankment, the suspect sat strapped to a steel chair. Her face was red and swollen, and through a dirty bandage, her shoulder wound oozed crimson and brown. A detective sergeant in shirtsleeves, face shining with sweat, backhanded the woman. The impact sent blood spraying. It flew across the room and dribbled down the olive green tiles.

David lit a cigarette. 'Any links to the Soviet Embassy?'

'She's refusing to talk. Background checks and informants lead us to believe that they were a small cell, acting alone.'

'Does Hitler know all this?'

'He knows what we know which isn't much. They were all British except for the woman we have in custody.'

'What is she? A Czech? French?' David's voice lowered. 'Is she American?'

'No,' groaned the prime minister, shrinking into the sofa, 'she's Polish.'

'Damn,' David muttered, getting up and pacing the room. 'Damn!' he repeated, only much louder. 'Did you tell Hitler that she's Polish?'

Chamberlain crossed his legs and looked sheepish. 'We thought it important that he should—'

David didn't wait for him to finish. He picked up a Ming Dynasty vase and threw it against the flocked wallpaper, the pieces clattering over a chiffonier. 'Fucking, fucking damn!'

Wallis rushed in. 'What's going on?'

David's face was brick, rendered as a war mask and twisted by lines she'd never seen before. Chamberlain quickly shuffled his documents and placed them in a folder.

David stumbled to the drinks table and struggled to open the whisky decanter. 'It's all ruined, I just know it.'

Wallis took his arm. 'Boysie, are you alright?'

'Ruined! Everything ruined—all the work, all that effort.'

Watson and a couple of pages appeared at the door.

'Herr Hitler wasn't harmed,' said Chamberlain, noticing the growing crowd of Palace staff.

David gave him a look of infinite loathing. 'Not harmed?'

Chamberlain got the message. 'I really must be going. I shall talk with you further at our regular meeting on Tuesday.' The prime minister picked up his briefcase and went to leave.

'You really haven't got a clue, have you?' said Wallis.

Chamberlain ignored her and turned directly to his king. 'Might I suggest you do your country a favour and keep your mistress quarantined from confidential affairs of state.'

'How dare you,' said David, approaching the prime minister with menace.

Wallis stepped in front of him. 'It's okay,' she soothed, 'his opinion means nothing.' Then glaring at Chamberlain, she added: 'He's just a glorified civil servant.'

The prime minister smoothed his greying hair, and as he left, turned to the butler and said softly: 'Thank you, Watson, I can find my own way out.'

Wallis turned on the staff. 'Well? What are you all staring at?'

Watson and the other servants made a hurried exit. David poured himself a large scotch, his eyes wild, possessed. Wallis felt his pain because it was as much hers as his, maybe more. She gently took away his drink and asked: 'Where do we go from here?'

Chapter Six, the Royal Right of Reply

The spine of the Palace of Westminster was designed along a north-south axis. Starting at the northern end, it led from the House of Commons, through its lobby and along the Commons Corridor, to the hub of the building, the octagonal Central Hall. Then it continued along the Peer's Corridor to the Peer's Lobby and the chamber of the House of Lords. If all the doors were open, David sitting on the throne in the Lords, could see all the way to the speaker's chair in the Commons. Though it would constitute an act of treason for any of his or her subjects to do so, the monarch could sit on the throne of the Lords any time he or she might please. Except for the annual state openings of parliament, few since the Stuarts had been so pleased, but on the evening of the fourth of April 1939 King Edward VIII changed all that.

There were separate entrances to the parliament for the members, peers and public, but the king took the Sovereign's Entrance, which lay at the base of the Victoria Tower. Having more important matters on his mind and caring little for the normal pomp, he did not employ any of the ceremonial coaches. Instead, he arrived in his Rolls Royce, emerging dressed in the uniform of the Grenadier Guards, the crossed batons, oak leaves and crown of a field marshal emblazoned on his epaulets. He saluted the officer commanding the household cavalry unit that had been hastily assembled to guard his passage and ascended the Royal Staircase, his way lined by sword-wielding troopers of the Life Guards and the Blues and Royals.

At the top of the staircase, David passed through the Norman Porch and into the King's Robing Room. This was located at the southern extremity and ceremonial end of the north-south axis. Due to the short notice given by the Palace, the robes, crown, sword of state and other regalia of a royal visit to Westminster had been rushed in by armoured car not ten minutes earlier, delivered from their home at the Jewel House in the Tower of London.

After putting on his official parliamentary robes of state, David sat on a hurriedly fetched office chair to receive the Imperial State Crown. Like his father and grandfather before him, he shunned the Chair of State, not wanting to shift the little footstool that had stood untouched for forty years. Though its owner had long since passed, the stool remained at its post, ever ready to prevent Queen Victoria's petite legs from dangling.

As soon as he was dressed, the king went to leave. However, though impatient to be gone, he took a moment to do something he had never bothered to do before: he paused beside the Robing Room's northeast door, waylaid by the glass-topped cabinet standing there. Stepping back and peering down, he took the time to study the document displayed within. It was a facsimile of his Stuart ancestor, Charles I's death warrant. Adorning the parchment lay the names of Oliver Cromwell and 58 of the other commissioners who convicted him, each man's signature accompanied by his seal. The spattering of red wax blobs reminded David of the floors of field hospitals he had visited during the war. Unimpressed by parliament's grizzly but enduring reminder of the sovereign's mortality, the king entered the Royal Gallery. This room was the largest in Westminster Palace. It led north along the axis and was quite a trek. If it were the opening of parliament, he would have been expected to walk its length at a ceremonial pace, taking his place in a little procession of office bearers, with spectators lining the route. However, this day, he rushed past the faded frescoes of the battles of Trafalgar and Waterloo, and was quickly in the next room. It was the Prince's Chamber. Decorated with paintings of Tudor kings and queens, and reminiscent of a superior London club, the Prince's Chamber lay immediately behind the throne of the House of Lords. His brothers were there to greet him. A handful of functionaries were also present, standing a few yards away and gathered before a marble statue of Queen Victoria. These included the Earl Marshal, Bernard Marmaduke Fitzalan-Howard, 16th Duke of Norfolk; the Lord Great Chamberlain, Gilbert Heathcote-Drummond-Willoughby, 2nd Earl of Ancaster; and Lieutenant General Sir Guy Williams, GOC Eastern Command; the latter already holding the Sword of State.

All three of the king's brothers were in military uniform: Bertie, Henry and Georgie representing the Royal Navy, the army and the Royal Air Force. David passed the text of his speech to the Duke of Kent. 'Georgie, you look after this, I shan't need it.'

'Are you sure?' he asked, folding the paper and shoving it inside his blue-grey jacket.

'Of course I'm sure,' David insisted. 'I wrote the damn thing. I should be able to remember what it says. Oh, one thing I mustn't forget—it was wobbling a bit—is my crown on straight?'

Georgie took a close look and nodded. 'Yes, it's fine.'

'Good. Bloody thing always wants to lean to one side. A crown can appear ridiculous at the best of times, but lopsided it makes one look like a drunk at a costume party.'

David heard the evening session of the Lords being brought to order by the Lord Chancellor. Without further ado the king sent Ancaster, Norfolk and Williams into the House and quickly followed, his brothers behind him.

As the royal procession filed in, the lords temporal and spiritual rose from their red-upholstered seats. The king mounted the steps of the dais, crossed to his throne and sat down. His brothers filed in behind him and took their positions, standing in front of their chairs of state; all three were to his immediate right, but on a lower level of the dais. From his throne, and to his near right, David looked on the bishops of the Established Church of England. In their ceremonial white rochets with black chimeres, these were the men who had colluded with his ministers to prevent his marriage. Standing at the benches further down on his right were the government peers. Down the centre of the chamber were the law lords: the Lord Chief Justice and the high court judges in scarlet and white fur, the Lord Chief Justices of

Appeal in black silk damask with gold embroidery; all were bewigged and stood in rows to his front, the crossbenchers behind them. His Majesties Loyal Opposition stood at the benches to his left. The king rested his elbows on the arms of his throne and instructed: 'My lords, pray be seated.' He glanced sideways and saw the queen's throne; it was the only empty seat in the House.

Once everyone was settled, David motioned to the Lord Great Chamberlain who, in response, lifted his white wand of office, thus signalling Black Rod to summon the members of the House of Commons. There was then something of a wait while the ritual of knocking on doors, bowings and such was played out—yet another reason for David to be annoyed with his Stuart ancestor.

Passing the time, the king looked across the chamber and saw his friends the Duke of Westminster, The Duke of Wellington, Baron Redesdale, The Earl of Galloway, and of course, Lord Norman, who got away from the City just in time. Up in the public gallery, guarded by a watchful police detective, he caught a glimpse of Wallis—the lonely little petunia in the king's union patch.

There came a clatter of feet as the members of the Commons sauntered down the Peer's Corridor and crossed the lobby. Upon entering the chamber, the House Speaker, the Commons Clerk, Black Rod and the Sergeant at Arms took their positions at the rail that formed the Bar of the House of Lords. There they bowed. The prime minister and the other members of the Commons followed, but were not required to bow. Instead, they were left to crowd in as best they could, politely jostling for position. Normally at this time, the Lord Chancellor would approach the sovereign, and on bended knee, produce from a satchel a vellum scroll bearing the 'Speech from the Throne', reflecting His Majesty's government's legislative agenda. Today the chancellor's satchel remained empty.

David sat up straight, his elbows still resting on the arms of his throne. With no notes to hold, his hands formed into fists. He stared ahead as though waiting for the sun to rise over the sea, his audience so silent he could almost hear its collective heartbeat. Into this auditory void, and without the use of his Neumann microphone, he began to speak, his voice projecting firmly, his diction razor sharp.

'As you all know, the assassination attempt on the visiting chancellor of Germany, Herr Hitler, was perpetrated by members of the British Communist Party.'

A murmur of concern rolled across the chamber as David continued. 'But this assault is not just an act of treason by home grown agitators, it must be at the behest of the Communist International, the Soviet Union, Joseph Stalin— the true enemies of the British Empire.'

A few peers felt compelled to ignore the long-established convention of remaining silent during occasions of royal attendance in the Lords. They gruffly shouted: 'Hear, hear!'

Gratified for the vocal support, the king pressed on. 'Yet what is the trajectory of our foreign policy but to pick a fight with Germany. To risk another war that would lay waste the land, bankrupt the exchequer and scythe another grim harvest from our youth.'

David subtly shifted the pitch of his delivery from warlord to priest. 'Some say war is in the nature of mankind, but I say only if we let it be. We owe our children a world made better by our deeds, not worse. We must shield them from the storms that we have seen. We owe our children nothing less. We owe our children peace.'

This time, all the peers and most of the members ignored convention and shouted: 'Hear, hear.' Wallis found the power of their resonating voices deeply moving.

David scanned the chamber, saw the many nodding heads, and went in for the kill. 'Why risk all protecting Stalin with British blood. Better to let Germany do our dirty work and rid the world of communism.'

There was shocked silence as the king's meaning sank in. The lull was short-lived. Applause in the Lords was normally forbidden, but that night it was deafening.

David noticed Churchill. He stood, ruddy-faced, in the midst of the other members of the Commons. Unlike those around him, he remained stock-still, declining to be swept up by the emotion of the moment. Not only did Churchill not agree with the words of the king, he coldly envied the panache with which they had been delivered. Like many a prima donna, he was prone to jealousy, and loathed the thought of sharing the limelight with a pretender to his oratory mantle. His king knew this would be the case. David gave his head a tilt in Churchill's direction, a salute of acknowledgement, player-to-player, and proceeded to his call to action.

'My lords, ladies and gentleman, Britannia and her empire have, numerous times, stared down the threat of annihilation, the death of our culture, our traditions, our values and our birthright; and yet, by dint of extraordinary effort, and yes, sacrifice, we have beaten back those darkening waves to end the day triumphant. I urge you to show that same skill, fortitude and courage today. Not the skill and courage to make war, but the strength and will to keep peace.' David lowered his voice, almost in supplication. 'It is a noble pursuit.' With his voice again rising, he declared: 'I believe I speak for the people of my realm when I urge you, the privileged and the powerful, to do all within your gift to maintain that peace, that glorious peace, in this our sceptred isle. Let nothing distract you from your holy quest. This I beseech of you, sitting before you as your anointed king.'

Lord Redesdale shouted: 'God save the King!'

The chamber responded, thundering three times: 'God save the King!'

David departed the chamber, but now owned the stage.

The next morning there was consternation in the Cabinet Room. Not a single minister had contemplated or knew how to deal with a king who was so unflinching in his resolve to test the limits of his constitutional powers. He had broken the shackles of convention and they feared he would never submit to them again. Yet more worrying was the knowledge he had harnessed the power of the Lords to his cause. He also had the backing of the press. Under the editorship of Geoffrey Dawson, the Times led the way, calling the king's speech courageous. All the leading newspapers were full of praise. Dissenting voices were rejected. Even the Labour-leaning

Daily Herald echoed the others. Winston Churchill wrote a piece critical of the speech, as did the foreign correspondent for the News Chronicle, Vernon Bartlett, but neither could get his opinion published. A ragtag assortment of pamphleteers provided the only voices of dissent. His majesty's government had been comprehensively outmanoeuvred.

Overnight and through the morning the Palace received hundreds of telegrams. The messages of support arrived from the journalist, A. K. Chesterton; the writer and philosopher, G. K. Chesterton; the explorer, St John Philby; symphony conductor, Reginald Goodall; former England cricket captain, Arthur Gilligan; race car driver, Sir Malcolm Campbell; Major General John Fuller; George Bernard Shaw; and the pacifists: Aldous Huxley, Bertrand Russell and Siegfried Sassoon. Over the ensuing days, mountains of mail from across the length and breadth of the nation and empire overwhelmed the Palace post office. A platoon of staff was seconded to the Private Secretary's Office to open and read it all, sorting the opinions into either favourable or critical. Almost all the correspondence was fulsome in its praise of the king's speech.

At noon a hastily convened parliamentary delegation visited the Palace. Three of the politicians represented the Lords: the Earl of Glasgow, Baron de Clifford and the Duke of Bedford; while the other three spoke for a large portion of the Commons backbench: William Scott, Archibald Ramsay and John Mackie. They were there to humbly suggest the creation of a 'King's Party', dedicated to the cause of peace. David was flattered but demurred. Though, to some, it may have seemed otherwise, he had not abjured pragmatism.

Having pushed his luck to the brink, he well knew he must now pull back. With the delegation crowding the audience chamber, he put aside his drink and spoke candidly. 'Every decent man and woman, highborn or low, city and country, desires peace. It is not political. Therefore, I believe I stand on firm ground when I speak for peace. On this I am my people's voice. However, if I were to speak on other matters, I should risk being seen as political. I must be above party politics. Henceforth, I shall cease all utterances, observations and reflections on industry, poverty, job creation, public works, defence and the like. I must go back to my kennel for fear of making my commentary commonplace. A guard dog need only bark when necessary; if it yaps incessantly, it loses its purpose. This dog will only bark for peace. Beyond that, I am, as always, at the disposal of my government.' After the usual pleasantries, the delegation left with his blessing, and his fervent hope they would work tirelessly for the cause.

A little later in the day there was a phone call from Sir Oswald Mosley, the leader of the British Union of Fascists. He asked David's private secretary, Alexander Hardinge, if he might speak to the king. David declined to take the call, telling Hardinge to say he was in a meeting, and offering his apologies.

That evening Chamberlain and Wilson met with Kennedy. The prime minister seemed dazed. Leaning against his armrest, he absentmindedly used his fingertip to draw circles on his forehead. 'I fear we are in for a torrid summer.'

The leather creaked as Kennedy shifted in his chair. 'Do

you think the Germans will be satisfied with just a Polish corridor or do you think they'll want the whole shebang?'

Chamberlain sighed: 'With the way his majesty's behaving, I think they'll risk going for the whole…' He cleared his throat. 'Shebang.'

Kennedy allowed himself another wry smile. 'Ah, yeah, Mr Saxe Coburg and Gotha. Sorry, I mean Mr Windsor.'

Chamberlain sighed again. 'Indeed.'

The American ambassador reached into his briefcase. 'Which brings me to the purpose of my visit.' He removed a file and handed it to the prime minister. 'You're going to have to keep this under wraps. It's from the FBI on Wallis Simpson, FKA Spencer, FKA Warfield, maybe, one day, AKA Windsor. It's top secret. If it gets out, I'll know who to blame.'

Wallis gripped the bedhead as she thrust her pelvis into David's face. The four-poster shook, and he almost suffocated as she climaxed. Exhausted, she rolled off and collapsed beside him, exhaling her breath like a struck tent. From the opposite wall, Victoria's portrait stared down, not amused. Wallis didn't care. Don't give me that look, she thought. You couldn't have conceived *all* your nine children from the missionary position. Or maybe you did and that's why you look so cross.

She ran the back of her hand gently down David's chest and over his stomach. 'What do you think will happen?'

David stretched and crossed his arms behind his head, enjoying the afterglow and happy to talk shop. 'The next move is Hitler's. If he wants war he will have war, but only with Poland.'

'And Churchill?'

'I wish he'd stick to writing his book: "A History of the English Speaking Peoples"! If that's not a subject big enough to keep a person distracted, then I'm not Edward the Eighth.'

Wallis kept staring at Victoria's portrait. 'While Churchill has a voice, disaster is always close at hand.'

'He's lost his opinion column at the Evening Standard.'

'Yes, but now he's over at the Daily Telegraph.'

'He is indefatigable.'

'No, he's intolerable, don't trust him.'

David looked at Wallis, a small crease of concern between his eyebrows. 'Winston and I may have our differences on issues. Right now, we find ourselves on opposing sides of the fence, but as I have said many times, he is and will always be a loyal friend.'

'Perhaps,' Wallis conceded, 'but a war can set friend against friend, brother against brother. He's champing at the bit, even though Britain would probably lose if it came to a fight.'

'You underestimate my people,' said David, turning away onto his side. 'If the unthinkable occurred and we found ourselves at war, we'd not be left empty handed.'

Wallis sat up, displaying an earnestness that a less trusting man than David could well have found suspicious, daring to hope she might hear a morsel of information important enough to release her from the grip of Ribbentrop's henchmen.

David turned back impressed by her reaction, wallowing in her curiosity like a boy with a tit-bit of schoolyard gossip.

'Does that surprise you?'

Wallis belatedly attempted to display a cool reserve. 'No, nothing these days would surprise me.' She paused to light a cigarette, using the break in conversation to calmly collect her thoughts. 'So what's this secret weapon?'

David felt sufficiently confident to boast: 'We haven't shown Hitler everything in our box of tricks—have you ever heard of Radar?'

'Yes, we are aware of it,' said Dorfman.

The little flat was again shrouded in darkness, curtains drawn and the window shuttered firmly.

'The British have made significant advances,' Wallis declared, for the first time feeling confident in the agents' presence. 'They have a chain of Radar stations along the coast. All are equipped with an electron tube they call a resonant-cavity magnetron.'

'It sounds like something from Mr H. G. Wells!'

Wallis continued, though annoyed by the agent's sarcasm and worried he might consider her information of no importance: 'With it, a ground station can detect enemy aircraft during the day or night, no matter what the weather.'

The German scratched the back of his shaved head. 'Do you have the specifications, blueprints?'

'Hell, no,' Wallis shouted, 'I'm not Mata Hari!' She glanced behind her at the second agent. 'Haven't I done enough?' The gray-suited man offered her a cigarette and lit it with a gold Dunhill lighter.

Dorfman sneered, 'We will decide when your debt to the

Fatherland has been repaid.'

Wallis exhaled a long plume of smoke. It glowed white in the inky blackness. 'No way!' she insisted, 'I'm never coming here again. And don't summon me with more damned flowers!'

'Oh, my dear lady,' came a familiar voice, 'I am most sorry, next time we'll bring you chocolates.'

Wallis looked up to see Ribbentrop emerge from the shadows.

Hitler returned to Berlin a publicly outraged but privately satisfied man, his designs on Polish territory reinforced by the fact that a member of the assassination team was a citizen of that country. He mourned the loss of his trusted staff, but welcomed the fact he now had a perfect excuse to increase German pressure on Warsaw. As soon as Reinhard Heydrich's SD had deftly manufactured the necessary evidence—forged papers showing the young assassin was acting under orders from her government—he issued a series of harsh demands on Poland. These he argued were essential for German security in the face of unwarranted Polish aggression.

In response Chamberlain issued a guarantee to Warsaw. However, within hours of the guarantee being given, an editorial page of The Times declared that 'the new obligation didn't bind Britain to defend every inch of the existing frontiers of Poland.' The Times went on to comment that, 'the guarantee involved no blind acceptance of the status quo.'

To this Churchill replied in the Commons: 'We must not let ourselves be deluded into thinking that we can still afford ourselves the comfort of further territorial negotiations. Our first duty is to re-establish the authority of law and public trust in Europe.'

On 20th April Hitler celebrated his fiftieth birthday with the biggest military parade ever seen in Germany. If the invitation to Britain had been an attempt to intimidate him, it had failed. At the same time, during a visit to Paris, Churchill was informed by the chief of staff of the French army, General Joseph Georges, that the Germans had benefited from the time gained at Munich, saying, 'Hitler's capture of the Czech arms manufacturer, Skoda, was a major disaster.' His artillery could no longer guarantee its technical superiority over that of the Germans nor could it maintain its numerical advantage.

A month later Britain put pressure on Poland to make some concessions to the German demands for the annexation of the lands taken from them after the end of the Great War, including the Free City of Danzig. With strong Cabinet support, Chamberlain continued an ongoing dialogue with all parties. He told Warsaw that Hitler would be prepared to compromise provided he didn't feel humiliated in the process. The Poles ignored him.

In late June, Churchill ventured up Whitehall to the War Ministry. He had arranged to see his old supporter, Leslie Hore-Belisha. A former transport minister who had introduced the Belisha Beacon, the driving test and the 30 mph speed limit, he had a year earlier been promoted to secretary of state for war. This senior appointment was opposed by many of his Cabinet colleagues who disliked his energy, seeing him as too pushy, some even privately suggesting he was a

Bolshevik. Believing war to be inevitable, Hore-Belisha had encouraged his friend, Churchill, to send him ideas. Acting on Churchill's suggestion, he had tried to reintroduce conscription, but Chamberlain rejected this as too costly. He then tried to put British industry on a war footing and to coordinate the three services into a ministry of supply, but again was rebuffed. Fed up with these frustrations and horrified by Britain's abandonment of Czechoslovakia at Munich, he had considered resigning from Cabinet. Churchill urged him to remain, arguing that the cause of appeasement could only be enhanced by his departure. Hore-Belisha had taken his friend's advice.

Churchill was ushered into the War Secretary's office and was surprised to find the Inspector-General for Overseas Forces, Sir Edmund Ironside.

Hore-Belisha rose from behind his desk. 'Winston, good to see you, I hope you don't mind, but I thought it might be wise to invite Sir Edmond to join us.'

General Ironside stood to shake hands. 'Winston, it's been too long since our last meeting.'

Churchill looked up at the General's towering presence. 'Yes, Edmond, I agree. How was your visit with the Polish high command?'

'A very good question,' Hore-Belisha interrupted, 'one that will elicit a thought-provoking answer. So let us settle down before hearing it. I've organised some coffee.'

The three men walked to a sideboard where the Secretary of State for War did the honours. Once they were settled in their enormous art deco club chairs, he opened the discussion by inviting Ironside to answer Churchill's earlier question.

'The Poles were most hospitable,' said the general, 'I was able to make a very thorough assessment of their military capability, and I'm afraid to say, I found their entire situation most concerning. While their army is large—it is almost as large as the German's—its command structure is chaotic and their weaponry antiquated. They have several divisions of cavalry, but practically no armour. Their air force is old and not trained for close tactical support. If we were fighting a war with them as our allies, they would be excellent—provided it was the Crimean War.'

Churchill cleared his throat as he lit himself a cigar.

'I'm sorry, Winston,' Ironside continued, 'but should they be invaded, Hitler's panzers would cut through them like butter. Brave as they most certainly would prove to be, you can't fight tanks with horses. If Hitler attacks, the country will be quickly overrun. It's also doubtful we could get across the Baltic to support them. The Germans would make sure to first take the port of Danzig and cut the Poles off from the sea. The threat to Germany's eastern front would last a matter of weeks, if not days.'

'And what about the Russians?' Churchill asked. 'You were part of the anti-Soviet military intervention back in 1919.'

'Archangel was a cold and miserable place. Bloody bastards tried to assassinate me. I wouldn't entrust any part of our defence policy—no matter how small—to the communists. Besides, Polish antipathy to Russia is centuries old.'

Churchill put down his coffee. 'Overall, Sir Edmond, I

would account your assessment as grim.'

'But accurate and realistic,' said Hore-Belisha. 'I have the report here if you'd like to read it. It's most thorough. Oh, by the way, Winston, I am recommending Sir Edmond to the post of Chief of the Imperial General Staff.'

Churchill smiled. 'Congratulations, Edmond, I dare say that you are the right man for the job. The position requires a strong personality. I might even say a domineering personality.'

'I agree,' said Hore-Belisha. 'General Gort is out of his depth in such a position.'

Ironside adjusted his uniform, but said nothing.

Churchill rose slowly from his chair and walked to the window. He could see outside all the bustle of Whitehall and wondered how bleak, even bombed out, it could be in a very short while. He turned back to his colleagues. 'So, Edmond, Leslie, you're both telling me that in the event that we go to war, the western front will meet the full force of Hitler's massed divisions?'

'Yes, we will,' said Ironside. 'We, and I presume, the French.'

Churchill returned to his chair. 'Leslie, do any of your fellow members of the Cabinet realise how dire the situation has become?'

The War Secretary inhaled as if about to speak, but thought better of it and simply shook his head.

'Right,' Churchill pronounced, 'then the government's reluctance to switch British industry to a war footing must be swept away.'

'I couldn't agree more,' said Hore-Belisha, 'but it's like banging my head against a brick wall. Chamberlain still seems to think that war might actually be avoided.'

'Oh, yes, of course,' said Churchill, his tone sarcastic, 'I'm sure Hitler would quite happily leave us alone. He'd not bother Britain in the least—until we are bereft of a single ally, all of them gobbled up piecemeal! We must immediately press for the fullest cooperation with France and for the introduction of conscription.'

'I'd support you to the hilt on that,' said Ironside. 'We cannot depend on volunteers as we did at the start of the last war.'

'The prime minister will not hear of it,' said Hore-Belisha. He finished his coffee before delivering more bad news. 'Chamberlain believes—and he has the backing of many in Cabinet on this matter—that to call for compulsory military service would send to the Germans the wrong signal.'

Ironside pounded his fist on the arm of his chair. 'Then why did we put on that bloody air show for them, if not to send precisely that same signal, if not to scare them witless? Was all that nothing but a sideshow, a circus?'

'I don't know,' sighed Hore-Belisha, 'I refused to attend. I like my clowns to be funny, not nauseating. However, my feelings are not at issue. The problem is there's great sympathy in the Lords and elsewhere in high places, great sympathy for Hitler's point of view. Most feel immense embarrassment that an attempt was made on his life on British soil. Some even believe a mea culpa would be in order.'

'Damn shame the assassins missed.'

'Yes, Winston, I heartily agree,' said the war secretary, his eyes widening at the thought of what might have been, 'but the king articulated the view of the establishment and much of the nation with his speech to parliament. Those agents, no doubt inspired by their communist beliefs, were almost certainly aligned with Stalin. The one assassin who survived admitted as much under interrogation. You know, the one who was Polish.'

Churchill sniffed.

'Yes, Winston,' Hore-Belisha slowly nodded, 'again I agree with your sentiment. But her nationality remains an irrefutable if most regrettable fact, and an extra element in this sorry saga that has done little more than encourage Hitler's megalomania, if such encouragement were ever needed.'

Ironside rubbed his fist into his palm. 'Are either of you privy to the identity of the damned fools who thought it wise to invite the German leader to these shores.'

'It was officially a German initiative,' Hore-Belisha growled, 'but word has it that it was not originally their idea. Notwithstanding such talk of conspiracy, the assassination attempt has taken the wind from our sails. I'm afraid His Majesty's reaction to the event has given the Germans carte blanche.'

'Leslie,' said Churchill, silently mourning the king's drift to appeasement, 'unless we lead the way, any resistance in Europe to Nazi domination will collapse. Every small nation would make the best terms they could with the Nazi behemoth, falling like dominos, until we found ourselves entirely alone to face the combined force of all the fascist dictators; not only Hitler, but Mussolini, Franco and who knows what other horror might emerge from under a slimy rock?'

Though he feared it to be folly, Hore-Belisha undertook to try to convince his Cabinet colleagues of the urgency of the matter. All three men knew that such would be an uphill battle and that precious time was running out.

After the meeting Churchill left for the House of Commons, the black dog of depression creeping back into his soul. On the street outside Westminster Palace he was greeted by a solemn group of demonstrators, all carrying placards calling for his return to Cabinet. They cheered when they saw him approach, one even handed him a cigar. It was not a Cuban but its smoke and the cheers of the mob blew away the old man's despondency. It was warming to know he enjoyed such support, but he despaired that the Cabinet was blind to a threat that even ordinary citizens could see so clearly. With a wave to the crowd he entered Westminster Palace reinvigorated and ready to once again do battle in the bear pit of the Commons.

In July Major Ewalt von Kleist-Schmenzin met secretly with the British ambassador to Germany. He told him that the Government should return Churchill to the Cabinet saying: 'He is the only Englishman that Hitler fears. Churchill's presence might avert war as the German leader would know that Britain was determined to resist further acts of aggression.' The British ambassador sent the information to Downing Street. It landed on the desk of Horace Wilson who filed it.

In August Hitler ordered Ribbentrop on a top secret mission to Russia. The unfortunate yet timely attempt on the Fuhrer's life had done nothing to hurt the foreign minister's standing with his leader. In fact, Hitler held him in higher regard than ever before. Luck was still on Ribbentrop's side. The intelligence information, regularly received from Wallis, remained his greatest weapon against his enemies, but knives were being drawn, illustrating—if proof were ever needed—that though success may breed success, jealousy is bred much faster.

It was a warm August night. In London's St. James's, a black cat prowled the length of a townhouse roof. Beyond its path lay a sea of dormers, chimneys and slate, ebbing away to Buckingham Palace. In his drawing room David sat with Wallis, reading the evening papers. The radio was playing in the corner. It was Churchill giving his weekly broadcast.

'There is a hush all over Europe, nay, over all the world,' Churchill announced sotto voce. 'It is the hush of suspense. It is the hush of fear. Listen! No, listen carefully. I think I hear something.'

A little over a mile away in Portland Place, Churchill sat alone. He was behind the microphone, in a small BBC radio studio. His only company was a solitary engineer beyond the sound proof glass. 'Don't you hear it?' he asked. 'It is the tramp of armies. It is the sound of two million German soldiers, going on manoeuvres. That's right, just manoeuvres, all along the Polish frontier from Danzig to Cracow, only on manoeuvres.'

Wallis looked up from her Vogue magazine. 'Is there anything else on the radio?'

David got up and adjusted the dial to a Mozart concerto. 'I love Winston,' he said, 'but the man does go on at times.'

Twelve hours later, Churchill lay in bed snoring, his eyes covered by a sleep mask. He was woken by Inches, his Butler.

'Sir, there's a phone call for you.'

'What time is it?'

'Half past seven, Sir, Friday morning.'

'I know what blasted day it is. Tell them to bugger off.'

'Sir, I think it's important. It's a Count Raczynski, the Polish ambassador.

'What?' Churchill yelled, jumping out of bed and tearing off his sleep mask. 'Why didn't you tell me sooner.'

Inches rolled his eyes as he helped his boss pull a dressing gown over his naked body. Pushing in his dentures, Churchill raced downstairs to his study and picked up the phone. 'Count Raczynski, Edward, it's me, Winston.'

The Polish Ambassador to the Court of St. James was at his London desk. 'German troops crossed the border several hours ago. Bombs are falling on Warsaw.'

'Hmm,' Churchill growled, 'so it has started. Does Downing Street know? The Foreign Office?'

'No, There's nobody answering in Whitehall. I thought it best to phone you.'

Churchill thanked the ambassador and immediately made several calls. The first was to General Ironside at the London district army headquarters at Horse Guards. The general was eating breakfast at his desk. He hated having his meals interrupted by the phone. At first he tried to ignore it but the ringing was insistent. Finally, he could stand it no more. He put down his fork, knowing that by the time he returned to his bacon and eggs it would be greasily cold. 'Ironside,' he answered harshly.

'Edmond, it's Winston. Nobody at the War Office knows about it, have you heard?'

'Bloody well heard what?'

'Bloody Hitler, the madman's done it. He's invaded bloody Poland.'

Churchill quickly dressed and drove from Chartwell to London, stopping only to pick up a box of Havana cigars from an importer he knew in Croydon. Arriving at Whitehall he embarked on what would prove to be a long and exhausting day, fruitlessly traipsing through crowds of worried Londoners who had gathered there, eager for the latest news. He politely fended off questions from those who recognised him, and for once, avoided making comments to the many reporters. Instead he saved his energy for the various government departments he dropped in on, arguing himself hoarse, pressing for an emergency sitting of the Commons, urging his colleagues to act. The first positive response he received came from Hore-Belisha, who joined him on his journey. In the end, they garnered a small group of supporters: Anthony Eden, Duff Cooper, Bob Boothby, Brendan Bracken; but elsewhere found little enthusiasm for action. Chamberlain, huddled with

Horace Wilson, claimed to be too busy to see them. In the lobby of Number 10, Churchill expressed his concerns to his colleagues: 'Downing Street has blockaded itself from the outside world. The prime minister is hamstrung by moral confusion and scared of his own shadow. Impervious to any call for action, he hasn't even thought to convene a meeting of the Cabinet, let alone sound out the idea of forming a war cabinet. Only spoken to Halifax and Hoare!' All Churchill and his group could learn was that Sir Neville Henderson, the British Ambassador in Berlin, had been instructed to tell the Germans that unless they suspended their aggressive action against Poland and were prepared to withdraw to within their own borders, the British government would fulfil its obligation to Poland. None of the Churchill group could find out what 'fulfil' might entail, and all were alarmed by rumours that the ambassador had been instructed to make it clear Britain was not making an ultimatum.

Late that evening Churchill and his colleagues retired to his flat in Morpeth Mansions. Over a few quiet scotches they bemoaned the country's lack of resolve, all creeping around the key issue, none daring to say it, until Churchill growled the obvious. 'The king's address to the joint sitting of parliament was back in the spring, but it has cast a long shadow. It stretches all the way to this first day of autumn. And the darkness of its shade has proved such to blind the government, delude the people and befuddle the national will. What we have is not so much cowardice as strategic incoherence. Without a concerted effort against Hitler, the drift to catastrophe becomes certain. A declaration of war is the one and only answer. Yet no war, not even the threat of war, is going to be declared any time soon.'

'There must be something we can do,' lamented Bracken. 'We aren't without means.'

There was a moment's silence as they all looked to Churchill.

The old man took a sip of his drink and put down his glass.

Within days, film footage of the Polish invasion reached Britain. The celluloid hadn't come from the Polish because the Wehrmacht had quickly captured Danzig, closing off the country's access to the outside world. Rather, it had been processed and produced by Joseph Goebbel's propaganda ministry: a dozen separate prints individually canned, flown to London in the diplomatic bag and released to Whitehall through the German embassy. British audiences were able to watch the war in their Odeon Cinemas a mere forty-eight hours after moviegoers in Germany. The fact they were allowed to do so was due to Cabinet not seeing any point in seizing and censoring the footage; they simply made sure His Majesty's government dictated the tone and content of the narration. In any case, the film had arrived without a soundtrack; Goebbels was not naïve enough to think Westminster would accept a single word his office might write. The propaganda minister was happy for the British to pen their own English words, because it wasn't the words that mattered, it was the pictures. Goebbels also surmised Chamberlain would feel as certain the images would hurt the

German cause as the propaganda minister felt they would do the opposite. By the first Thursday after the commencement of hostilities British audiences were able to watch German tanks rolling over the Polish countryside and Stukas dive-bombing villages. They were left shocked but in awe, hearing but not listening to the condemnatory British voiceover. However, a cinema patron in Coventry did throw his ice cream at the screen when Hitler's smirking face appeared in close-up.

A world away from the chaos of international relations, David and Wallis took a Saturday afternoon walk in the Palace garden.

'Do you think Chamberlain will involve Britain,' Wallis asked.

'What? Declare war?'

'Yes, or at least threaten it.'

'No, I don't think so. Can you imagine old Neville, sword aloft, rallying the nation to arms? The image is laughable. The Poles should negotiate a peace deal while they still can, before they've lost too much. Just give Hitler what he damned well wants—the land that twenty years ago was stolen from Germany, territory that had been part of Prussia for centuries. All the man is asking for is a Polish corridor and a gateway to the Soviet Union.' David looked at the flowerbeds. 'Your chrysanthemums are doing well.'

'Yes, they add brightness and warmth to a garden in the fall.'

'Good,' said David, 'we need it. Bloody Poland!'

Churchill stood on the balcony at Chartwell, the ever-present cigar in his mouth, and looked out over the Weald of Kent. If the Germans invaded, it would be across this land they would march, landing on the southern beaches to strike north, like the Normans and the Romans before them. Tanks would grind up the pasture and rip out the hedgerows, the peaceful villages would burn, blood would stream in the gutters and black smoke darken the sky, a plague of death would lay to waste his 'little world, this precious stone set in the silver sea.' The view had all but reduced the old man to tears before he dragged himself back to the present. Captain Brian Gorton stood beside him.

'I've just been speaking to Hore-Belisha,' Churchill said, without looking away from the pastoral paradise that lay before him. 'They're still not doing anything about this Nazi aggression. Summoned the German ambassador, registered a protest, that sort of thing… government by inertia.'

Gorton watched a bullfinch glide past. 'Meanwhile Germany strikes deeper into Poland. Who will be next?'

'Precisely! Everyone knows that Hitler won't stop at Poland any more than he stopped at Czechoslovakia.'

Gorton put his hands in his pockets and bowed his head. 'These are dark days.'

'Poor Poland,' said Churchill, 'friendless and wedged between tyrants.'

'I'm afraid I've more bad news for you. Only rumours you understand, but they're from high up.'

'Churchill pulled his cigar out of his mouth. 'Really? Come into the study.' He closed the door and offered Gorton a seat.

'What have you heard?'

'Wallis Simpson. Chamberlain has received an FBI report linking her with Ribbentrop.'

'She's met him several times,' Churchill shrugged. 'I mean, so have I.'

'I doubt that your relationship would have been as—how shall I put it—as intimate as theirs.'

'Oh, how people talk.' Churchill whined. 'There's all sorts of scuttlebutt. I've even heard it suggested the woman's an hermaphrodite!'

The phone rang and Churchill answered it. 'Yes…Yes… Good afternoon, Prime Minister.'

Churchill covered the mouthpiece and whispered to Gorton: 'Chamberlain.' Taking his hand away, he continued. 'Yes, Neville, I'm as well as can be expected, considering the circumstances in which we find ourselves. And yourself?'

The mood in Britain, in the pubs and around the kitchen tables, was tense, and with every passing day the tension amplified. People were scared, but they were also angry; their stress was matched by their disgust. Letters to the editors of the national press reflected a shift in public opinion, demanding the nation make a stand. One reader quoted Milton: 'Remember the country it is of which thee are.' Though slow to sense the country's mettle, the government did show some spirit of its own: it recalled parliament and passed the Emergency Powers Defence Act, putting the country onto a war footing. The new powers dealt with the coordination of emergency services and the rehearsal of evacuation plans for children in high-risk industrial areas. They imposed security crackdowns on the use of radio communications, carrying a camera in certain areas and even the owning of homing pigeons. They also dealt with public safety. The City Engineers Office had for months been identifying potential bomb shelters, going from building to building assessing their cellars, their capacity and the level of protection they might provide. The government even ordered the street kerbs painted white in preparation for possible blackouts.

The ever-mounting anxiety turned to alarm on Sunday 17th September. On that day the Soviet Union declared that Poland had ceased to exist and invaded the country from the east. Ribbentrop's mission to Moscow had resulted in what would soon be known as the Molotov-Ribbentrop Pact, named after the foreign ministers of the respective nations. To the amazement of all, the treaty renounced warfare between the two countries. The pact seemed to many as counterintuitive, given the Nazi's frequent diatribes against communism and their obvious lust for Slavic land. Even if sometimes grudgingly, all sides acknowledged the move as a masterstroke by Hitler and Ribbentrop, and importantly for the king, legitimised his warnings on the evils of communism. Ribbentrop could now revel in the prestige of having been an integral part of a plot that had completely outfoxed the world. He was at the height of his power.

This reversal deprived Britain of a potential ally and put paid to any hope for the creation of an eastern front against Germany. The odds were stacking the wrong way. The only good news for the British people occurred as a result of the prime minister's call to Chartwell. Chamberlain had reshuffled his cabinet, making Winston Churchill Secretary of State for Defence and First Lord of the Admiralty.

After placing in his new minister's hands his seals of office, the king counselled: 'Now that the communists have attacked Poland, we have two enemies. Surely even you can see a declaration of war is unthinkable against their combined power.'

'With war nothing is unthinkable,' Churchill replied, his answer as enigmatic as it was terrifying. David immediately changed his plans for the following night.

On the evening of Monday 18th Wallis found herself unexpectedly alone in the Belgian Suite. Bored to distraction by the wireless and needing release from the nervous energy born of her pent-up fears, she chose to wander the Palace's endless corridors. Though she knew the building teemed with staff, they were largely invisible to her, moving like shadows in other rooms and scurrying through hidden passageways, leaving her to roam free in a capsule of solitude, her footsteps echoing from the ceilings and high walls. After some time she chanced to pass by the Yellow Drawing Room and noticed a white flash, followed by the crash of thunder. Far from intimidated by the sound, for she had always adored storms, she entered the room to stare out the towering windows. She was looking down Birdcage Walk when the darkened room again glowed white, a bolt of lighting bursting in a dozen zigzags, several coming to ground in the vicinity of the clock tower. Once more, there was thunder. It rolled over the Palace roof, making the furniture shake, the crystal chandelier tinkling like a wind chime. But none of this mattered to Wallis for her thoughts were of nothing save her view of the dark immensity that was the Palace of Westminster.

The raging storm that illuminated Wallis was matched within parliament; the crowded House of Commons was in uproar. A barely tethered riot was taking place, a tumult not seen or heard since the time of cavaliers and roundheads. If men still carried cutlasses they would have gleamed, brandished from either side of the chamber.

The prime minister battled to be heard as he spoke from the despatch box. 'Chancellor Hitler gave a speech today in Danzig. There he requested a new round of peace talks, in light of the new situation.'

The room filled with heckling, threats and muttered oaths. The secretary of state for war, Hore-Belisha, walked out in disgust at his leader's feebleness. The prime minister didn't notice. He looked to the Speaker who eventually brought the house to order. Chamberlain resumed his speech.

'Friends… I hope I still have friends in this place.' A few voices rose in the affirmative. 'Friends, the German leader has appealed for peace.'

The members erupted again, the prime minister's detractors yelling from all parts of the chamber, from behind him and in front, from the benches to the right as well as to the left. This time, Chamberlain didn't bother referring to the Speaker. Instead, he tried to bellow louder than his opposition:

'The Soviet Union,' he pronounced, summoning up as much passion as his reserved nature might endure. 'The Soviet Union has been quick to occupy the eastern parts of Poland. With their forces concentrated against the Germans in the west, the Poles had little in reserve with which to stop the massed Russian armies. We have just received news through the Foreign Office that the Red Army has linked up with German troops in Brest-Litovsk. For all practical purposes the Polish campaign is over.' The pandemonium died down as the room absorbed the immensity of the news. It had been expected but was no less shocking for that. A nation had been snuffed out.

Chamberlain continued. 'Herr Hitler—' Again the room erupted, filled with boos and cries of 'shame'. The prime minister doggedly pressed on. 'Adolf Hitler proposes that we and the other western powers recognize the new status quo in Eastern Europe. I would ask this house to consider the opportunity this represents for lasting peace.' The members were astounded into silence.

Chamberlain collapsed back into his seat as the Speaker called on the member for Portsmouth North. Admiral Sir Roger Keyes rose to his feet. He was dressed in full uniform. 'The Government has dithered while Hitler and Stalin have divided, slicing up Poland between them, as if she were no more than a salami sausage. Prime Minister, I call you and your government cowards!'

A group of Conservative members hurled abuse at the admiral. The Speaker called for order. Keyes continued. 'I accuse you of the most outrageous timidity. No wonder these despots ignore you. Your response in the face of this aggression is to hide beneath your bed and whimper!'

A Labour member jumped up. 'Let the House hear from the first lord of the admiralty.'

A second member got up. 'Yes, let's hear from Mr Churchill.'

Members began to chant: 'Churchill! Churchill! Churchill!'

The Speaker called on the member for Epping. Winston Churchill rose and walked to the despatch box. An enormous bolt of lightning struck, blinding, the chamber skylight seeming to explode, seeming to curse those below. A boom of thunder pounded in its wake. Churchill's thunder was no less. 'An appeaser is a man who would feed a crocodile hoping it will eat him last.'

The members yelled, 'Hear, hear!'

'Is Poland to be sacrificed for nothing? Who next will be attacked? Lithuania? Denmark? Belgium? France? Great Britain? The time for talking is over.'

'Hear, hear!' was yelled again and the chamber once more descended into uproar.

Churchill stepped away from the despatch box, the position retaken by Chamberlain. As the two men passed one another Chamberlain snapped: 'You are now part of the government, a minister of the Crown—are you not aware of Cabinet solidarity?'

'Yes,' replied Churchill, 'but I believe that it is I who now speaks for the Cabinet.'

Churchill resumed his seat as the prime minister clutched the despatch box.

'Order! Order!' yelled the Speaker.

Chamberlain looked to either side of him. He knew Churchill was right. In the deepening crisis of the past few weeks he had slowly lost the support of his front bench.

The House finally settled down.

Chamberlain began to speak, now almost pleading: 'Friends, I call on you to back the government's policy position, a policy of negotiation on Poland.' There came a blizzard of rebuke. The prime minister instinctively backed away, forced by the cacophony to fall into his seat.

The Speaker, eyes bulging, jettisoned his last vestiges of decorum, yelling above the racket: 'The House will come to order. The House will come to order!' He seemed on the point of apoplexy as he screeched: 'The member for Birmingham South has the floor.'

The room fell suddenly silent—even the outside storm took pause—as the former minister and now backbencher, Leo Amery, stood up. He stared at Chamberlain and quoted Oliver Cromwell: 'Prime Minister, you have sat here too long for any good you are doing. Depart, I say, and let us have done with you. In the name of God, go!' With that the sky again flashed.

Outside, the city shook beneath the tempest. The buildings dazzled with every lightning stroke, their windows dark as gunshot wounds and the ink-black sky broken by fleeting mosaics of phosphorescence, like a windscreen shattering again and again. Within and without, Westminster was in collision with a brutal force beyond all reason. A bolt struck the flagpole on top of the Victoria Tower, connecting for an instant the summit of British imperialism with a cataclysm beyond its grasp.

The London storm was just a gentle rain in Oxford. David sat at high table in Merton College. A string quartet played Haydn. The fellows, dressed in their academic gowns, passed around the port before the dean rose to propose the loyal toast. 'Gentlemen.'

Everyone stood except David. The dean raised his glass. 'Gentlemen, the King.'

'The King,' they all repeated before sitting down and lighting their cigars.

David walked to the lectern and addressed his audience. He went through the normal formalities and then began the substance of his speech. 'As you all know, my government, the Cabinet, had been considering whether or not to request an armistice between Poland and Germany. This could then have been followed by a conference where various territorial claims could be discussed. Now I am afraid all that has been forgotten. And why? Because Stalin has entered the fray, but do we ask the Russians to withdraw from Polish soil? Do we threaten them with war? No, we close our eyes and look away.

'I have fought long and hard for peace, but I say to you here tonight, and to the whole nation and empire, that if Britain declares war on Germany, we should surely be condemned as hypocrites if we fail to declare war on the Soviets—the communists—as well.'

The assembled dons muttered among themselves.

David looked on, hoping the muffled debates gravitated

to his support. He continued, resolutely driving home his argument. 'No, you don't agree? Good! Neither do I. Such a policy would prove suicidal. It is unthinkable. I ask you here tonight: why go to battle for Poland, a country so very far away? Do we go to battle over China, though war has raged in that far place for years and years? I say again tonight, as I have said so many times before, we must choose the road to peace. It is not blocked to us. It lies wide open. We can do naught but take it. Fail and we condemn our children to another bloody war, a murderous conflict that will be ours to fight till the final gasp. A twilight of the gods where good men stood aside, doing nothing to avert it.'

The next day Chamberlain and Churchill met in the Cabinet Room. The prime minister swirled the scotch in his glass. 'I might as well tell you, for I know you would find out anyway, you were not my first choice. I made my first approach to Halifax.'

Churchill sipped his drink and stared into his glass, seeming unusually circumspect. 'You did survive the motion of no confidence.'

'Yes, but not by anywhere near enough; in a time of crisis the leader must know he has, at the very least, the full backing of his own party.'

Churchill drained his glass. 'The foreign secretary is an ambitious man. What did he say?'

Chamberlain sniffed. 'Halifax told me he had no doubt in his own mind that his becoming PM would create an impossible situation. He compared your qualities favourably to his own and asked me what would be his position? He is convinced that with you running defence, he should rapidly become no more than a honourary prime minister, an irrelevancy, with the nation looking to you as its de facto leader. You would be the one who mattered.'

Churchill pursed his lips before taking the liberty of getting up and bringing the scotch decanter to the Cabinet table. 'Edward,' he said, referring to the foreign secretary's Christian name as he played devil's advocate, 'why Edward enjoys the full support of the Conservative Party, while I am disliked and distrusted by almost all of them—I have more support amongst the Liberals and even the Labour Party. In addition, the fact that the foreign minister sits as a peer in the Lords is only a technical barrier. You know that.'

Churchill went to pour the prime minister a drink but he declined. 'No, I mustn't, I still have much to do today.'

The first lord of the admiralty had no such qualms, pouring himself a large one. 'I know Halifax said there would be "no more Munichs", and I commend his action in blocking German imports of military materiel, especially tungsten, but he has been a strong voice for appeasement, and therefore, he would be acceptable to the king. Despite my long friendship with His Majesty, Halifax holds views far more aligned to his position than I.'

Chamberlain reached for the decanter. 'I will have that drink.' He also poured himself a large one. 'Winston, please, may I be blunt?'

Churchill shrugged. 'It's your office, Prime Minister.'

'Yes, for a little while longer,' he accepted, 'but I must

inform you, my job would have proved far less taxing without the king's constant meddling and adoration for his own opinions. And as for that woman!'

'Yes,' Churchill was forced to agree, 'something of a mixed bag.'

Chamberlain looked out onto St James Park. 'Few could have experienced so rapid a fall from grace, but I regret nothing that I have done and I can see nothing undone that I ought to have done. I therefore am content to accept the fate that has befallen me.'

He turned back to the cabinet table. It was piled high with documents. 'Last night at Oxford, His Majesty suggested that if we go to war with Germany, we must go to war with the Soviets as well.'

Churchill grunted. 'Encouraging the king to remain on the throne is one of the few things I have done in my life that I regret.'

Chamberlain riffled through the mass of documents. 'The Labour Party would never agree to war with the Soviets.'

'That is true,' said Churchill, 'and Britain has not the strength to take on the combined force of both dictators. No, we should declare war only on Hitler and then wait. It will only be a matter of time before Hitler reneges and attacks Russia. That is his ultimate ambition, lebensraum and such. Then we shall have a valuable ally with which to defeat Nazism. We can save the removal of the Communists for later.'

Chamberlain found what he was looking for and sat down again. 'Forgive me if I am less sanguine; I received this file from Joe Kennedy.'

'The American ambassador?'

'Yes, of course, sorry, the ambassador, it's from the FBI. The subject, Wallis Simpson.'

Chamberlain handed over the file. 'I've been so busy of late I only just read it. Might be an idea to call Vernon Kell, over at MI Five.'

Chamberlain finished his drink and walked over to the coat stand. He put on his hat and sighed: 'Now I must have my final audience with the king.'

The prime minister's official car picked him up at the back of Downing Street and drove him to Buckingham Palace via Horse Guards Road and Birdcage Walk. As he travelled to his last appointment as head of government, his mind drifted. He looked out again at St. James Park and thought how it had been, along with Hyde Park and most of the West End, part of the king's private deer hunting forest, the name Soho, originally a deer hunter's rallying cry to summon the dogs. Now it was he who had been summoned, off to the Palace to deliver the news he must resign. As his car swung around the Victoria Memorial, he noticed for the first time the aspect of the marble statue of the queen and the gilded figure of Winged Victory. They both faced east, but he was going west, and headed for oblivion.

The prime minister's car entered through the Palace north gate, crossed the forecourt and passed under the north archway to the quadrangle. Chamberlain alighted at the King's door entrance and was greeted by Alexander Hardinge. With the gravel crunching under his feet, the outgoing prime minister took a moment to look around. Admiring the golden limestone of the quadrangle walls, he realised this would likely be the last time he would ever see them. His tenure as the head of government had aged him. He was exhausted, and of late, had been alternately plagued by constipation and diarrhea, his movements stained dark with blood.

Hardinge led Chamberlain into the north wing. From the lobby they took the old familiar route: walking down the long corridor that headed west to the Minister's Staircase, then up the wide steps to the King's Audience Chamber.

'I have lost the support of the Cabinet and the parliament,' he said. 'Therefore, it is with heavy heart that I come to you this evening to tender my resignation as prime minister of your government.'

David glanced out the door; he knew Wallis was just around the corner, listening.

Chamberlain turned and looked in the same direction to which the king was staring. He realised what was going on and turned back in disgust. 'You've never closed that door, have you?'

'There is nothing to fear in the Palace,' David replied, and noticing the old politician's face was as pale as the room's beige walls, he observed: 'You don't look well, Neville. You should take this opportunity for a well-earned rest.'

The king had not meant to be rude but Chamberlain recoiled at being addressed by his Christian name, finding the informality patronising and indicative of pity, even disrespect. He looked about the chamber and noticed that the shattered

Ming vase had been replaced.

'Yes,' said David. 'I thought you'd notice. It's a porcelain vase from the Manchu Dynasty. Part of my private collection.'

And no doubt cheaper than the original piece, thought Chamberlain. 'A tasteful choice, Sir,' he said. 'It complements the room's décor.'

The prime minister then rose to go and mentioned, almost as an afterthought: 'On the subject of my successor, I advise you to send for Mr Churchill.'

David frowned. 'Why not Halifax? He shares your views on opposition to war.'

'The people,' said Chamberlain, 'your people, will not wear it. Send for Churchill.' He took his briefcase, bowed and left, never to see the king again.

Half an hour later, when Churchill was there to 'kiss hands' in the King's Audience Chamber, David asked his new prime minister: 'Winston, you have experienced a long apprenticeship. Has it been worthwhile?'

'That is a decision for the British people,' he said flatly.

'Don't let them down, Winston. They are a trusting lot. Don't lead them into war. Don't bring down death upon them.'

'Sir, if there is a war, it will be the Germans who will do the dying.'

David handed Churchill his new seals of office.

The prime minister's car pulled up outside Number 10 Downing Street. Churchill emerged and waved to the crowd who thronged the opposite sidewalk. Turning away, he entered the building without saying anything beyond a simple 'Thank you'. Once inside, there was no such lack of words as he set about stamping his authority on the first Churchill ministry.

Forced to wait impatiently for the last of Chamberlain's effects to be removed from the Cabinet Room, the prime minister paced around outside, issuing orders on his feet, as if on the battlefield; grabbing whatever phone was nearest to him, briefing senior military personnel, sacking and replacing Cabinet Ministers, having his private secretary at the Admiralty organize the boxing and delivery of his files, and instructing his butler, Inches, to be driven to Croydon, there to pick up more cigars. The Cabinet Secretary Edward Bridges and his staff ran hither and yon, trying to keep up.

With Churchill's new broom there were many high-profile casualties. Several of those who were out the door would later be referred to as 'the guilty men of appeasement'. Off to the backbenches were Sir Samuel Hoare and Sir John Simon. Viscount Halifax was replaced as Foreign secretary, but for the sake of continuity, he, and also Chamberlain, remained in the Cabinet, both given nominal positions: the former made Lord President of the Council, the latter made Lord Privy Seal; both essentially ministers without portfolio, with nothing much to do, and as Churchill hoped, nothing much to say.

His new ministry received their seals the next morning, and an hour later they were assembled around the Cabinet table. The first order of business was the creation of a special subcommittee or War Cabinet. After a little cajoling and occasional bullying, Churchill got the people he desired. There would be six members: Churchill, the prime minister and minister for defence supply; Anthony Eden, restored to his previous portfolio as secretary of state for foreign affairs; Leslie Hore-Belisha, Churchill's long-time supporter, left in place as war minister; and three others who had for some time been in the new prime minister's camp—Duff Cooper as minister for information, Brendan Bracken taking over from Churchill as first lord of the admiralty and Sir Kingsley Wood, left as secretary of state for air; the latter had presided so successfully over his ministry that the country was producing 80 warplanes a month. The War Cabinet met just twenty-four hours after Churchill had taken office. All singing from the same hymnbook, they quickly created a new and far more robust foreign policy to take to the rest of the ministry. That evening the full Cabinet reconvened, and before any detractor might organise sufficient numbers to counter it, Britain's new stance was rammed home, Churchill telling his colleagues: 'I have thought carefully these last days whether it was my duty to enter into negotiations with that man, but it was idle to think that. If this long island story of ours is to last, let it end only when each one of us lies choking in his own blood upon the ground.'

Late that night, Churchill spoke to the House of Commons. His moment had finally arrived. He was the leader of the nation's government. It could not have come at a better time. It would be a moment writ large in history, as emblematic for the world as it was climactic for him.

'I declare the talking ended,' he pronounced from the despatch box. 'Now is the time for ultimatum. His Majesty's government demands the immediate and total withdrawal of all German troops from Polish soil.'

The House went strangely quiet. The German government was equally silent.

Chapter Seven, the Revelation

The radio was playing big band jazz and they were making love on David's desk. Wallis moaned, 'Boysie, never forget how much you mean to me.'

'Why would I do that?' he asked.

The music was cut short by a news bulletin. 'We interrupt this program to cross to Number Ten Downing Street for an important announcement by the prime minister.'

David instantly forgot his question, disengaged and got back to his feet. Holding up his unbuttoned pants with one hand, he shuffled across to the radio and turned up the volume. The telecast cut to the Cabinet Room and Churchill's sombre voice.

'This evening the British ambassador in Berlin handed the German government a final note…'

Wallis remained flat on her back, her legs apart, her evening gown scrunched around her hips. She looked up and saw her new portrait hanging on the wall. It stared down as disapprovingly as Queen Victoria had.

Churchill continued: 'that unless we heard from them by eleven o'clock tonight that they were prepared at once to withdraw their troops from Poland, a state of war would exist between us. I have to tell you now that no such undertaking has been received and that consequently this country is at war with Germany.

David stared at the radio. 'That's it then.'

Wallis rolled over and curled up like a foetus. Till then she could fool herself into believing her visits to the antique shop were an attempt to help prevent war, now everything had changed.

An hour later, the night was pierced by the wail of sirens being tested. Across London people were roused from their beds to shuffle down to their allocated air raid shelters. At the Palace there was no purpose built bomb shelter; however, the staff had acted quickly to make sure that something was organised.

The Palace administration was divided into several departments: the Lord Chamberlain's office, the Privy Purse, the Private Secretary's Office; but it was the department of the Master of the Household that was responsible for improvising an air raid shelter, the task delegated to Bernard Eldridge, the Page of Chambers.

A week earlier there was a meeting between David and Eldridge. Wallis, Watson and Freddy Smith, David's Lord in Waiting, were also present.

At the meeting the king felt somewhat embarrassed when he told Eldridge: 'Please don't think my summoning you here means that I consider actual fighting in this war to be anything but the remotest possibility; this is simply a precaution—Pascal's wager if you like. Bernard, what can you recommend by way of a bomb shelter for the residents here at the Palace?'

'Sir, my respectful advice is to open up a row of empty

rooms, located near the wine cellar. They are used to accommodate assistant house keepers and chambermaids who would normally serve family members residing in the Palace, but as you and Mrs Simpson are presently the only royal residents, the extra staff are not required and the bedrooms are therefore vacant.'

Freddy made sure to hide his reaction after Bernard referred to Wallis as a royal resident. Failing to make the same observation, David enquired. 'How would those rooms stand up to a bombing raid?'

'The windows are only small. For the moment, they could be covered and the outer wall reinforced with sandbags. How much protection that would afford against a direct hit I cannot say. However one of the maids' rooms enjoys a little known benefit.'

'What on earth could that be?' asked David, bemused by such a notion.

'Perhaps, Sir, if you have the time, I might take this opportunity to show you.'

The small party journeyed to the service areas in the south wing, taking a course that led through the extensive kitchen facilities. Wallis was impressed by their size. 'You could feed an army from this place.'

'Of course,' said David, grinning. 'What do you think the kitchen does when we have garden parties?' The question was rhetorical and Wallis laughed, but it forced the king to recall the promise he had made to blind Private Jenkins. 'I will use all the power that God might grant me to keep your children safe.' David's heart sank at the thought he might fail the old soldier.

The group followed Bernard Eldridge down a service staircase to a labyrinth of passageways. Outside the wine cellar they turned north, passing half a dozen rooms. All their doors were open, revealing a twin set of beds in each. Bernard then stopped at the end of the passage and invited David and Wallis to enter the last chamber. It was as plain as all the others, with two iron beds, a nightstand between them and an empty wardrobe. There was one tiny window: a horizontal slit, about six inches high, just below the ceiling.

'Sir,' Eldridge announced in the manner of a tour guide. 'We are almost at the north-western corner of the north wing; Your Majesty's audience chamber lies two floors directly above us. Mr Watson, if you would be so kind as to help me move the wardrobe.'

The two servants heaved the awkward piece of furniture several feet down the wall, revealing a small door. Everyone gathered around.

Eldridge used his handkerchief to wipe dust from his hands. 'This is the added feature of which I spoke.'

'A closet?' Wallis asked.

'Oh, no, Ma'am, much more than that.' With something of a flourish, Eldridge swung open the door, exposing to the light a stairway that descended into pitch darkness. 'What you see, Sir, Ma'am, is the access point to a top-secret underground passageway. I've taken it upon myself to have it cleaned by two highly trusted members of the staff—got rid of the cobwebs and such. The passageway leads down, quite some distance, to the London Underground. To be precise, to a recess in the tunnel of the Victoria line. It's not generally known, but the tube passes underneath the Palace.

'It does?' asked David, tapping the tile floor with his foot.

'Yes, Sir, directly beneath you.'

'My God, how extraordinary.'

'If the structure above this room should collapse, Your Majesty could avoid being trapped by taking advantage of this escape route.'

'Oh, I do like that,' said David, peering into the black hole. 'A secret passageway! I wonder if it was ever used by smugglers?'

'More likely used by mistresses for assignations,' countered Wallis.

David didn't care. 'It's positively "Every Boy's Annual". We must go down and explore.'

'It is rather damp, Sir,' Eldridge counseled as he poked his handkerchief back into his pocket.

'And still a bit sooty, I don't doubt,' said Wallis. 'Darling, perhaps you could inspect it another day. We could purchase you some overalls.'

'I say,' said David, 'what fun.'

'Sir,' suggested Watson, 'If you desire it, I could have this room decorated to your taste. Perhaps include a radio and cocktail cabinet.'

'Yes,' Eldridge agreed through hooded eyes, peeved at Watson's interruption and lack of regard for his seniority. 'The adjoining rooms could be appropriately furnished to accommodate guests who might be similarly inconvenienced by an air raid alert.'

The intervening week had passed, and now, due to the testing of the air raid sirens, David and Wallis had the opportunity to once again descend to their improvised shelter. It had since been freshly painted and furnished with a Persian rug, double bed and two armchairs. With inclusion of the cocktail cabinet and radio, it was a bit cramped, but this didn't prevent them from enjoying a nightcap, or two.

'I wonder how often we'll end up down here?' Wallis asked.

David admitted he hadn't the slightest notion but observed, 'it's good to know that we're just a short walk to the wine cellar.'

'Darling, perhaps we should move to Windsor Castle?'

'No, we can't be seen to be running away. We must put up with every inconvenience that the rest of London must endure. In any case, I refuse to believe this will all go on much longer. Someone will open the door to negotiation. I mean we must have learnt something from the Great War.'

'I'm sorry; I know he is your old friend, but I don't think Churchill will be interested in talking to the Germans. I suspect he has been looking forward to this war.'

David got up to mix them both another drink. 'I don't agree, I think you're wrong.'

'No,' Wallis replied. 'You don't think I'm wrong, you pray I'm wrong.'

The Observer Corps had installed an observation post on the roof of the palace, below the flagpole. As soon as the all clear was sounded, David insisted on taking Wallis almost as far up as the roof, leading her to the nursery. It was above the China Room, on the third level of the northeast corner of the Palace, and offered good views across to the West End and the City.

'What are you expecting to see?' Wallis asked.

David had Watson open the window. 'I just want to check how the city is coping. I am the king, after all.' Watson stepped aside and David stuck his head out. 'Hmm, it looks like any other night except the lights are out.'

'Then how can you see anything?'

'Full moon.'

Wallis felt uncomfortable surrounded by all the children's toys. 'Can you close the window; there's a draft'

'Oh, look. Come here, darling, and see the sky.'

Wallis crept toward the window and peeked out.

Like people all over London, David had noticed barrage balloons were already flying overhead, guarding the capital.

'That didn't take long,' said Wallis.

'No, top marks for that. Let us pray that they'll never be needed.'

The next morning, outside Number 10 Downing Street, workmen were filling sandbags, piling them up against the front wall's soot-stained bricks, reinforcing the building as best they could. Up in the Cabinet Room, Churchill was doing something similar; he and Brian Gorton were meeting with Vernon Kell. The director general of MI5 was a no nonsense military man, a 66 year old senior army officer, fluent in French, German, Italian, Polish, Russian and Mandarin. His report delivered bad news and he took no joy in giving it.

'The antiques shop is leased in a private capacity to the manager of IG Farben's London office. We know it's from there that Mrs Simpson has been passing information to the German embassy.'

Churchill leafed through a thick folder full of photographs, reports and other documents. 'My God, what kind of information?'

'Information of a highly sensitive nature.'

'Well, out with it, man, what?'

'The Germans think they've recruited a spy in Whitehall but he's actually a double agent working for us. Since Ribbentrop's departure they've been using him as their primary British contact with Wallis Simpson. He has been working with a German foreign agent known as Dorfman.'

Churchill's face was growing darker by the minute. 'What has she revealed?'

'According to our agent, pillow talk mostly. The king has discussed with her top secret information and she has leaked it to the Germans.'

'What information?'

Kell shifted in his seat and said: 'Radar.'

'That's a highly complex subject,' admitted Churchill. 'I have, myself, only just been briefed on the latest advances, and though they are impressive, I haven't the least comprehension of the physics.'

'Our agent informs us that the details she gave on radar were purely verbal, none of the necessary technical details, but still enough to tip off the Germans on a vital element in our defence strategy.'

'Why was this allowed to go on?'

'It only happened three weeks ago.'

'Three weeks!'

'The radar information, yes,' said Kell. He cleared his throat before continuing. 'With respect, Prime Minister, we must handle this matter with the utmost delicacy. Lives are at stake. We cannot risk compromising our man.'

Churchill put the folder on the Cabinet table. 'Is this the full dossier?'

'Yes, almost; I might also mention that she has given them photos of documents from the code and cipher school at Bletchley Park.'

'Bletchley Park?' the prime minister roared.

The director general remained calm in the face of the storm. 'I'm afraid so, but that information was of a nature that will only serve to confuse the Germans; she did us rather a favour there.'

'Thank you, Mr Kell,' Churchill sniffed, somewhat mollified. He closed the dossier. 'Good afternoon.'

The head of MI5 rose from his seat, but before leaving, he bowed his head slightly. 'Prime Minister, if you would indulge me for a moment.' Without waiting for an answer, he turned to Gorton and shook his hand firmly. 'Brian, let me take this opportunity to once again congratulate you on your transfer to Number 10.'

Gorton closed his eyes and nodded discretely.

Kell then turned back to Churchill. 'Prime Minister, we've all got our work cut out for us now, and I fear for some time yet. Therefore, I'd just like to say: you won't regret having Brian on board. He will be an asset as no other could possibly be.'

Gorton blushed. Churchill grunted. 'Hope he does a better job than Horace Wilson. Cleared him out with the rest of Chamberlain's people. Shifted him sideways to Treasury.'

The Director General of MI5 collected his files and took his leave. As soon as the door had closed behind him, Churchill turned to Gorton and pointed accusingly in the direction of Kell's departure. 'Remind me to sack that man next week.'

'I shouldn't be too critical,' Gorton responded with his usual equanimity. 'He's a good soldier.'

'But what action has he taken?'

'Since identifying the Palace security breach all government documents regarding defence and foreign policy have been screened before being forwarded to the king. He has actually been sent some disinformation.'

Churchill pulled a cigar out of his breast pocket. 'Why didn't you tell me this before?'

'Would you trust me now if I had?'

'I've shown you Wallis's FBI file. I've been forthcoming in other ways.'

Gorton looked at the prime minister with raised eyebrows.

'Yes, well,' Churchill blustered, 'I suppose you're right, but I'm still not happy. How Chamberlain could have been so relaxed about this intelligence is beyond my reckoning.'

'Winston, Wallis Simpson's sordid conduct is small beer,

while the existence of our double agent is anything but. It is absolutely top secret.' Gorton allowed himself a small grin. 'As you are well aware, his identity is known to only a handful of people.'

Churchill lit his cigar, and between puffs, growled: 'I dare say.'

Later that day, together with Hore-Belisha, Churchill left for an emergency session of the House of Commons. The news of Wallis's betrayal, mingled with all the intense passions and excitements of the previous days, should have left the new prime minister angry or depressed but instead his mood gave way to serenity and an uplifted detachment from human and personal affairs. When the war secretary mentioned his calm expression, Churchill confided: 'I feel strangely good.'

'Don't say that too often,' Hore-Belisha advised, 'they're already calling us both warmongers.'

'Let them talk, but at this moment in history I feel inspired by the glory of old England. Peace-loving and ill-prepared, she has in an instant become fearless at the call to honour.'

Once in the Commons, Churchill stood behind the despatch box and spoke to his fellow members of parliament. 'At this solemn hour it is a consolation to recall and dwell upon our repeated efforts for peace. Though ill starred, they had been faithful and sincere which is of the highest moral value. The storms of war may blow and the lands may be lashed with the fury of its gales, but in our own hearts this afternoon there is peace. Our hands may be active, but our consciences are at rest.'

That evening the workmen's toil had left a high, thick wall of sandbags against Number 10's lower walls and windows. Upstairs, in 'the building out the back', Cabinet had just been informed of Wallis's activities.

The former foreign secretary, now lord president of the council, Lord Halifax, placed his hand flat on the table and leaned across to Churchill. 'Something must be done. This disloyalty must be addressed by the Government.'

'Edward is right,' said Hore-Belisha, 'she should be arrested for treason.'

Anthony Eden stated the obvious: 'Leslie, she can't be arrested for that; she is still an American citizen.'

'Fine,' replied Hore-Belisha, 'then she's a damn spy and should be shot!'

Churchill stared down his minister. 'Nobody will be shooting anyone. The last thing we want is to make an enemy of America. Public opinion in the United States is vitally important to British interests. She is an American citizen and should be quietly deported—nothing more, nothing less. Relations with America cannot be put at risk.'

Eden was incredulous. 'How could we ensure she doesn't sell her story to the American press?'

Churchill shrugged. 'That can be sorted out.'

'What about the king?' asked Halifax.

Despite the declaration of war, the Irish Guards still wore their full dress red and navy uniform. There were four, not two, standing at the palace entrance. Together with the Royal Standard fluttering on the flagpole, that number indicated the sovereign was in residence.

Following the Cabinet discussion, Churchill had called a special meeting with the king for the following morning. They now faced each other in the audience chamber. On the coffee table lay the open dossier of incriminating photos and reports.

'Radar was the ace up our sleeve,' said the prime minister, jowls hanging pendulously from his bulldog face.

David shook his head. 'I still can't believe it.'

'I don't care what you believe.'

'I trusted her with all my heart.'

'But not with all your brain.'

David burred at the prime minister's tone. 'It was you who convinced me to stay on, to be the strong king the nation would need.'

'I created a Frankenstein.'

'I was not the monster that declared war. A war that could lead to the death of millions.'

Churchill pointed to Wallis's dossier. 'We are masters of the unsaid word and slaves to those we let slip out. She must leave voluntarily or be arrested and charged as a spy. If charged she will be found guilty and shot.'

David closed the dossier and clutched it to his chest.

'There's no need to keep it from me,' Churchill sighed. 'They are only the carbons. The originals are at Curzon Street.'

David checked and found the prime minister was right. He hurled the dossier across the room, its contents flying everywhere.

Churchill picked up a photo from the floor. It was not blurred or grainy. It was a clear, sharp shot of Wallis leaving the antique store. He put it back on the coffee table. 'A first class cabin on the Queen Mary has been purchased in the name of Mrs Bessie Simpson. The ship departs from Southampton this evening.'

David stared in disbelief. 'I cannot live without her.'

Churchill's voice was harsh. 'You are an appeaser who has failed to protect state secrets. You have compromised the nation's defence through your irresponsibility and negligence. Think yourself lucky that you are not tried for treason.'

'What am I to do?' David asked.

'Abdicate,' said Churchill.

A raging tremor rose through David's body and catapulted him up from his chair and out of the room. In the lobby he caught Wallis listening in. Speechless, she panicked and ran off, bursting into the Picture Gallery and then the White Drawing Room.

Meanwhile, a page of the backstairs, on seeing the king depart, entered the audience chamber to clear the coffee cups. He stopped in his tracks when he saw the mess of papers. 'Leave it!' Churchill barked.

Wallis was pressed against the fireplace, bailed up below the portrait of Queen Alexandra. David was in her face, panting with such rage he could hardly speak. 'Why?' he asked breathlessly. 'Why?'

Wallis regained her composure. 'The sooner this stupid war with Germany is over, the better.'

David swallowed hard. 'Even if it means our defeat?'

'A short war lost is cheaper than a long war won.'

David was shocked into a fleeting calm. 'What?' he asked,

his face askew and frowning. 'You cannot be serious. We will never surrender.'

Wallis laughed. 'Listen to yourself; you sound like Churchill. We, you, this country could lose everything. All because of that misguided warthog.'

'You have broken a trust. You have passed on to Germany national secrets that I told you in the strictest confidence. I am implicated in an act of treason.'

'It has nothing to do with you,' Wallis insisted. 'It was my doing and mine alone.'

David grasped his hair and pulled back his head in exasperation. 'We are talking treason!'

'Not I. I'm still a citizen of the United States of America. And you? How can you commit treason? You're the king.'

'What?' David asked again, even more exasperated.

Wallis grabbed him by his arms. 'Listen to me, I've looked it up, treason is defined in the English statutes as compassing or imagining the death of the king, taking up arms against the king or giving aid to the king's enemies. How can you do that when you're the king? How can you take up arms against yourself?'

'My God,' David sniped, 'you have been doing your homework.' He pulled off her hands and took a step back, addressing her as though she were a crowd. 'But you're wrong. Do you know why Charles the First lost his head? Do you know the real reason? Hmm? It was because parliament argued successfully that the king is an office, not the man who holds it. I, as a man, can be found to have betrayed that office. I, like any other, can be condemned to death for treason. Is that the measure of your love?'

'So, this is the end?' Wallis asked, suddenly deflated.

'You heard what Churchill said, listening in as you always do.'

'No, David, don't.'

'I was a fool to have trusted you. Pack your bags and go.'

'Please, David,' Wallis cried as she tried to hold him.

He brushed her aside. 'Go. Get out of here. Get out of my home. Get out of my country. Get out of my life!'

The four wings of Buckingham Palace were arrayed around the Quadrangle. To the east was the ceremonial gate where the monarch entered or left on official business. To either side were the smaller eastern gates used by ministers, but only for state occasions. On the south wing lay the Ambassador's Court entrance. Approached from Buckingham Palace Road, it was the more frequently used thoroughfare. Here, at the bottom of the steps, Michael, the chauffeur, waited in the king's Rolls Royce. A few feet away, two police detectives leaned against a black sedan and also waited. Behind the Rolls Royce, a stream of footmen loaded trunks into a truck. It was far from full as Wallis had only been allowed three hours to pack for America. Most of her property would have to be shipped on later.

Once the last of the luggage had been loaded, the driver bolted shut the doors; and as soon as he was in the truck's cab, Wallis appeared. She descended the stairs alone. Michael got out of the king's car and opened the back door. David watched from a window as she was helped into her seat. He rubbed his eyes as if he couldn't believe what they were telling him.

Michael hopped behind the wheel and released the brake. He was about to pull away when there came a knock on his window. It was David.

'Michael, stop!' he ordered and opened Wallis's door. 'May I go with you to Southampton?'

Wallis nodded, not daring to speak for fear she might lose what little control of her emotions she had left.

David sat down beside her and said: 'Everything has changed, yet one thing remains the same, I cannot live without you.'

Wallis began to shake as tears brimmed in her eyes. David reached out and took her in his arms. 'But you must be honest with me. What was the real reason for your talking to the Germans?'

The route to Southampton took Wallis and David through Surrey and Hampshire. The little procession of David's Rolls Royce, the sedan of detectives and the small truck had reached Farnham before Wallis finished explaining what had happened. Over this time she told David all about her jealousy, her asking Ribbentrop to investigate Susanna, the ambassador's discovery of the doomed girl's secret love letters, his leaking them to the press, her time with Ribbentrop in Paris, their one and only intimacy, her meeting him again at Notting Hill, the extortionate demands he made of her, the meetings with his agents and all the many betrayals, both large and small; and the more she told, the more she felt herself sinking into a cesspit of her own filth, sliding deeper with every

276

revelation. In the end she told David everything, everything except the one thing she would never dare admit: the baby. The baby, born small and premature, but healthy just the same. The baby she had seen just once. The baby, so tiny, her pregnancy was barely noticeable. Her body, the only part of her left undamaged by its unwanted birth.

For a long while David was silent. He turned and looked out at the passing fields and farms, everything about him strangely still, collecting himself like an actor waiting for his cue. Finally he spoke. 'It was blackmail, pure and simple. You should have told me. I would have understood.'

Wallis fell upon him, clutching, pressing her head against his chest and crying with relief, her gratitude unfathomably deep, the joy she felt so strong it almost hurt.'

But Wallis had forgotten that the aristocracy was not hidebound by the morality of the middle classes. She had forgotten about David's ancestors. There was Alexandra, his grandmother, Queen to King Edward the Seventh. Her portrait, hanging in the White Drawing Room, had borne silent witness to her passionate reunion with David. And the dead queen would have understood; Alexandra had always turned a blind eye to her husband's wandering one. She even invited his last mistress to her husband's deathbed. Wallis had also forgotten Charles the Second's final words, devoted not to his wife or his dozen illegitimate children, but to his mistress: 'Let not poor Nelly starve.' King George the fourth had bedded almost every lady in London except his wife. King Henry the eighth had probably died of the pox—as had many others. Wallis had forgotten that an almighty chunk of

Britain's aristocracy was the bastard progeny of David's ancestors, the legitimate family merely that part of an iceberg appearing above the surface of the sea and not the bulk in the depths below. The king's calm reaction to Wallis's betrayal was a quality she could never hope to understand. It was a confidence for which he had been trained his entire life, a rationalism so ingrained it was oxymoronically spiritual.

However, though he always understood that nobody was expected to be immune from the carnal delights of the bedchamber, discretion was—he had learnt the hard way—still demanded, and honour defended to the death.

'I blame myself for what has happened,' he admitted, 'but you should have been forthcoming with the truth. Were you afraid of me?'

'No,' Wallis wept. 'No,' she repeated, trying to be convincing, though she knew it wasn't true.

David knew it too, and wasn't buying it. 'What have I ever done to make you feel so scared? Your courage is the quality I most respect in you. It's the highest in a suite of attributes I love. This burden of knowledge has encumbered you since France, has it not? It's the reason for your strange behaviour these past few months, isn't it?'

Wallis nodded, but couldn't speak.

David spoke for her. 'So, you were never falling out of love with me?'

Wallis burst into another bout of tears. 'No, no, no, never,' she sobbed.

'It was my blind stupidity, my arrogance,' he almost snarled.

'No,' she begged, 'I always understood.'

David took a deep breath. 'If I had not left you alone in Paris, we would never have come to this sorry juncture. Now, you are being sent away again.' His feelings of guilt metamorphosed to anger. 'There was nothing I could do, other than what I did. Not if I was to keep the crown.' And then his mood softened. 'You do understand that, don't you, my darling? You do understand?'

'Yes, of course,' she averred, not wishing to elicit such a display of his remorse. 'I always understood.'

Despite the pain of revelation and admission, David felt immediately cleansed. Their shared catharsis had revived him completely, and he resolved to step once more into the ring. 'This fight is far from finished,' he declared. 'We are not in the tumbril yet.' David took his hanky and gently wiped away his lover's tears. 'It's alright,' he said, smoothing the moisture from her cheeks. 'It's alright.'

'But, there's Susanna. Not a day goes by when I don't ache for her.'

'David gave her his handkerchief. 'It wasn't your fault.'

'But—'

'It wasn't your fault,' he said firmly; there was no point in wallowing in the past—that could not be altered—but the future was there for the taking. He had to think clearly and quickly. 'Did Ribbentrop make any other threats?'

Wallis's face went blank.

David rolled his eyes. 'Wallis, darling, we haven't time for all of this. Were there any other threats, even little ones? I must know.'

Her forehead creased. 'No,' she lied, her stomach churning, 'there's nothing more.' She then scolded herself by adding: 'As if more were ever needed,' delivering the critique with righteous anger, as if talking of someone else; remorse or self-pity would not have been as convincing.

David swallowed it. 'Alright, then we can deal with this'

Ten minutes later, they had crossed the soft fields of Hampshire and were almost at Winchester. David pressed his index finger against his lower lip. He had a plan. He turned to Wallis and spoke excitedly. 'The situation is far from hopeless. Who knows how long the war will go before we fire a shot in anger? As soon as you get to New York you must contact Charlie Lindbergh—'

'And Henry Ford?' Wallis interrupted in support.

'Yes,' David replied, 'that's it, as many of our friends as you can muster. We have to do everything we can to influence American opinion. Roosevelt must put pressure on Churchill to end this madness. You can be a lightning rod for peace. We can still save the day.'

'Can Churchill make you abdicate?'

'Not if I'm prepared to risk all.'

'Oh, David, please be careful.'

'Don't worry, I won't lose my head.'

'Churchill is sharpening the axe.'

'He should watch he doesn't cut his fingers. We have powerful friends who will support our efforts to end the war.'

David looked out at the passing spires of Winchester Cathedral. The town of Winchester was the old capital of

England. It was the burial place of ancient kings: Saxon, Danish and Norman. 'But I am not dead,' he whispered, and then muttering: 'King Edward the Eighth is very much alive. I have never felt *more* alive.'

One hundred yards ahead, hidden beyond a bend, a Friesian cow had found a gap in a hedgerow. It wandered along the shoulder of the highway. The Rolls Royce was travelling at fifty miles an hour when the animal suddenly came into view. Oblivious to the oncoming danger, it decided to cross the road to greener pastures. Michael quickly applied the brakes, but the lumbering animal was already too close. The chauffeur swerved to the right. David and Wallis were thrown across the back seat. Their car missed the bovine mass by millimetres. But then, to their horror, they found they were stuck on the wrong side of the road, a truck approaching from the opposite direction, travelling at high speed and heading straight for them. In that instant, with the tyres screeching in her ears and the truck's grill growing ever larger in her eyes, Wallis knew it was all her fault; she had cursed them with her lies.

Michael wrenched the steering wheel counter clockwise and crunched down on the accelerator. David and Wallis were thrown in the opposite direction as the car turned sharply to the left. With its horn blaring, the truck whooshed by, the Rolls Royce shuddering in the slipstream.

David glanced back at the scene of the near disaster and let out a slow whistle. 'Damn, that nearly put a spanner in the works. Good driving, Michael.'

His chauffeur calmly nodded; it was all part of the job.

Wallis looked down and noticed her hands were shaking uncontrollably.

Southampton was one of Britain's most important ports and had been a centre for trade since medieval times. The largest vessels in the world could enter or leave at any point in the tide. It was the only British Port that could make such a claim. Following the Great War, Cunard transferred its express service to Southampton, and when the 'New Docks' was completed, the first ship to berth there was the Mauritania. That had been five years ago, but on this day in September, the Queen Mary waited.

The noisy hubbub of departing passengers could barely be heard behind the thick glass windows of the VIP room, the privacy of this exclusive area made available as soon as Michael told the terminal manager that the king was waiting outside in his car. With the porters carrying her luggage from the wharf onto the ship, David and Wallis stood arm in arm in this strangely silent space, not noticing or caring about the leering customs officers who whispered furtively at the door that led to the first class gangway.

'I'll see you soon,' said David. 'We'll get through this.'

Wallis stared up at the rows of decks. 'That's it, isn't it? Life's something you have to get through.'

'There can be great moments,' he countered, trying to be reassuring.

She turned back to him. 'And this—is this a great moment?'

'It's one I'll never forget.'

They embraced, while beyond them, passengers waved from the decks and the air was filled with multicoloured bolts of flying streamers. A whistle blew and the third-class gangway pulled back from the ship.

Wallis clung to David. 'All I've ever wanted is to have what so many take for granted—the right to be with the one I love.' She kissed him as hard as she could.

The Queen Mary's foghorn blasted. The second-class gangway pulled away. Dockers stood ready at the bollards and took up the mooring ropes.

Wallis could not let go of David. The foghorn blasted again. The Dock Master approached. 'Sir, with the deepest respect, Mrs Simpson has to board.'

'Yes, of course,' said David, gazing into Wallis's eyes. 'Darling, you have to get going.'

'Why?' she persisted. 'Why can't we have that simple life? That, instead of... instead of this constant wrenching, Why?'

He sucked in a small breath. 'It's the price of duty.'

She turned and stared wanly at her ship.

David touched her cheek. 'We won't be apart for long. I swear, one day we'll have it all.'

Wallis wasn't listening. She kept staring at the ship and all the passengers. 'A war has just begun, yet look at all the streamers.'

He turned her face to his. 'My darling, we will have peace one day, you have my word to that.'

Steam erupted from the foghorn as it blew for the final time. The first-class gangway pulled back and the Queen Mary slipped its moorings. Wallis braced herself against the railing.

She could see David standing alone on a gantry as the ship drifted by. The severed streamers flapped in the wind as she gave an uncertain wave. Then he was gone.

Two hours later David arrived in Whitehall, his Rolls Royce coming to a halt outside the black oak entrance to Number 10. He did not wait for Michael. He swung open his car door, got out and marched straight up the steps, ignoring the bobby, who barely had time to salute. His detectives were still getting out of their car when the king was let into the building. In an instant he had crossed the checkerboard floor of the entrance hall and was ascending the grand staircase.

Churchill was working with Edward Bridges and his private secretary, Jock Colville, when David burst into the Cabinet Room. 'Winston, we need to talk.' He glared at the civil servants. 'In private!'

Churchill nodded to his staff. They hurriedly departed, shutting the door behind them. 'Your Majesty,' he said, 'I do believe I am the first prime minister to enjoy the honour of entertaining the king in this august room.'

David pulled up a seat and sat down. 'Winston, you have known me since my investiture as Prince of Wales; we have played on the same polo team, conspired in politics, been colleagues and friends. Often, over many years, I have sought out and accepted your advice, but this time it's different. This time your advice is rejected. You will not now, nor will you ever make me abdicate.'

Churchill smiled. 'Then there must be two wars. The one that rages outside and the one in here.'

David bristled. 'No English king has ever abdicated and I won't be the first.'

'Perhaps I shall propel your departure by other mechanisms.'

'Do not toy with me!' said David, a little too loudly for his purpose. 'I cannot be deposed without the assent of the House of Lords and that you will never get.'

'I see,' said Churchill as he puffed on his Cuban.

David pointed toward Horse Guards Parade. 'And you cannot use the military or the constabulary for it is to me they owe their sworn allegiance.'

'True,' agreed Churchill.

'Finally, you cannot use the will of the people for it is I who…' David lifted his feet and rested them on the Cabinet table. 'I am their champion.'

Churchill looked askance at his guest's bootheels. 'Since becoming prime minister I have held from you top secret and sensitive government papers.'

David's eyes flashed. 'The impertinence! You have no constitutional right to do that to your—'

'King,' the prime minister interrupted, 'who stands before me, accused of high treason!'

David took his feet off the table and straightened his jacket. 'You would not dare.'

Churchill picked up a file from the table. 'Let me show you something.' He removed a sheet of paper and handed it to David. 'You are holding a transcript of Hitler's battle orders, intercepted by operatives within the Foreign Office.

David stared at the text, dyslexic with anger.

'Please, allow me,' offered Churchill, reaching out. 'Let me read it to you.' David gave him the transcript.

'Now, let me see,' said the prime minister, fiddling with his glasses. 'Yes, this is the best bit, the Fuhrer giving orders to his Wehrmacht commanders to, and I quote: "Send to death mercilessly and without compassion, men, women and children of Polish derivation and language." Unquote.'

'I don't believe it,' said David, taken aback. 'Not genuine—Polish disinformation.'

Churchill put aside the transcript. 'As we speak, reports are coming to us from throughout Poland. Reports of lovely chaps called Einsatzgruppen who follow in the wake of Hitler's panzers. They are committing unimaginable atrocities, liquidating the entire Polish intelligentsia, murdering the nobility, teachers, priests, judges and… the Jews. Ah, yes, what of them? They are being herded like cattle into pens, the Nazis killing, raping, pillaging as they go. This is what you, by your wanton vanity, have aided and abetted.'

David's face went pale and he murmured: 'I will not abdicate.'

'Oh, yes you will,' said Churchill.

'You are a stubborn man,' David countered, 'and that will be your undoing.'

'It takes one to know one, but as you can see, I'm rather busy at the moment.' Churchill walked to the door and pulled it open. 'Too busy to entertain you further.' He smiled and bowed. 'Good night, Your Majesty.'

'Why the servile grin?' asked David.

The prime minister kept smiling as he spoke. 'When you

have to kill a man it costs nothing to be polite.'

David marched to the door. 'Now that is treason!'

Churchill stood and waited, listening to the king's footsteps fade away down Treasury Passage. He then returned to the Cabinet table and picked up the phone. 'Your Majesty,' he said to himself, 'may have the people, the military and the peers, but you neglect the fourth estate.' He dialed a number he had long since memorised. Up The Strand on Fleet Street, the phone rang on Lord Beaverbrook's desk.

Big Ben tolled the hour. It was eight o'clock in the morning. David was eating his breakfast and reading one of his morning newspapers. He was pleased to see in The Times of London that the government of the United States of America had just declared its neutrality. On the breakfast table, beside the teapot, were several other newspapers to which he subscribed. He hoped to enjoy just as much what they had to say.

The phone rang. Watson stood at his post by the door. He picked up the phone, walked across the room and placed it on the table.

David picked up the receiver. 'Hello,' he answered—for security reasons, making sure he didn't identify himself.

The shaken voice of his younger brother came down the line. 'David, it's Georgie. Have you got the morning papers?'

'Yes,' said David, 'they're all in front of me. Whatever is the problem?'

'Have you seen the Daily Express?'

'Wait a second.' David put down the phone and reached for the pile of papers, sorting through them he muttered: 'The

Daily Mail, the Telegraph, Financial Times… No, the Daily Express isn't here. Watson, where's the Express?'

The butler's face remained as calm as always, betraying nothing of his thoughts. 'Excuse me, Sir,' he said as he bowed and backed out into the hall.

Inside the receiver, David heard Georgie's voice asking: 'Have you got it, is it there?'

David picked up the phone again. 'Just a minute, coming now.'

Watson returned with The Daily Express. 'My apologies, Sir, I sought to keep it from you until after you'd eaten.'

David grabbed the newspaper and saw the headline. It read: 'WALLIS SIMPSON SECRET BABY TO TOP NAZI'

David was suddenly gripped by an attack of tinnitus: a ringing that drilled from his eardrums into the middle of his brain, a sound like the screaming silence that followed the cessation of an artillery barrage. He then heard a distant voice. It was Georgie again. 'David? David, are you there?'

The receiver slipped from David's hand and clattered on the breakfast table.

The four smaller bells of the Westminster clock tower chimed the quarter hour. Outside on the street corners, the newsboys were busy as commuters crowded around, grasping for a copy of the Daily Express. Beaverbrook stood at his office window, high above Fleet Street, and watched the antlike people scurrying away with the grains of sugar he had fed them: a sensational feast of scandal. This would be a benchmark day in his flagship publication's growing circulation, a benchmark day for the share price and the principal shareholder: him.

In the embassy of the United States of America, Joe Kennedy sat at the breakfast table, staring at the Daily Express front page. His cheese omelette ignored, he whispered: 'Holy shit, it's leaked.' He clicked his fingers at a steward, indicating the phone. 'Get me Washington on the line, the White House.'

Churchill lay in his bed at Morpeth Mansions, a copy of the Daily Express at his side. He patted his overweight cat and then got up. Puffing contentedly on his cigar, he walked out onto the terrace and looked at the view; a view he loved as much as that of the Weald of Kent. The clock tower shone in the morning light as its bells chimed the half hour.

On Pall Mall, in Marlborough House, Queen Mary sat, her face as chalky as the cliffs of Dover, the Daily Express in her lap. She got up from her armchair, letting the newspaper fall to the floor, and walked across to the fireplace. A framed photo of David sat on the mantelpiece. She held it and stared at her son's smiling, young face. The glass shattered as she threw the picture into the hearth. As if in response, the mantelpiece clock chimed the ninth hour.

Night had fallen and all the windows in Buckingham Palace had been blacked out, the building appearing ghostly under a waning, gibbous moon. In David's study lay his copy of the Daily Express, but David wasn't there; he was in the garden, stumbling along the footpath. His tie undone, his shirt hanging out, he had a bottle of scotch in one hand and a glass in the other. He stopped when he saw Wallis's chrysanthemums, no longer bright, but grey in the moonlight. He gulped down the dregs from his glass and noticed something in the sky. It was the massive fleet of barrage balloons. They sat, fat in the stillness of the evening, brooding, reminding David of his nemesis.

The glass of whisky slipped from his hand and smashed on the path. He took a swig from the bottle and lost his balance, falling on the broken shards. Blood flowed from a deep cut. It gleamed in the moonlight, flowing over his wrist and down to his arm, spreading like wet soot across his linen shirt. At this David laughed: 'Wallis, you were wrong. My blood isn't blue at all.'

Burning magnesium sunlight shone through the gaping windows of the music room. Holding a single page document in his bandaged hand, David squinted, trying to focus on the text. He sat at a small table, set up under the main chandelier. His eyes were bloodshot and dark ringed, his face looked ready to be embalmed, and he'd grazed his face shaving. The document he struggled to read was headed: 'Instrument of Abdication'.

David lay it down on the little table and looked across to his brothers: Bertie, Georgie and Henry. The three princes stood a few feet away, waiting with a small group of government officers and Palace functionaries. A photographer was also close by.

Georgie stepped forward. 'Sign and all our efforts will have been in vain. Please fight on.'

Bertie stammered: 'Heaven knows, I'm not up to the job and L-L-L...'

David got up and walked over to him, but the Duke of York struggled on. 'I don't want the job. And as for poor little L-L-L...'

The king rested his hands gently on his brother's shoulders. Bertie suddenly became calm. He stopped shaking and spoke clearly. 'Lilabet.'

'Yes, Lilabet,' David reassured. Returning to his seat, he touched the cut on his cheek and noticed a spot of blood.

'They will be cheering in the Kremlin,' said the Duke of Kent, 'and weeping in the gulags.'

David gripped the edge of the table. 'Georgie, there is no other way out.'

'Yes, there is,' he countered. 'Force the government to try to depose you. I guarantee they won't have the stomach for it.'

'Yes,' David answered slowly, 'but what of the damage I should do to the crown, to all those who may succeed me?' He turned to face his brother. 'What of the damage to the nation and the empire?'

Georgie stared at the floor.

'At a loss for an answer?' David asked.

Georgie looked up. 'What would Wallis think? She'd blame herself all the more if you went through with this.'

David sighed. 'Wallis will not be permitted to reenter Britain. I cannot tell you why, but if I stay here, I will never be able to see her again. And yet I must see her again. Despite everything, and she and I will talk about everything, I can assure you it will be a very long discussion; but, despite all that, in the end she will know I must forgive her.' He turned to the others. 'As I keep telling everyone, I cannot live without her! I do wish people would listen. Without Wallis I am nothing.'

'And the people, are they nothing? Until you sign, they are still your people.'

'Oh, Georgie, they will walk away from me. It would be naïve, I dare say preposterous, for me to think otherwise. I have been cuckolded. There will be pub jokes about me. I have lost their respect.'

'But she is not your wife,' he protested.

'She might as well be. My actions have made sure of that. I have made her as much of a wife in the people's eyes as, for some, I have made her a queen. No, I can't have all that. I have lost the people's respect, and therefore their love. The love I've worked so hard to gain is now irretrievably lost. I am nothing without the people and I am even less without Wallis.'

David motioned for Georgie to come closer, and in a whisper, said 'When this business is settled, I will leave for America. There, I will be free to marry… finally.' David smiled and pointed at the instrument of abdication. 'I could have signed this document three years ago.' He picked up his fountain pen, and while removing the cap, continued speaking, though now absent-mindedly. 'Perhaps, it would have been better if I had signed it then.' He shook his head. 'No, I've helped the nation. People have jobs. I think I gave the people hope, and as for the war, not a single British life has yet been lost.' His voice rose as he turned to the others. 'Not a single life lost! Not one! There is still a chance for peace. Even though I am no longer the one at the helm, there are others of good will who might, on my behalf, keep my promise to Private Jenkins.'

David's pen had remained poised above the parchment long enough to give Georgie a glimmer of hope. 'David,' he begged, 'please don't sign just because of Wallis and her bastard child.'

Georgie's words ripped through the king like a battle-axe. He glared at his youngest brother, his voice breaking on his words. 'How could you say such a thing? I have always favoured you, held you closer than any in my court.' For the first time in his life, he sneered at the young prince. 'But now you are lost to me. If you cared for Wallis, you would never have uttered something so cruel.' David turned to the Duke of York. 'Bertie, I am glad you will succeed me.' He got up again and shook his hand. 'I have been foolish for looking down on you. I have ignored you and thought you incompetent. I was wrong and I am sorry. Please accept my apology.'

Bertie closed his eyes and bowed his head. The king returned to his little table, sat down and carefully signed the instrument of abdication.

Georgie groaned: 'Bloody hell, may God protect us all.'

David offered his pen to King George VI. 'Bertie? Your Majesty?'

The new king took it and signed. The pen then went in order of age to Henry. 'Damn poor show,' he said as his signature was added. He went to hand on the pen, but Georgie refused to accept it.

'I've already signed,' said David. 'I'm simply asking you to witness the document.'

Georgie looked at the former king and bit his lower lip to stop his chin from quivering. 'This is the end,' he declared, and took the pen. 'Whether or not we win all the battles, we will lose this bloody war. We will lose our empire and be forever beholden to others. The name Great Britain will become an empty boast.' He signed and handed the pen back to David. 'Hold onto this; one day it'll fetch a fortune at Sotheby's.'

Chapter Eight, the Consequences

There had been a submarine alert. It kept the Queen Mary held up overnight in Cherbourg. Running behind schedule, the ocean liner raced toward Ireland, soon to be in the Celtic sea and later making landfall in the port of Cobh.

Onboard, in the first class dining room, Wallis sat alone at her table. Picking at her Waldorf salad, she could feel the stares of the other diners in the crowded room, all of them gossiping like a colony of bats.

'May I join you?' asked a voice behind her back. Wallis looked up to see Thelma, and dropped her fork. 'My God, what are you doing here?'

'Same as you: going home to the States.' Thelma swung around and grabbed one of the empty chairs. 'You look lonesome here, sitting all by yourself. I thought you'd like some company.'

Without waiting for an invitation, Thelma pulled out the chair and sat down. She waved to one of the waiters and spoke to him breathlessly. 'Be a doll and get me a champagne cocktail.' As the young man left for the bar her eyes lingered on his backside, not bothering to look at Wallis as she asked: 'So, how've you been doing?'

'I think you can find that out from the newspapers,' said

Wallis stiffly.

Thelma looked back at her and smiled. 'Yeah, sweetie, I know that, but how are you coping?'

'I'll live.'

'That's the way, nil desperandum, don't let the bastards grind you down. You know, when I see your reputation being trashed by the press, I think to myself: there but for the grace of God go I. Really, it's true; I dodged a bullet. Back in the day I wanted to get my hands on old Ribbie too; he's a bit of a dish, but you beat me to him. Anyway, while you were counting his roses, I was otherwise involved with that other guy. What was his name? Oh, yeah, David.'

The waiter placed her cocktail on the table and Thelma took a sip. 'Girl, you really took me on my word when I asked you to keep an eye on him. Come to think of it, you kept a lot more than an eye on him. You jumped in, boots and all. I swear, you poured yourself all over that hunk of prime beef like hot gravy.'

'Stop it!' yelled Wallis. The dining room went silent.

Thelma couldn't have hoped for a more attentive audience. 'Honey, take it easy; I don't care about all that anymore. I got a Vanderbilt now. Look at this for a rock.'

Thelma flashed a massive diamond engagement ring that sat beside her wedding band. 'That boy must have more money than all the British royal family put together, and icing on the cake, my guy actually married me.'

Wallis got up and left. She heard the laughter break out as soon as she was clear of the room.

That night, Sir John Reith, Director-General of the BBC, sat at the small table where David had signed the Instrument of Abdication. There was a BBC microphone set up before him. A radio crew was standing by, waiting for the cue. A technician in headphones gave a signal and the director-general announced: 'This is Buckingham Palace—His Royal Highness Prince Edward.'

Sir John rose and offered the chair. As he stepped forward David accidentally knocked the table with his foot. On the airwaves it sounded like the BBC Director General had walked out in anger, slamming the door, but David didn't know that. He sat down and looked at his brothers. They were all still there from the afternoon and were gathered around him. Without further ado he began, speaking clearly and precisely, with emotion but not theatricality.

'A few hours ago I discharged my last duty as King and Emperor, and now that I have been succeeded by my brother, the Duke of York, my first words must be to declare my allegiance to him. This I do with all my heart.'

On the Queen Mary, Wallis heard the BBC broadcast; a radio had been brought to her cabin. She chewed her nails as she listened to her lover's voice. The distance between them seemed at once immense yet intimately close.

'You all know the reasons which have impelled me to renounce the throne. However, I want you to understand that in making up my mind I did not forget the country or the empire, which as both Prince of Wales and king, I have for twenty-eight years tried to serve. I take full responsibility for any harm that might have been done, but you must believe me when I tell you that I would have found it impossible to carry out the heavy burden of responsibility and to discharge my duties as king without the help and support of the woman that I love.

'Wallis Simpson was there beside me in all my efforts to create new industries, to bring hope to Britain's unemployed, to make this nation's defences strong and to fight for peace. A peace I dare to hope will soon return.'

Wallis's eyes burned, tears streaming salt from a bottomless sea. She struggled to tune the radio. The shortwave signal ebbed and flowed through the crackling static. Then as if by divine providence the sound of David's voice returned, pellucidly clear. 'I want you to know that this decision I have made is mine and mine alone. This was a thing I had to judge entirely for myself, and most importantly, for the nation.

'It is a decision that has been made less difficult for me by the sure knowledge that my brother, with his long training in the public affairs of this country and with his fine qualities, will be able to take my place most capably in these crucial times. And he has a matchless blessing not enjoyed by me—a happy home with his wife and children.

'During these hard days I have been much comforted by my family and also by the ministers of the crown. In particular Mr Churchill, the prime minister, has always...' David hesitated and then continued, 'has always treated me with full consideration.

'I now quit altogether public affairs and I lay down my burden. If at any time in the future I can be found of service to His Majesty in a private station, I shall not fail.

'Today, we have a new king. I wish him and you, his people, happiness and peace with all my heart. God bless you all. God save the King.'

Wallis turned off the radio, and sat stunned by what she'd heard. She whispered to herself: 'It will be alright.' Then, glancing around her cabin as though some dark force might have snuck in to listen, she grabbed her coat and walked out onto the deck. Feeling the bracing air she thought on the reception she would receive upon her return to the States; her behaviour had been totally exposed. Like Eve she saw her nakedness and was ashamed. Fearful too, for having been gone so many years, she had not the slightest inkling as to how she would be greeted by the folks back home, by the government, the press. Would her friends still talk to her or would she be ignored—a pariah?

The breeze ran through Wallis's hair and caressed her face. Leaning on the railing, she looked out at the dark, rolling waves and the star filled sky. There she was, alone again, beneath the dome of the firmament. She breathed deep and walked along the empty deck. But dark figures lurked in the shadows.

Wallis stopped again and removed from her pocket a silver case. She snapped it open and took a cigarette. A hand reached out from the darkness and flicked on a flame from a gold Dunhill lighter. She turned in surprise and beheld the grey-suited man from the flat above the antique shop. 'Why,' she asked, suddenly afraid, 'what are you doing here?'

The grey-suited man dropped the lighter. Wallis watched it fall. Suddenly, his hands were around her throat, cutting off her windpipe. Wallis kicked and punched and scratched and gasped for air, desperate to live, desperate for a little more of everything. She tore herself free but her scream faded as she fell, swallowed up by the beat of the waves on the Queen Mary's hull.

The Dunhill lighter was picked up from the deck and used to ignite a cigarette. Its flame illuminated the face of the grey-suited man. It was Captain Brian Gorton. Wallis's story would never be released to the American press. Her body floated on the Irish Sea as Churchill rose to speak in the House of Commons.

'I say to the house as I have said to ministers who have joined this government. I have nothing to offer but blood, toil, tears and sweat. We have before us an ordeal of the most grievous kind. We have before us many years of struggle and suffering. You ask, what is our policy? I say it is to wage war by land, sea and air. War with all our might and with all the strength that God has given us. To wage war against a monstrous tyranny never surpassed in the dark and lamentable catalogue of human crime. That is our policy.'

Immediately following his abdication speech, David tried to contact Wallis by wireless but she could not be found. She wasn't in her cabin or any of the public rooms. David was asked to call again in the morning. He spent a restless night in the Palace and phoned back at dawn. Wallis was still not in her cabin. David requested that the wireless operator notify the ship's master. When told of the disappearance, the captain was horrified to realise how little had been done. He ordered a search of the entire ship from stem to stern. This was completed without success. In Wallis's cabin they found her purse and wallet and other personal effects, but no trace of her. The cabin steward said he had seen her leave her stateroom, heading in the direction of the deck at around dinnertime, but had not seen her since. He added she was wearing a mink coat—the coat was not in her cabin nor was her cigarette case. By noon the captain was left with no other choice but to report her as officially missing, feared overboard.

David was beside himself with worry. He refused to eat or shave, smoked incessantly and ploughed through a bottle of Hennessy Brandy. He was supposed to meet with the lawyers to negotiate the sale to Bertie of Balmoral and Sandringham, the titles being still in his name. He had also to discuss his royal allowance, a new residence and a hundred other matters, including whether or not he would return to active duty in the army, but he refused to see anyone. Finally, after two long and horrible days, the news was reported to him, in person, by the secretary of state for war, Leslie Hore-Belisha. The minister had no time for the former king and he didn't mix his words.

'Your Royal Highness, I come to you bearing the gravest possible news.'

David had leapt from his seat when the war secretary entered his drawing room, but now he collapsed back down, his bones disjointed by dread. When he spoke his voice seemed disembodied, as if uttered by someone else who shared his brain. The voice asked: 'What is your news, Mr Hore-Belisha?'

'Mrs Wallis Simpson is dead,' said the minister without emotion. 'Her body was found by fishermen on a beach in County Cork. She is, as we speak, being flown back in secret by the Royal Air Force to be buried in a remote place somewhere in England. The exact location will remain unknown to the public and there will be no confirmation of her death. Under the Emergency Powers Defence Act the press have been ordered to suppress the story. Mrs Simpson will remain officially missing for as long as it is deemed necessary, and any rumours as to her fate will be denied or simply ignored. You have been entrusted with this knowledge at the instruction of the king and the prime minister, contrary to my advice, and in the expectation that you will do your duty and never speak of it.'

'A faceless, nameless nothingness,' said David, his eyes as cold and clear as ice.

'No, a missing person,' the minister corrected.

David sat, frozen but seething, a panther about to pounce. Two words hissed from behind his clenched teeth: 'Get out.'

Hore-Belisha needed no prodding and was gone in an instant. David slammed the door behind him and proceeded to smash to pieces every object in the room. He remained locked up in the Belgian Suite until the day of the funeral.

Above the former king, across the royal apartments on the piano nobile, there was a flurry of activity as Bertie, Elizabeth and their daughters moved into their Palace home. The new king was happy to leave his brother locked up below in his self-imposed dungeon. So long as he did not roam about and upset his daughters, he'd let David wallow alone until he could bring himself to leave. 'I just hope,' he said to his wife, 'indeed, I pray the poor man hasn't lost his mind.'

David was doing all but losing his mind. He paced about like a lion, roaming from yellow drawing room to blue bedroom to white bathroom and then back again, around and around, addressing his reflection in the many mirrors he stumbled past, or swearing to the many portraits hanging from the walls. The people in those paintings would probably have thought him mad. 'Charlotte,' he lectured to his great-grandmother's grandmother, pointing to her husband's portrait, 'you think me more addled than George over there, but I am not going insane. Far from it, I am steeling myself for what is to come.' David opened a fresh bottle of Hennessy. 'Yes, I know. George lost all the people of America, while I have lost just one, but she is more to me… more to me than all the rest.' He began to blubber. 'She's gone, snatched away, and we were almost free… free.' He took a deep breath and sighed. 'Why am I so surprised? I, more than any other, should know how things are done in high places. The history of British royalty is a saga written in blood. It has only recently been staunched by the diminution of the power of the sovereign. I snatched back a tiny little morsel of that power, and now Wallis has paid the age-old price.'

It was Georgie who finally went to see him. He found his brother lying on the floor, half asleep and surrounded by empty bottles, shattered ornaments, old photos and a spray of vomit.

'David, pull yourself together and get cleaned up. There's

a driver here to collect you.'

'What for?' he asked, not attempting to open his eyes.

'The funeral—I've managed to get permission for you to attend Wallis's funeral.'

'Where?'

'I don't know. They won't tell me. You're to be taken there alone.'

'How did you know her body had been found?'

'Bertie told me, and it must remain a family secret. You cannot reveal the location of Wallis's burial place.'

To Georgie's amazement, David began to laugh. 'Is there a closet large enough to hold such a skeleton?'

Rain drizzled as David stood at Wallis's graveside, the cemetery set in the grounds of a lonely little church. He was dressed in his khaki battle dress uniform. The only other members of the funeral party were seven guardsmen and an army chaplain.

The service finished, the coffin was lowered into the ground. David took a handful of earth and threw it on the polished pine.

The gravestone was already engraved and sitting nearby, waiting to be set in place. It read: 'Bessie Wallis Beloved of David—Peace at Last—19th June 1896 - 26th September 1939.'

After a moment's reflection, the former king signalled for the soldiers to fill in the grave. He thanked the chaplain and the captain of the squad of guards. As he turned to leave, the young officers saluted. David returned the salute; he had not yet been demoted, and still wore the rank insignia of a field marshal.

The formalities, such as they were, now over, he walked down the drive to his waiting car. As the driver opened the back door there was a roar of warplanes. David looked up and saw a squadron of Hawker Hurricanes fly past. After the sound of the planes had faded away, he got into his car and said to the driver: 'I don't feel like going back just yet. I want to see more of this valley. How about we drive north?'

'I don't think I have orders to allow that, Sir.'

'Alright, then I shall walk.'

The driver, an agent from MI5, ceased his protest and did as his former king requested.

Beyond the village the ground rose gradually to a range of hills. David's black Humber Pullman sped in that direction, travelling along a county lane so old and worn it lay several feet below the level of the adjacent fields, the hedgerows so high and overhanging they almost formed an arch, blocking out much of the light. From this tube of darkness the lane broke through to open country along the spine of the range. The views to either side stretched out for miles, and for the former king, the memories came flooding back.

The Humber pulled over and the driver opened the back door. 'Wait here,' said David as he got out of the car. 'I shan't be long.' He left the roadside, climbed a small ridge and at its summit saw the solitary elm he knew from years before. Beneath its branches he and Wallis had spread their picnic blanket, eaten cakes and drunk a thermos of American coffee.

The rain cleared and patches of sunlight broke on the valley floor. They dappled a patchwork of woods, hedgerows and lush green fields. David took from his pocket a gold wedding band. He stared at it for a moment then slipped it on his finger. At that exact moment the sun came out all around. He felt drenched by its warmth. In the distance a rainbow appeared, arcing perfectly over the valley. David gazed at the sight and removed from his holster his service revolver. It sat, dull and cold in his hand, untouched for twenty years. He put the weapon to his temple. His finger slid lightly across the trigger and then froze. David's eyes widened as he saw a falcon swoop down and snatch a bullfinch.

The driver had his nose buried in the early morning edition of the Daily Express. The lead story concerned the German pocket-battleship Admiral Graf Spee. The night before, she had sunk the British steamship Clement. The German commander, Captain Langsdorff, had ordered the steamer's entire crew into lifeboats before sinking her. In a separate story there was the news that elements of the first British army corps had begun landing in France. The war with Germany was intensifying. It was only a matter of time before British lives were lost, and with every ton of merchant shipping sent to the bottom, the chances of a negotiated settlement diminished.

Clack! The back door of the Humber opened. The MI5 agent jumped out of his skin. David sat down behind him. 'Take me home.'

'Still Buckingham Palace, Sir?'

'What to you think?' said David, 'I'm not a bloody Gypsy.'

Two hours later the black Humber pulled up at the Ambassador's Entrance. David got out and marched through the portico into the Palace. Walking across to the northern side of the quadrangle, he took the King's door and progressed to the first floor via the Minister's Staircase.

'Your Majesty, I mean, Your Royal Highness,' squeaked a flustered footman as he stumbled to get out of the way. David brushed past and stormed into the audience chamber.

Bertie and Churchill were in the middle of their first Tuesday meeting. The two men were sitting opposite one another, the new king on the sofa where David had once sat. Both were rendered speechless by the former king's sudden appearance.

David walked around behind Bertie, made himself comfortable on the sofa and asked the prime minister: 'Why not drown me too?'

Churchill refused to be ruffled. 'Impossible; there's insufficient tea in my cup.'

'You could always help yourself to more,' suggested David.

Churchill took the advice, reached across and poured himself a fresh brew.

At the same time David leaned over the prime minister's bowed head and whispered: 'Why not show some courage? Instead of having me assassinated by your goons, have the backbone to order me shot?'

Churchill sat up and stirred his tea. 'I don't turn kings into martyrs.'

David pulled out his service revolver. 'No, better that title for you.'

Bertie retreated to the end of the sofa. 'Ste-steady on!'

David pointed the gun loosely at Churchill. In a relaxed voice he explained: 'With you gone, Halifax will take over, he'll cut cards with the devil and we'll avoid your thrilling little war.'

The prime minister remained defiant. 'You've not the strength to change my destiny.'

'Destiny?' asked David. 'What of Wallis? Did she not have a destiny?'

Churchill sipped his tea and declared: 'Your Royal Highness, history is not written by whores.'

David smiled. 'Then why have you written so much?'

The prime minister put down his teacup, annoyed by the former king's smirk as much as by the childish nonsense with the gun. 'What are you grinning about?'

'When you have to kill a man, it costs nothing to be polite.' David steadied his gun, took careful aim and pulled the trigger.

Churchill looked down through the smoke to see a hole beneath his bow tie.

David lay down the gun and nodded to the dying statesman. 'I know, life is precious.'

The footman raced in to see Churchill's startled eyes.

David turned to his brother and said: 'It's over.'

'You'll hang for this,' replied Bertie, without any trace of a stammer.

A death rattle escaped from Churchill's lungs as he collapsed to the floor.

'No, not that,' yelled Bessie, tossing and turning, frantic, delirious. 'I don't want to see it. I don't want to see David hang.'

Alice stopped and shut the old book. Clasping her daughter's hand, she soothed: 'It's alright, sweetie, it's alright, we don't have to go on; I've got something else to read—it's much nicer.'

Bessie settled. Her mother kissed her on the forehead and reached into her handbag, pulling out another book.

The light switched on. Alice saw a nurse walk into the room. She looked down at Bessie and asked: 'What's all the noise about? Are you in pain?'

Bessie shook her head, holding her breath in fear. The nurse checked her drip and scanned the monitors. 'You're getting plenty of morphine so please don't make such a commotion; you'll disturb the other patients. Try to relax and get some sleep.'

The nurse reached through Alice's chest to check Bessie's pulse. She grunted, and without saying anything more, left as quickly as she had entered. On her way out she switched off the light, the room returning to soft darkness.

'Gosh,' said Alice, 'it's easy to see nothing has changed around here.'

Bessie let go her breath and struggled to get oxygen into her drowning lungs. Her body gave way to a spasm of coughing so severe she almost lost consciousness. Alice rolled her daughter's shrunken frame to one side, amazed at how little she weighed; she was just a husk. The thought filled the old woman with horror. She slapped Bessie on the back, trying to dislodge the phlegm. Her baby girl's ribs were as sharp as the bars on a radiator grill. Finally, Bessie coughed up the muck, and after a moment, the spasm passed. Exhausted, she regained her breath.

Alice eased her daughter over. 'Would you like a sip of water?'

'No,' Bessie wheezed, 'you have something else to read?'

Alice quickly angled the new book in front of her daughter. Bessie was startled when she saw the front cover; it featured a colour photo of David and Wallis, taken on a tropical island. They looked blissfully happy together, but were obviously much older.

Alice read aloud the title: '"Edward and Wallis: the Later Years".' She turned the pages of the book, showing Bessie pictures of the couple enjoying life together. 'It's full of lovely photos,' her mother added enthusiastically. 'Here are Wallis and David in the Caribbean. I think it's the Bahamas. Here they are in Paris, here's Miami and New York, Washington and—'

'But the old book said Wallis died.'

'Yes, sweetie, it did. It also said she had a daughter.'

Bessie's eyes swivelled up to her mother. 'What happened to her?'

'She's sitting beside you. I'm Wallis's little girl and you're her grandchild.'

'Huh?' Bessie shook her head in disbelief, struggling to exhale a derisory laugh. 'No, no way, it can't be.'

Alice took off her reading glasses and rubbed her eyes. 'I'm sorry, I should have told you sooner. I never realised I'd go so quickly. You never had the chance to say goodbye. If I'd only been able to last a little longer you might have had the benefit of my deathbed confession. You would never have cursed yourself for letting me die alone. Your troubled life was made worse by the poison of guilt. Your self destruction was my doing.'

Bessie swallowed hard, trying to extinguish the anguish she felt for her mother's remorse. 'My life was mine to live, the choices I made were my own.' Her voice broke into a rasp and she clawed at the shiny dust jacket of the book. 'If Wallis is my grandmother, the old book is the ugly truth; the new book, a beautiful lie.'

Alice leaned against the bed and once more took her daughter's hand. 'It's a lie only if you make it so. When I read you the old book, I asked you at one point what David should do. Should he abdicate or go on. You said he should "play for time".'

'But that was in the book already.'

'No, it wasn't.' her mother said, shaking her head. 'Look at this old book again!' Alice flung open the leather bound cover and flicked through the pages till she got to the point where Bessie had yelled for her not to go on. 'See, here is where David shot Churchill. Here is where he falls to the ground. This is where we stopped reading. We stopped because you could not bear to hear anymore. Now, my darling, sweet child, turn the next page.'

Bessie shook her head. 'What's the point? It doesn't matter. Your glossy book says this old book is wrong. I don't know what to believe, anymore.'

'Please, Darling, turn over the page.'

'I'm too tired. I don't need this, not now.'

'I know, Bessie. I know I'm being cruel, but it's only to be kind. I want you to have the chance to do what I failed to do. What I couldn't do. Not then when I was—I'm sorry, but I have to say it—when it was I who was dying.'

Bessie stared at her mother and knew she had nothing to lose. She turned to the next page. It was blank.

Her mother grabbed the book and her fingers flew through the succeeding pages. All were empty. 'This is a book of life,' she urged. 'A story you write as you read and read as you write. You told David to follow his ambition and have it all. But what if he hadn't taken your advice? What if, instead, he gave up his crown for love and married Wallis? If he had followed his heart and not his ambition, then the old book would be the same as the new.'

'But then Wallis would never have had her baby,' Bessie insisted. 'I, you, we wouldn't exist.'

Alice regained her composure. 'That's why I am here. You can be the author of this new book. I've come back to give you a choice I never had the chance to take: our lives or a life for Wallis and David, this horrible place or a world reborn, a sunny world that you can create.'

'Does it matter anymore?' said Bessie. 'I'm dying and you're dead.'

'Then it should be an easy choice to make.'

'I don't even know if this is really happening.' Bessie looked around the grimy room in confusion. 'Maybe this is just a dream.'

'Then what have you to lose?'

Bessie looked at the two books before her.

'It's up to you,' Alice whispered, 'but whichever book you create, remember, I'll always love you and we'll always exist. We exist for eternity, no matter how often we live, no matter what choices we make.'

Bessie began to drift into unconsciousness. 'Thank you for coming back for me.'

Alice smiled. 'Sweetie, I was never gone.'

Bessie reached toward the glossy new book. Her fingers fell lightly on the sun-filled photo of David and Wallis.

Outside, the rain stopped falling, the clouds burnt away and the first glowing shafts of morning cracked through the now-broken window. The golden sunlight ran across the floor, filling the room with light. Alice and Bessie weren't there, nor was the bed, the chair or the medical equipment. Instead, the room was filled with dust-covered shelves and old packing cases. There was a sound of cooing as a pigeon flew past. Its wings flapped as it darted out the window.

www.ingramcontent.com/pod-product-compliance
Lightning Source LLC
Chambersburg PA
CBHW071203100726
47908CB00002B/498